DEBBIE MACOMBER
SHERRYL WOODS
ROBYN CARR

That Holiday Feeling

MIRA®

ISBN-13: 978-0-7783-2837-7

Recycling programs
for this product may
not exist in your area.

THAT HOLIDAY FEELING

www.MIRABooks.com

Printed in U.S.A.

CONTENTS

SILVER BELLS

Debbie Macomber

Christmas 2009

Dear Friends,

Since the six Manning books were republished in 2008, one of the questions I've been getting from readers is "What happened when Carrie Weston grew up? Shouldn't there be a story about her, too?" Funny you should ask, because Carrie—the teenage daughter in *Bride on the Loose* (which appears in *The Manning Grooms*)—does indeed have her own story. It's called "Silver Bells"—and here it is.

With the publication of my backlist, I have a chance to revisit characters and stories I wrote as long as twenty years ago. It thrills me to discover that my readers, both new and old, enjoy these books, perhaps even more than when they were originally published.

I'm delighted to have "Silver Bells" included in this volume, along with novellas by Sherryl Woods and Robyn Carr (who just happen to be wonderful friends as well as talented authors).

My wish for you this Christmas is that you'll have time to relax with a good book or two—hope this is one of them!—and that you and your family receive all the blessings of Christmas.

Debbie Macomber

P.S. I love hearing from my readers. You can reach me at www.debbiemacomber.com or at P.O. Box 1458, Port Orchard, WA 98366.

To DORIS LaPORT and TERESA COLCHADO,
who keep my house clean and my life sane.

One

"Dad, you don't understand."

"Mackenzie, enough."

Carrie Weston hurried through the lobby of her apartment complex. "Hold the elevator," she called, making a dash for the open doors. Her arms were loaded with mail, groceries and decorations for her Christmas tree. It probably wasn't a good idea to rush, since the two occupants appeared to be at odds—which could make for an awkward elevator ride—but her arms ached and she didn't want to wait. Lack of patience had always been one of her weaknesses; equally lacking were several other notable virtues.

The man kept the doors from closing. Carrie had noticed him earlier, and so had various other residents. There'd been plenty of speculation about the two latest additions to the apartment complex.

"Thanks," she said breathlessly. Her eyes met those of the teenager. The girl was around thirteen, Carrie guessed. They'd moved in a couple of weeks earlier, and from the scuttlebutt Carrie had heard, they'd only be staying until construction on their new home was complete.

The elevator doors glided shut, as slowly as ever, but then the people who lived in the brick three-story building off Seattle's Queen Anne Hill weren't the type to rush. Carrie was the exception.

"What floor?" the man asked.

Carrie shifted her burdens and managed to slip her mail inside her grocery bag. "Second. Thanks."

The thirtysomething man sent her a benign smile as he pushed the button. He stared pointedly away from her and the teenager.

"I'm Mackenzie Lark," the girl said, smiling broadly. The surly tone was gone. "This is my dad, Philip."

"I'm Carrie Weston." By balancing the groceries on one knee she was able to offer Mackenzie her hand. "Welcome."

Philip shook her hand next, his grip firm and solid, his clasp brief. He glared at his daughter as though to say this wasn't the time for social pleasantries.

"I've been wanting to meet you," Mackenzie continued, ignoring her father. "You look like the only normal person in the entire building."

Carrie smiled despite her effort not to. "I take it you met Madame Frederick."

"Is that a real crystal ball?"

"So she claims." Carrie remembered the first time she'd seen Madame Frederick, who'd stepped into the hallway carrying her crystal ball, predicting everything from the weather to a Nordstrom shoe sale. Carrie hadn't known what to think. She'd plastered herself against the wall and waited for Madame Frederick to pass. The crystal ball hadn't unnerved her as much as the green emeralds glued over each eyebrow. She wore a sort of caftan, with billowing yards of colorful material about her arms and hips; it hugged her legs from the knees down. Her long, silver-white hair was arranged in an updo like that of a prom queen straight out of the sixties.

"She's nice," Mackenzie remarked. "Even if she's weird."

"Have you met Arnold yet?" Carrie asked. He was another of the more eccentric occupants, and one of her favorites.

"Is he the one with all the cats?"

"Arnold's the weight lifter."

"The guy who used to work for the circus?"

Carrie nodded, and was about to say more when the elevator came to a bumpy halt and sighed loudly as the doors opened. "It was a pleasure to meet you both," she said on her way out the door.

"Same here," Philip muttered, and although he glanced in her direction, Carrie had the impression that he wasn't really seeing her. She had the distinct notion that if she'd been standing there nude he wouldn't have noticed or, for that matter, cared.

The doors started to shut when Mackenzie yelled, "Can I come over and talk to you sometime?"

"Sure." The elevator closed, but not before Carrie heard the girl's father voice his disapproval. She didn't know if the two of them were continuing their disagreement, or if this had to do with Mackenzie inviting herself over to visit.

Holding her bags, Carrie had some difficulty unlocking and opening her apartment door without dropping everything. She slammed it closed with one foot and dumped the Christmas ornaments on the sofa, then hauled everything else into her small kitchen.

"You'd been wanting to meet him," she said aloud. "Now you have." She hated to admit it, but Philip Lark had been a disappointment. He showed about as much interest in her as he would a loaf of bread in the bakery window. Well, what did she expect? The fact that she expected *anything* was because she'd listened to Madame Frederick one too many times. The older woman claimed to see Carrie's future and predicted that, before the end of the year, she'd meet the man of her dreams when he moved into this very building. Yeah, right. She refused to put any credence into that prophecy. Madame Frederick was a sweet, rather strange old lady with a romantic heart.

Carrie pulled out the mail, scanned the envelopes and, except for two Christmas cards and a bill, threw the rest in the garbage. She'd just started to unpack her groceries when there was a knock at the door.

"Hello again," Mackenzie Lark said cheerfully when Carrie opened the door. The quickness of her return took Carrie by surprise.

"You said I could come see you," the teenager reminded her.

"Sure, come on in." Mackenzie walked into the apartment, glanced around admiringly and then collapsed onto the sofa.

"Are you still fighting with your dad?" Carrie asked. She'd had some real go-rounds with her mother before Charlotte married Jason Manning ten years earlier. At the time, Carrie and her mother had been constantly at odds. Carrie knew she was to blame, in part, but she was also aware that her mother had been lonely and unhappy.

Hindsight told her that the root of their problem had been her parents' divorce. Carrie didn't remember a lot about her father—her parents had separated when she was four or five. As she grew older, she came to resent that she didn't have a father, and for reasons that were never clear, she'd blamed her mother.

"Dad doesn't understand." Mackenzie lowered her eyes, her mouth turned down.

"About what?" Carrie asked gently.

The girl stood and walked over to the kitchen and watched Carrie put away groceries. She folded her arms on the counter and then rested her chin there. "Everything. We can't talk without fighting. It's tough being a teenager."

"You might find this difficult to believe, but it's just as difficult raising one," Carrie said.

Mackenzie sighed. "It didn't used to be like this with Dad and me. We got along really well. It wasn't easy when Mom left, but we managed."

"So your parents are divorced?" Although she didn't mean to pry, she was definitely curious.

Mackenzie wrinkled her nose. "It was awful when they split."

"It always is. My parents divorced when I was just a kid. I barely remember my dad."

"Did you see him very much afterward?"

Carrie shook her head. It had bothered her when she was younger, but she'd made her peace with it as an adult. She'd felt hurt that her father didn't want to be part of her life, but ultimately she'd decided that was his choice—and his loss.

"I'm spending Christmas with my mom and her new husband." Mackenzie's eyes brightened. "I haven't seen her in almost a year. She's been busy," she said. "Mom works for one of the big banks in downtown Seattle and she's got this really important position and has to travel and it's hard for her to have me over. Dad's a systems analyst."

Carrie heard the pain in Mackenzie's voice. "You're

fifteen?" she asked, deliberately adding a couple of years to her estimate, remembering how important it was to look older when one was that age.

Mackenzie straightened. "Thirteen, actually."

Carrie opened a bag of fat-free, cheese-flavored rice cakes and dumped them onto a plate. Mackenzie helped herself to one and Carrie did, as well. They sat across from each other on opposite sides of the kitchen counter.

"You know what I think?" Mackenzie said, her dark eyes intense. "My dad needs a woman."

The rice cake stuck midway down Carrie's throat. "A…woman?"

"Yeah, a wife. All he does is work, work, work. It's like he can forget about my mother if he stays at the office long enough." She grabbed another rice cake. "Madame Frederick said so, too. *And* she says he's going to meet someone, but she couldn't be any more specific than that."

"Madame Frederick?"

"She looked into her crystal ball for me and said she saw lots of changes in my future. I wasn't too happy—except for the part about my dad. There've been too many changes already with the move and all. I miss my friends and it's taking way longer to build the new house than it was supposed to. Originally we were going to be in for Christmas, but now I doubt it'll be ready before next Thanksgiving. Dad doesn't seem to mind, but it bugs me. I'm the one who's going to a strange school and everything." She frowned, shaking her head. "I want my life back."

"That's understandable."

Mackenzie seemed caught up in a fantasy world of her own. "You know, I think Madame Frederick might've stumbled on something here." Her voice rose with enthusiasm.

"Stumbled on something?" Carrie repeated cautiously.

"You know, about a relationship for my dad. I wonder how I could arrange that?"

"What do you mean?"

"Finding a new wife for my dad."

"Mackenzie," Carrie said and laughed nervously. "A daughter can't arrange that sort of thing."

"Why not?" She seemed taken aback.

"Well, because marriage is serious. It's love and commitment between two people. It's…it's…"

"The perfect solution," Mackenzie finished for her. "Dad and I've always liked the same things. We've always agreed on everything…well, until recently. It makes sense that I should be the one to find him a wife."

"Mackenzie…"

"I know what you're thinking," she said, without a pause. "That my dad won't appreciate my efforts, and you're probably right. I'll have to be subtle."

Carrie laughed. "I can't believe this," she whispered. This girl was like a reincarnation of herself eleven years earlier.

"What?" Mackenzie demanded, apparently offended.

"Take my advice and stay out of your father's love life."

"Love life?" she echoed. "That's a joke. He hasn't got one."

"He doesn't want your help," Carrie said firmly.

"Of course he doesn't, but that's beside the point."

"Mackenzie, if you're not getting along with your dad now, I hate to think what'll happen when he discovers what you're up to. My mother was furious with me when I offered Jason money to take her out and—"

"You were willing to *pay* someone to date your mother?"

Carrie didn't realize what she'd said until it was too

late. "It was a long time ago," she murmured, hoping to leave it at that. She should've known better. Mackenzie's eyes grew huge.

"You actually paid someone to date your mother?" she said again.

"Yes, but don't get any ideas. He refused." Carrie could see the wheels turning in the girl's head. "It was a bad idea, and like I said, my mother was really mad at me."

"Did she ever remarry?"

Carrie nodded.

"Anyone you knew?"

Again she nodded, unwilling to tell her it was the very man she'd tried to bribe.

Mackenzie's gaze met hers and Carrie looked away. "It was *him,* wasn't it?"

"Yes, but I didn't have anything to do with that."

Mackenzie laughed. "You offered him money to date your mother. He refused, but dated her anyway. That's great! How long before they got married?"

"Mackenzie, what happened with my mother and Jason is…unusual."

"How long?" she repeated stubbornly.

"A few months."

She smiled knowingly. "They're happy, aren't they." It was more of a comment than a question.

"Yes."

Carrie only hoped she'd find a man who'd make her as truly contented as Jason Manning had made her mother. Despite ten years of marriage and two children, her mother and stepfather behaved like newlyweds. Carrie marveled at the strength of their love. It inspired her and yet in some ways hampered her. She wanted that kind of relationship for herself and wasn't willing to settle for anything less. Her friends claimed she was too picky, too demanding when it came to men, and she suspected they were right.

"My point exactly," Mackenzie declared triumphantly. "You knew your mom better than anyone. Who else was more qualified to choose a husband for her? It's the same with me. I know my dad and he's in a rut. Something's got to be done, and Madame Frederick hit the nail on the head. He needs a love interest."

Carrie's smile was forced. "Madame Frederick is one of my favorite people, but I think it's best to take what she says with a grain of salt."

"Well, a little salt enhances the flavor, right?" Mackenzie added. Excited now, she got to her feet. "What about you?" she asked.

"Me?"

"Yeah, you. Would you be willing to date my dad?"

Two

"She's pretty, isn't she, Dad?"

Philip Lark glanced up. He sat at the kitchen table, filling out an expense report. His daughter sat across from him, smiling warmly. The way her eyes focused on him told him she was up to *something.*

"Who?" he asked, wondering if it was wise to inquire.

"Carrie Weston." At his blank look, she elaborated. "The woman we met in the elevator. We talked this afternoon." Mackenzie rested her chin in her hands and continued to gaze at him adoringly.

Philip's eyes reverted to the row of figures on the single sheet. His daughter waited patiently until he was finished. Patience wasn't a trait he was accustomed to seeing in Mackenzie. She usually complained when he brought work home, acting as though it was a personal affront. He cleared his mind, attempting to remember her question. Oh, yes, she wanted to know what he thought of Carrie Weston. For the life of him, he couldn't remember what the woman looked like. His impression of her remained vague, but he hadn't found anything to object to.

"You like her, do you?" he asked instead, although he wasn't convinced that pandering to Mackenzie's moods was a smart thing to do. She'd been impossible lately. Moody and unreasonable. Okay, okay, he realized the move had been hard on her; it hadn't been all that easy on him, either. But they'd be here for only six to eight weeks. He'd assumed she was mature enough to handle the situation. Evidently, he'd been wrong.

Mackenzie's moods weren't all he'd miscalculated. Philip used to think they were close, but for the past few months she'd been a constant source of frustration.

Overnight his sane, sensible daughter had turned into Sarah Bernhardt—or, more appropriately, Sarah Heartburn! She hadn't whined this much since she was three. Frankly, Philip didn't understand it. Even her mother's defection hadn't caused this much drama.

"Carrie's great, really great."

Philip was pleased Mackenzie had made a new friend, although he would have been more pleased if it was someone closer to her own age. Still, as he kept reminding her, the situation was temporary. Gene Tarkington, a friend of his who owned this apartment building, had offered the furnished two-bedroom rental to him for as long as it'd take to complete construction on his Lake Washington house. The apartment wasn't the Ritz, but he hadn't been expecting any luxury digs. Nor, truth be told, had he expected the cavalcade of characters who populated the building, although the woman with the crystal ball looked fairly harmless. And the muscle-bound sixty-year-old who walked around shirtless, carrying hand weights, appeared innocuous, too. He wasn't as certain about some of the others, but then he didn't plan on sticking around long enough to form friendships with this group of oddballs.

"Dad," Mackenzie began in a wistful voice, "have you ever thought of remarrying?"

"No," he answered emphatically, shocked by the question. He'd made one mistake; he wasn't willing to risk another. Laura and the twelve years they were together had taught him everything he cared to know about marriage.

"You sound mad."

"I'm not," he said, thrusting the expense report back inside his briefcase, "just determined."

"It's because of Mom, isn't it?"

"Why would I want to remarry?" he asked, hoping to put an end to this conversation.

"You might want a son someday."

"Why would I want a son when I have you?"

She grinned broadly, obviously approving his response. "Madame Frederick looked into her crystal ball and said she sees another woman in your life."

Philip laughed at the sheer ridiculousness of that. Remarry? Him? He'd rather dine on crushed glass. Wade through an alligator-infested swamp. Or jump off the Space Needle. No, he wasn't interested in remarrying. Not him. Not in this lifetime.

"Carrie's a lot like me."

So *this* was what the conversation was all about. Carrie and him. Well, he'd put a stop to that right now. "Hey." He raised his hand, palm out. "I guess I'm a little slow on the uptake here, but the fog is beginning to lift. You're playing matchmaker with me and this—" person he couldn't recall a single thing about "—neighbor."

"Woman, Dad. Carrie's young, attractive, smart and funny."

"She is?" He hadn't noticed that earlier, but then how could he? They'd met for about a minute in the elevator.

"She's perfect for you."

"Who says?" As soon as the words left his lips, Philip knew he'd made a strategic error. He'd all but invited an argument.

Mackenzie's smile blossomed like a rose in the sun. "Madame Frederick, for one. Me for another. Just think about it, Dad. You're in the prime of your life and all you do is work. You should be enjoying the fruit of your labors."

"I'm building the house," he said, wondering where she'd heard *that* expression.

"Sure, to impress Mom, just so she'll know what a mistake she made leaving you."

His daughter's words brought him up short. Philip sincerely hoped that wasn't true. He wanted a new home for plenty of reasons, none of which included his ex-wife. Or so he believed.

"Why would your mother care about a home I'm building?"

"Think about it, Dad."

"I am."

She shot him a knowing look, one tempered with gentle understanding, which only irritated him further. "Let's leave Laura out of this, all right?" His feelings for Mackenzie's mother were long dead. He'd tried to make the marriage work, as God was his witness. Even when he discovered she was having an affair—the first time— he'd been willing to do whatever was necessary to get them back on track. It'd worked for a few years, but for the most part he'd been deluding himself.

The divorce had come well after there was any marriage left to save. He'd berated himself for a long time before, and since. He had his daughter and his dignity, and was grateful for both. The last thing he intended to do at this point was risk that hard-won serenity.

"I want you to ask Carrie out."

"What?" He couldn't believe her nerve. "Mackenzie, for heaven's sake, would you stop? I'm *not* dating Carrie Westchester or anyone else."

"It's Carrie Weston."

"Her, either." He stalked into the kitchen and poured himself a cup of coffee. He took one sip, cringed at the bitter taste and dumped the rest in the sink.

"Please? She's in Apartment 204."

"No! Case closed! I don't want to hear another word about this, understand?" He must have added just enough authority to his voice because she didn't pursue the subject again. Philip was grateful.

The next time he glanced at his daughter, he saw her sitting in the middle of the living room, her arms folded tightly around her. The sour look on her face could have curdled cream.

"Say, why don't we go out and buy a Christmas tree?" he suggested. Despite what Mackenzie might think, he didn't enjoy fighting with her.

She turned to stare at him disdainfully and consider his proposal. With what seemed to require an extraordinary amount of effort, she said, "No thanks."

"Fine, if that's the way you want to be."

"I thought you said a Christmas tree would be too much trouble this year."

It would be, but he was willing to overlook that if it'd take his daughter's mind off her present topic of interest. "We could put up a small one." He figured a compromise would go a long distance toward keeping the peace.

"She likes you," Mackenzie said with a righteous nod.

Philip didn't need to ask who she was talking about. He pressed his lips together to keep from saying something he'd later regret. Such as…how did this Carrie person know enough about him to either like or dislike him?

"She told me what happened to her when she was about my age," Mackenzie continued undaunted. "Her parents divorced when she was around five and her mother didn't date again or anything. She closed herself off from new relationships, just the way you're doing, so Carrie felt she had to take matters into her own hands. And who could blame her? Not me, that's for sure." She paused long enough to draw in a breath. "By the time Carrie was a teenager, her mother had shriveled into this miserable, unhappy shrew." She stared pointedly at him before saying, "Sort of like what's happening to you."

"Come on now!"

"So," she went on, ignoring his outburst, "Carrie felt she had to do something. She offered to pay this guy to date her mother. Out of her own meager savings from babysitting jobs and walking the neighbor's dog. She took everything she'd managed to scrape together to pay this man. She told me she would've done anything to give her love-starved mother a second chance at happiness."

Philip restrained himself from rolling his eyes at her melodramatic rendition. All she needed was a violin playing softly in the background. "How noble of her."

"That's not the end of the story," Mackenzie informed him.

"You mean there's more?"

She paid no attention to his sarcasm. "When her mother found out what she'd done, she was furious with Carrie."

"I can well imagine." Philip crossed his arms and leaned against the doorjamb. He glanced at his watch, indicating that there was only so much of this he was willing to listen to and he was already close to his limit.

"But she withstood her mother's outrage. Knowing she was right, Carrie gladly accepted the two-week restriction her mother placed on her."

The strains of the violin grew distinctly louder.

"Carrie didn't pick just any Tom, Dick or Harry for her mother, though. She carefully, thoughtfully surveyed the eligible men around her and chose this really cool guy named James…or something like that. His name isn't important—what *is* important is that Carrie knew her mother well enough to choose the perfect man for her. She chose the very best."

Now his daughter was beginning to sound like a greeting-card commercial. "This story does have a point, doesn't it?"

"Oh, yes." Her eyes gleamed with triumph. "Not more than three months later, four at the most, Carrie's mother married Jason."

"I thought you said his name was James."

"I also said his name doesn't matter. The point is that he married her and they're both happy."

"That must have cost her a pretty penny, since Carrie had already paid him everything she'd saved just for that first date."

"He married her for free."

"Oh, I see, she was on sale."

Mackenzie frowned at him. "You're not funny. Carrie told me that meeting Jason was the best thing that ever happened to her mother. Once a year, on the anniversary of their first date, her mom sends her flowers out of gratitude that her daughter, the very one she'd restricted for two whole weeks, had cared enough to find the man of her dreams."

As her voice rose victoriously, the violin faded and was replaced with a full choral arrangement of *God Bless America.* Philip could just about hear it. His daughter was Sarah Heartburn during her finest hour.

"Now," she said, "will you ask Carrie out? She's perfect for you, Dad. I know what you like and what you don't, and you're gonna like her. She's really nice and fun."

"No." He yawned loudly, covering his mouth.

"I've never said anything, but I'd really love to be a big sister, the way Carrie is to her two half brothers."

"Thanks, but no thanks." The kid was actually beginning to frighten him. Not only was she telling him he should date a woman he'd barely met, now she was talking about them having children together.

"Don't do it because I asked it of you. Do it for yourself. Do it before your heart turns into a hardened shell and you shrivel up into an old man."

"Hey, I'm not dead yet. I've got a good forty or fifty years left in me."

"Maybe," Mackenzie challenged. "*If* you're lucky." With her nose pointed at the ceiling she exited the room with all the flair and drama of an actress walking offstage after the final curtain call.

Grinning to himself, Philip opened his briefcase. He removed a file, then hesitated, frowning. It was one thing to have his daughter carry on like a Shakespearean actress and another for an adult woman to be feeding her this nonsense. While he couldn't remember much about Ms. Carrie Weston, he did recall that she'd appeared interested in him, judging by the intent way she'd studied him. Perhaps he'd better set the record straight with her. If she intended to use his daughter to get to him, then she was about to learn a thing or two.

He slammed his briefcase shut and marched toward the door.

"Where are you going?" Mackenzie asked, returning— of course—at that very instant.

"To talk to your friend," he snapped.

"You mean Carrie?" she asked excitedly. "You won't be sorry, Dad, I promise you. She's really nice and I know you'll like her. If you haven't decided where to take her to dinner, I'd suggest Henry's, off Broadway. You took me there for my birthday, remember?"

Philip didn't bother to inform his daughter that inviting Carrie to dinner wasn't exactly what he had in mind. He walked out the door and nearly collided with the old biddy clutching the crystal ball.

"Good evening, Mr. Lark," Madame Frederick greeted him with a tranquil smile. She glanced at him and then at the crystal ball and her smile grew wider.

"Keep that thing away from me," he told her in clear tones. "I don't want you doing any of that hocus-pocus around my daughter. Understand?"

"As you wish," she said with great dignity and moved past him. Philip glared at her, then sighed, exasperated. He headed for the stairs, running down to the second floor.

When he reached Carrie Weston's apartment, he was winded and short-tempered. She answered his knock almost immediately.

"Mr. Lark." Her eyes widened with the appropriate amount of surprise, as though she'd spent the past five minutes standing in front of a mirror practicing.

"It seems you and I need to talk."

"Now?" she asked.

"Right now."

Three

Carrie Weston was lovely, Philip realized. For reasons he didn't want to analyze, he hadn't noticed how strikingly attractive she was when they'd met in the elevator. Her eyes were clear blue, almost aquamarine. Intense. Her expression warm and open.

It took him a moment to recall why he'd rushed down here to talk to her. Maybe, just maybe, what Mackenzie had been saying—that he was shriveling up emotionally—contained a grain of truth. The thought sobered him.

"I need to talk to you about Mackenzie," he stammered out.

"She's a delightful young lady. I hope I didn't keep her too long." Carrie's words were apologetic as she reached into the hallway closet for her coat.

"It's about your discussion with her this afternoon."

"I'm sorry I can't chat just now. I feed Maria's cats on Wednesdays and I'm already late."

It could be a convenient excuse to escape him, but he was determined to see this through. "Do you mind if I tag along?"

She looked mildly surprised, but agreed. "Sure, if you want." She picked up a ten-pound bag of cat food. Ten pounds? Philip knew the older woman kept a ridiculous number of animals. Gene had complained to him more than once, but the retired schoolteacher had lived in the building for fifteen years and paid her rent on time. Gene tolerated her tendency to adopt cats, but he didn't like it.

"You might want to get your coat," she suggested as she locked her apartment.

"My coat?" She seemed to imply that the old lady kept her apartment at subzero temperatures. "All right," he muttered.

She waited as he hurried up the stairs. Mackenzie leaped to her feet the second he walked in the door. "What'd you say to her?" she demanded.

"Nothing yet." He yanked his coat off the hanger. "I'm helping her feed some cats."

The worry left his daughter's eyes. "Really? That's almost a date, don't you think?"

"No, I don't think." He jerked his arms into the jacket sleeves.

"She asked me if I wanted to bake Christmas cookies with her and her two brothers on Saturday. I can, can't I?"

"We'll talk about that later." Carrie Weston was wheedling her way into his daughter's life. He didn't like it.

Mackenzie didn't look pleased but gave a quick nod. Her worried expression returned as he walked out the door.

Philip wasn't sure why he'd decided to join Carrie. He needed to clarify the situation, but it wasn't necessary to follow her around with a bag of cat food to do so.

"Maria has a special love for cats," Carrie explained as they entered the elevator and rode to the ground floor.

"I just don't feel it's a good idea for her to be going out alone at night to feed the strays."

So *that* was what this was all about—feeding stray cats.

"Maria calls them her homeless babies."

Philip sure hoped no one at the office heard about this. They stepped outside and his breath formed a small cloud. "How often does she do this?" he asked, walking beside Carrie.

"Every day," she answered. Half a block later she turned into an almost-dark alley. Carrie had said she didn't think it was safe for Maria to venture out alone at night. Philip wasn't convinced it was any less risky for her. He glanced about and saw nothing but a row of green Dumpsters.

They were halfway down the dimly lit alley when he heard the welcoming meow of cats. Carrie removed a cardboard container from a Dumpster and left a large portion of food there. The cats eagerly raced toward it. One tabby wove his way around her feet, his tail slithering about Carrie's slender calf. Squatting down, she ran her gloved hand down the back side of a large male. "This is Brutus," she said, "Jim Dandy, Button Nose, Falcon and Queen Bee."

"You named them?"

"Not me, Maria. They're her friends. Most have been on their own so long that they're unable to adapt to any other way of life. Maria's paid to have them neutered, and she nursed Brutus back to health after he lost an eye in a fight. He was nearly dead when she found him. He let her look after him, but domesticated living wasn't for Brutus. Actually, I think he's the one that got Maria started on the care and feeding of the strays. I help out once a week. Arnold and a couple of the others do, too. And we all contribute what we can to the costs of cat food and vet care."

All this talk about cats was fine, but Philip had other things on his mind. "As I explained earlier, I wanted to talk to you about Mackenzie."

"Sure." Carrie gave each of the cats a gentle touch, straightened and started out of the alley.

"She came back from her visit with you spouting some ridiculous idea about the two of us dating," Philip continued.

Carrie had the good grace to blush, he noted.

"I'm afraid I'm the one who inadvertently put that idea in her head. Mr. Lark, I can't tell you how embarrassed I am about this. It all started with an innocent conversation about parents. My parents got divorced, as well—"

"When you were four or five, as I recall," he said. He hated to admit it, but he enjoyed her uneasiness. Knowing Mackenzie, he was well aware of the finesse with which his daughter manipulated conversations. Poor Carrie hadn't had a chance. "Mackenzie also said you paid a man to date your mother."

"Oh, dear." She closed her eyes. "No wonder you wanted to talk to me." She glanced guiltily in his direction. "Jason was far too honorable to accept my offer."

"But he did as you asked."

"Not exactly… Listen, I do apologize. I'd better have another talk with Mackenzie. I'll try to set the record straight. I was afraid she might do something like this. Actually, I should've realized her intent and warned you. But I didn't think she'd race right upstairs and repeat every word of our conversation."

"My daughter has a mind of her own. And she's taken quite a liking to you." For that, Philip was grateful. Mackenzie needed a positive female role model. Heaven knew her mother had shown little enough interest in her only child. Philip could do nothing to ease the pain of that, and it hurt him to hear Mackenzie make excuses for Laura's indifference.

As they chatted, Carrie led him into a nearby vacant lot. He learned quite a bit about her in those few minutes. She worked for Microsoft, had lots of family in the area and doted on her two half brothers.

The minute they stepped onto the lot, ten or so stray cats eased out of the shadows. They'd obviously been waiting for Carrie. Talking softly, issuing reassurances and comfort, she distributed the food in a series of aluminum pie plates situated about the area.

"I saw a lot of my teenage self in Mackenzie," she said when she rejoined him. She looked at him, but didn't hold his gaze long. "It wasn't just the fact that my parents were divorced—broken homes were prevalent enough— but I'd been cheated out of more than the ideal family. In some ways I didn't have a mother, either."

"Are you trying to say I'm not a good father?" he asked tightly.

"No, no," she said automatically. "I think I should keep my mouth shut. I do apologize for what happened with Mackenzie. Don't worry, Mr. Lark, I have no intention of using your daughter to orchestrate a date with you."

"Do you still want her to come over to bake cook- ies?" he asked. He'd be in trouble with Mackenzie if she didn't.

"You don't mind?"

"Not if you and I are straight about where we stand with each other. I'm not interested in a relationship with you. It's nothing personal. You're young and attractive and will make some man very happy one day—it just won't be me."

"I wouldn't... You're not—" She stopped abruptly and glared up at him. "Rest assured, Mr. Lark, you have nothing to fear from me."

"Good. As long as we understand each other."

Carrie removed her gloves and viciously shoved them into her pockets. She hung her coat in the closet and sat down, crossing her arms and her legs. She uncrossed both just as quickly, stood and started pacing. She couldn't keep still.

Philip Lark actually believed she'd tried to use his daughter to arrange a date with him! Talk about an egomaniac! This guy took the prize as the most conceited, egotistical, vain man she'd ever had the displeasure of meeting. She wouldn't date him now if he were the last man on the face of the earth.

The phone rang and she frowned at it, then realized she was being ridiculous and picked up the receiver.

"Carrie?" Her name was whispered.

It was her stepfather, Jason Manning. "Yes?" she answered. "Is there a reason you're whispering?"

"I don't want your mother to hear me."

"Oh?" Despite her agitation with Philip Lark she grinned.

"I ordered Charlotte a Christmas gift this afternoon," he boasted. From years past, Carrie knew buying gifts didn't come naturally to Jason, since he'd been a confirmed bachelor until he met her mother. The first Christmas after they were married he'd bought Charlotte a bowling ball, season tickets to the Seattle Seahawks and a vacuum cleaner. After that, Carrie had steered him toward more personal things.

"You know how your mother likes to go to garage sales?"

"I'm not likely to forget." Jason had given her mother

a lot of grief over her penchant to shop at yard sales. He liked to joke that Charlotte had found priceless pieces of Tupperware in her search for treasure.

"Well, a friend of mine started a limousine service and I hired him to escort your mother to yard sales on the Saturday of her choice. What do you think?" His voice rose in excitement. "She'll love it, won't she?"

"She will." Carrie couldn't keep from smiling. "She'll have the time of her life."

"I thought so," he said proudly. "Jeff's giving me a twenty-percent discount, too."

"I also think it's really sweet that you're taking Mom Christmas shopping in downtown Seattle on Saturday."

"Yeah, well, that's the price a man pays to please his wife." He didn't sound very enthusiastic.

"Doug and Dillon are coming to stay with me. We're baking cookies."

"I can't believe I'm voluntarily going Christmas shopping. There isn't another person in the world who could drag me into the city during the busiest shopping season of the year. Your mother's got to know I love her."

"She does know." Carrie had never doubted it, not from the first moment she'd seen her mother and Jason together. Rarely had any two people been more right for each other. While Jason might not be the most romantic man alive—she smiled whenever she recalled the look on her mother's face when she unwrapped that bowling ball—he was a devoted husband and father.

Jason Manning loved and nurtured Carrie as if she'd been his own child. A teenager couldn't have asked for a better stepdad. After some of the horror stories she'd heard from other girls in her situation, she appreciated him even more.

She heard a persistent pounding. "There's someone at my door," she told Jason.

"I'll let you go, then," he said. "Promise me you won't say anything to your mother."

"My lips are sealed." A limo to escort her to garage sales! Carrie smiled. She replaced the receiver and hurried across the living room to answer the door. It'd been a long day and a busy evening; she was hungry, tired and in no mood for company.

"Hi," Mackenzie said, her eyes wide. "So how'd it go with my dad?"

Carrie frowned.

"That bad, huh?" The girl laughed lightly. "Don't worry, it'll get better once he gets used to the idea of dating again."

"Mackenzie, listen, you and I need to talk about this. Your father's—"

"Sorry, I can't talk now. Dad doesn't know I'm gone, but I just wanted to say don't be discouraged. All he needs is time." She beamed her another wide smile. "This is going to be so great! Wait until Jane hears about how I found my dad a wife. Jane's my best friend. I'll see you Saturday." Having said that, she promptly disappeared.

Carrie closed the door and shut her eyes, feeling mildly guilty at what she'd started.

There was an abrupt knock at the door.

"Now what?" she demanded, her patience gone.

Madame Frederick smiled back at her. Arnold, muscles bulging in his upper arms, stood beside her. Both regarded her with open curiosity.

"Has she met him yet?" Arnold asked. "Has she met the man of her dreams—and do you know who it is?"

Madame Frederick's face glowed. "You can see for

yourself." She lifted her crystal ball and ran her hand over the smooth glass surface. "One look should tell you."

But Carrie couldn't see anything at all.

Four

A thin layer of flour dusted her small kitchen. Carrie fanned her hand in front of her face in an effort to clear the air. The scent of baking gingerbread men drifted through the apartment, smelling of spices and fun.

Dillon stood on a chair, leaning over the electric mixer, watching intently as it stirred the cookie dough. Doug was at the counter, his sleeves up past his elbows, a rolling pin in his hand. Mackenzie used a spatula to scoop the freshly baked cookies from the baking sheet and placed them on the wire rack to cool.

"Do you think anyone will taste the eggshell?" she asked.

"The recipe said two eggs," Dillon muttered defensively, "and Carrie said the whole egg. How was I supposed to know she didn't mean the shell?"

"You just should," his older brother informed him with more than a hint of righteousness.

"I already said we don't need to worry about it," Carrie inserted, hoping to soothe Dillon's dented ego. She'd gotten most of the shell out and the remainder had been pulverized to the point that it was no longer distinguishable.

Mackenzie rolled her eyes expressively, but it was clear she was enjoying herself. More and more she reminded Carrie of herself eleven years earlier. She'd taken to Doug and Dillon immediately and they were equally enthralled with her. Within an hour they were the best of friends.

"I want to decorate the cookies, too," Dillon cried, when he saw that Carrie had finished making the frosting.

"You can't lick the knife," his older brother remarked snidely. "Not when we're giving the cookies to other people."

"There'll be plenty of frosting for everyone," Carrie reassured them.

"Who's going to taste the first gingerbread man?"

The three kids looked at one another. "Dillon should," Doug said.

"Okay." Her youngest brother squared his shoulders bravely. "I don't mind. Besides, Carrie said no one would be able to taste the eggshell, anyway." He climbed off the chair and reached for a cookie. "Maybe you should put a little frosting on, just in case," he said to Carrie.

She slathered some across the cookie and handed it back to him. Dillon closed his eyes and opened his mouth while the others waited for the outcome. One bite quickly became another.

"Maybe I should eat two just to make sure," the six-year-old told her.

Carrie winked and handed her youngest brother a second cookie, also slathered with frosting.

"I better try some, too," Doug said and grabbed one. He gobbled it up, head first, then nodded. "Not bad," he mumbled, his mouth full of cookie. "Even *without* the frosting."

"We're saving some for us, aren't we?" Dillon asked, reaching across the counter for the frosting knife.

"Of course, but I promised a plate to Arnold, Maria and Madame Frederick."

"Can I frost now?" Dillon asked, pulling the chair closer to the counter where Carrie stood.

"I want to decorate, too."

"Me, too," Mackenzie chimed in.

An hour later, Carrie was exhausted. Doug and Dillon finished drying the last of the dishes and threw themselves in front of the television to watch their favorite DVD. Carrie sat on a bar stool, her energy gone, while Mackenzie painstakingly added tiny red cinnamon candies to the cookie faces.

"Dad's late," she said with a knowing sigh as she formed a pair of candy lips, "but then he's always longer than he says he's going to be. He has no life, you know." She glanced up from her task to be sure Carrie was paying attention.

"We agreed," Carrie reminded the girl, wagging her index finger.

"I remember." Carrie had insisted Mackenzie keep Philip Lark out of the conversation. It seemed drastic, but was necessary, otherwise Mackenzie would use every opportunity to talk about her poor, lonely father, so desperate for female companionship that he was practically shriveling up before her eyes. Carrie could repeat the entire speech, verbatim.

It had taken the better part of two days to convince the girl that Carrie wasn't romantically interested in Philip, no matter how perfectly matched they appeared to be in Mackenzie's estimation.

Carrie suspected that Mackenzie was hearing much the same thing from her father. Philip wasn't thrilled with the idea of his daughter playing matchmaker any more than she was. In the three days since their first meeting, they'd made an effort to avoid seeing or talking to each other. The last thing Mackenzie needed was evidence that her plan was working.

"It's a real shame," Mackenzie said, eyeing her carefully. "Madame Frederick agrees with me and so do Arnold and Maria."

"Enough!" Carrie said, loudly enough to draw the boys' attention away from the TV screen.

When Mackenzie had finished decorating the last of the cookies, Carrie set them on three plastic plates, covered each with clear wrap and stuck a bright, frilly bow to the top.

"I want to deliver Arnold's," Doug told her. The oldest of her brothers had developed an interest in the former weight lifter. Arnold fit the stereotype. From his shiny bald head to his handlebar mustache and bulging muscles, everything about him said circus performer. Sometimes, as a concession to holidays or other special occasions, he even wore red spandex shorts over his blue tights. Doug was entranced.

"Will Maria let me pet her cats?" Dillon wanted to know.

"Of course she will."

"I guess that leaves me with Madame Frederick," Mackenzie said, not sounding disappointed. She cast a look toward the kitchen and Carrie guessed she wanted to make sure there'd be enough cookies left to take home to her father. Carrie had already made up a plate for the Larks, and told her so.

"Thanks," Mackenzie said, her eyes glowing.

All three disappeared, eager to deliver their gifts, and Carrie collapsed on the sofa. She rested her head against the cushion and closed her eyes, enjoying the peace and quiet. It didn't last long.

Doug barreled back in moments later, followed by Mackenzie. Dillon trailed behind.

"She's in here," Carrie heard her brother explain as he entered her apartment. Philip walked with him.

Carrie was immediately aware of how she must look. Flour had dusted more than the kitchen counters. She hadn't bothered with makeup that morning and had worn her grungiest jeans. She'd hardly ever felt more self-conscious in front of a man. She probably resembled a snowman—snow woman—only not so well dressed.

"Dad!" Mackenzie cried, delighted to see him.

Carrie stood and quickly removed the apron, certain the domestic look distracted from any slight air of sophistication she might still possess. Perhaps it was her imagination, but it seemed Philip's gaze zeroed in on her.

"I should've knocked," he said, and motioned to Dillon, "but your friend here insisted I come right in."

"Oh, that's fine." Each word seemed to stick to the roof of her mouth like paste. She clasped her hands together, remembering how uneasy her mother had been around Jason those first few times. Carrie had never understood that. Jason was the easiest person in the world to talk to.

Now she understood.

"Mackenzie behaved herself?" Once again the question was directed to Carrie.

"Dad!" Mackenzie burst out. "Way to embarrass me."

"She was a big help," Carrie assured him.

"Mom didn't call, did she?" Mackenzie advanced one step toward her father, her eyes hopeful.

Philip shook his head, and Carrie watched as disappointment settled over the girl. "She's really busy this time of year," Mackenzie explained to no one in particular. "I'm not surprised she didn't call, not with so much else on her mind…and everything."

Carrie resisted the urge to place her arm around Mackenzie's shoulders.

"How about a movie?" Philip suggested abruptly. "I can't remember the last time we went together."

"Really?" Mackenzie jerked her head up.

"Sure. Any one you want."

She mentioned the current Disney picture. "Can Doug and Dillon come, too?"

"Sure." Philip smiled affectionately at his daughter.

"And Carrie?"

"I…couldn't," she interjected before Philip could respond.

"Why not?" Doug asked. "You said we're all done with the cookies. A movie would be fun."

"You'd be welcome," Philip surprised her by adding. His eyes held hers and the offer appeared genuine. Apparently he felt that with three young chaperones, there wouldn't be a problem.

"You're positive?"

"Of course he is," Mackenzie said. "My father doesn't say things he doesn't mean, isn't that right, Dad?"

"Right." He sounded less confident this time.

Carrie was half tempted to let him take the kids on his own but changed her mind. Doug had a point; a movie would be a great way to relax after the hectic activity of the morning.

The five of them would be at the show together—and what could be more innocent? But the moment they entered the theater and had purchased their popcorn, the

three kids promptly found seats several rows away from
Philip and Carrie.

"But I thought we'd all sit together," Carrie said,
loudly enough for Doug and Dillon to hear. Desperation
echoed in her voice.

"That's for little kids," six-year-old Dillon turned
around to inform her.

With the theater filling up fast, the option of sitting
together soon disappeared. Carrie settled uneasily next to
Philip. Neither spoke. He didn't seem any happier about
this than she was.

"Do you want some popcorn?" Philip offered, tilting
the overflowing bucket in her direction.

"No, thanks," she whispered, and glanced at her watch,
wondering how much longer it would be before the movie
started. "I certainly hope you don't think I arranged this,"
she whispered.

"Arranged what?"

"The two of us sitting together." She'd hate to have him
accuse her of anything underhanded, which, given his
apparent penchant for casting blame, he was likely to do.
On the other hand, she was the one who'd unwittingly put
the matchmaking notion in Mackenzie's head. What a
fool she'd been not to realize the impressionable teenager
would pick up on the ploy she'd used on her own mother.

"Why would I blame you?" he asked, sounding exasperated.

"Might I remind you of our last conversation?" she
said stiffly. "You seemed to think there was some danger
of me, uh, seducing you."

Philip laughed out loud and didn't look the least bit
repentant. "It wasn't myself I was worried about," he
explained. "I was afraid of Mackenzie making both our

lives miserable. If I seemed rude earlier, I apologize, but I was protecting us from the wiles of my headstrong daughter."

That wasn't how Carrie remembered it....

"I'm not going to let my daughter do my courting for me," he said, as though that explained everything. "Now relax and enjoy the movie." He tilted the popcorn her way again, and this time Carrie helped herself.

The theater lights dimmed as twenty minutes of previews began.

Somewhat to Carrie's surprise, she loved the movie, which was an animated feature. She was soon completely immersed in the plot. Philip laughed in all the places she did and whatever tension existed between them melted away with their shared enjoyment.

When the movie ended, Carrie was sorry there wasn't more. While it was true that she'd enjoyed the story, she also found pleasure sitting with Philip. In fact, she liked him. She'd almost prefer to find something objectionable about him—a nervous habit, a personality trait she disliked, his attitude. *Something.* Anything that would distract from noticing how attractive he was.

He'd made it as plain as possible that he wasn't interested in a relationship with her. With anyone, if that was any comfort. It wasn't. She wanted him to be cold and standoffish, brusque and businesslike. The side of him she'd seen at the movie was laid-back and fun-loving. But she knew Philip hadn't developed a sudden desire to escort his daughter to the movies. He'd offered because of Mackenzie's disappointment over her mother's lack of sensitivity. He loved his daughter and wanted to protect her from the pain only a selfish parent could inflict on a child.

"This was a nice thing you did," she said as they exited

the theater. The kids raced on ahead of them toward the parking lot. "It helped take Mackenzie's mind off not hearing from her mother."

"I'm not so sure it was a good idea," he muttered, dumping the empty popcorn container in the garbage can on their way out the door.

"Why not?"

He turned and stared at her. "Because I find myself liking you."

Her reaction must have shone in her eyes, because his own narrowed fractionally. "You felt it, too, didn't you?"

She wanted to lie. But she couldn't. "Yes," she whispered.

"I'm not right for you," he said.

"In other words, I'm wrong for you."

He didn't answer her for a long time. "I don't want to hurt you, Carrie."

"Don't worry," she answered brightly, "I won't let you."

Five

"What do you think?" Mackenzie proudly held up a crochet hook with a lopsided snowflake dangling from it. "Carrie's whole tree is decorated with snowflakes she crocheted," she added. "Her grandma Manning taught her to crochet when she was about my age." She wound the thread around her index finger and awkwardly manipulated the hook.

"It's lovely, sweetheart."

"Mom'll be pleased, won't she." Mackenzie turned the question into a statement, so certain was she of his response.

"She'll be thrilled." Philip's jaw tightened at the mention of Laura. His ex-wife had contacted Mackenzie and arranged a time for their daughter to visit her. Ever since she'd heard from her mother, Mackenzie had been walking five feet off the ground. Philip didn't know what he'd do if Laura didn't show. He wouldn't put it past her, but he prayed she wouldn't do anything so cruel.

"Carrie's been great," Mackenzie continued. "She taught me everything." She paused long enough to look up at him. "I like her so much, Dad."

The hint was there and it wasn't subtle. The problem was that Philip had discovered that his feelings for Carrie were similar to those of his daughter. Although he avoided contact with Carrie, there was no escaping her. Mackenzie brought her name into every conversation, marching her virtues past him, one by one.

Carrie had become a real friend to Mackenzie. It used to be that his daughter moped about the apartment, complaining about missing her friends—although she spent plenty of time on the phone and the Internet with them—and generally making his life miserable. These days, if she wasn't with Carrie, she was helping Maria with her cats, having tea with Madame Frederick—and having the leaves read—or lifting weights with Arnold.

"I'm going to miss the Christmas party," she said matter-of-factly. "It's in the community room on Christmas Eve." She glanced up to be certain he was listening. "Everyone in the building's invited. Carrie's going, so is Madame Frederick and just everyone. It's going to be a blast." She sighed with heartfelt regret. "But being with Mom is more important than a party. She's really busy, you know," Mackenzie said, not for the first time.

"I'm sure she is," Philip muttered distractedly. He'd forgotten about the Christmas party. He'd received the notice a day or so earlier, and would've tossed it if Mackenzie hadn't gone into ecstasies when she saw it. From her reaction, one would think it was an invitation to the Christmas ball to meet a bachelor prince. As for him, he had better things to do than spend the evening with a group of friendly oddballs—and Carrie.

Philip reached for his car keys and his gym bag. "I'll only be gone an hour," he promised.

"It's okay. It'll take me that long to finish this." She

looked up. "Oh, I almost forgot," she said, putting everything aside and leaping out of the chair as if propelled
upward by a loose spring. She ran into her bedroom and
returned a moment later with a small white envelope.
"It's for you," she said, watching him eagerly. "Open it
now, okay?"

"Shouldn't I wait until Christmas?"

"No." She gestured for him to tear open the envelope.
Inside was a card in the shape of a silver bell.

"Go ahead and read it," she urged, and would have
done so herself if he hadn't acted promptly. The card was
an invitation to lunch at the corner deli. "I'm buying," she
insisted, "to thank you for being a great dad. We've had
our differences this year and I want you to know that no
matter what I say, I'll always love you."

"I feel the same way, and I don't tell you that enough,"
he murmured, touched by her words. "I'll be happy to pay
for lunch."

"No way," she said. "I've saved my allowance and did
a few odd jobs for Madame Frederick and Arnold. I can
afford it, as long as you don't order the most expensive
thing on the menu."

"I'll eat a big breakfast," he said and kissed her on the
cheek before he walked out the door. He pushed the
button for the elevator and caught himself grinning. He'd
been doing a lot more of that lately. In the beginning he
thought moving into the apartment had been a mistake.
No longer. The changes in Mackenzie since meeting
Carrie had been dramatic.

The elevator arrived and he stepped inside, pushing the
button for the lobby. It stopped on the next floor and
Carrie entered, carrying a laundry basket. She hesitated
when she saw he was the only other occupant.

"I don't bite," he assured her.

"That's what they all say," she teased back. She reached across him and pushed the button for the basement, then stepped back. The doors closed sluggishly. Finally the elevator started to move, its descent slow and methodical, then it lurched sharply, dropping several feet.

Carrie gasped and staggered against the wall.

Philip maintained his balance by bracing his shoulder against the side. Everything went dark.

"Philip?" Carrie inquired a moment later.

"I'm here." It was more than dark, it was pitch-black inside. Even straining his eyes, he couldn't see a thing. "Looks like there's been a power outage."

"Oh, dear." Her voice sounded small.

"Are you afraid of the dark?"

"Of course not," she returned indignantly. "Well, maybe just a little. Everyone is— I mean, it wouldn't be unusual under these circumstances to experience some anxiety."

"Of course," he agreed politely, putting his gym bag down beside him.

"How long will it take for the power to come back on?"

"I don't know." He shrugged, although he realized she couldn't see him. "Give me your hand."

"Why?" she snapped.

"I thought it would comfort you."

"Oh. Here," she murmured, but of course he couldn't see it. He thrust his arm out and their hands collided. She gripped his like a lifeline tossed over the side of a boat. Her fingers were cold as ice.

"Hey, there's nothing to be afraid of."

"I *know* that," she responded defensively.

He wasn't entirely sure who moved first, but before

another moment passed, he had his arm around her and was holding her protectively against him. He'd been thinking about this since the day they'd attended the movie. He hadn't allowed himself to dwell on the image, but it felt right to have her this close. More right than it should.

Neither spoke. He wasn't sure why; then again, he knew. For his own part, he didn't want reality interrupting his fantasy. Under the cover of the dark he could safely lower his guard. Carrie, he suspected, didn't speak for fear she'd reveal how truly frightened she was. Philip felt her tremble and welcomed the opportunity to bring her closer into his embrace.

"It won't be long."

"I hope so," she whispered back.

Without conscious thought, he wove his fingers into her hair. He loved the softness of it, the fresh, clean scent. He tried to concentrate on other things and found that he couldn't.

"Maybe we should talk," she suggested. "You know, to help pass the time."

"What do you want to talk about?" He could feel her breath against the side of his neck. Wistful and provocative. In that instant Philip knew he was going to kiss her. He was motivated by two equally strong impulses—need and curiosity. It'd been a long time since he'd held a woman. For longer than he wanted to remember, he'd kept any hint of desire tightly in check. He'd rather live a life of celibacy than risk another failed marriage.

He would've ended their embrace then and there if Carrie had offered any resistance. She didn't. Her lips were moist and warm. Welcoming. He moaned softly and she did, too.

"I thought you wanted to talk," she whispered.

"Later," he promised and kissed her again.

At first their kisses were light, intriguing, seductive. This wouldn't be happening if they weren't trapped in a dark elevator, Philip assured himself. He felt he should explain that, but couldn't stop kissing her long enough to form the words.

"Philip…"

He responded by brushing his moist lips against hers. His gut wrenched with sheer excitement at what they were doing.

Carrie wrapped her arms around his neck, clinging tightly. He eased her against the wall, kissing her ravenously.

That was when the lights came back on.

They both froze. It was as if they stood on a stage behind a curtain that was about to be raised, revealing them to a waiting audience.

But the electricity flashed off as quickly as it had come on.

Philip plastered himself against the wall, his hands loose at his sides as he struggled to deal with what they'd been doing. He wasn't a kid anymore, but he'd behaved like one—like a love-starved seventeen-year-old boy.

For the first time since his divorce, Philip felt the defenses around his heart begin to crack. The barriers had been fortified by his bitterness, by resentment, by fear. This—falling in love with Carrie—wasn't what he wanted. After the divorce, he'd vowed not to get involved again. Carrie was young and sweet and deserved a man who came without emotional scars and a child in tow.

He was grateful that the electricity hadn't returned; he needed these few additional minutes to compose himself.

"Are you all right?" he asked, when he could speak without betraying what he felt.

"I'm fine." Her voice contradicted her words. She sounded anything but.

He thought of apologizing, but he couldn't make himself say the words, afraid she'd guess the effect she'd had on him.

"You can't blame a guy for taking advantage of the dark, can you?" he asked, callously and deliberately making light of the exchange.

The electricity returned at precisely that moment. He squinted against the bright light. Carrie stood with her back against the wall opposite him, her fingers fanned out against the panel, her eyes stricken. The laundry basket rested in the far corner where she'd dropped it, clothing tumbled all around.

"Is that all this was to you?" she asked in a hurt whisper.

"Sure," he responded with a careless shrug. "Is it supposed to mean anything more?"

Before she could answer, the elevator stopped at the lobby floor and the doors opened. Philip was grateful for the chance to escape.

"Obviously not," she answered, but her eyes went blank and she stared past him. Then she leaned over and stabbed the basement button again. She crouched down to collect her laundry as he stepped out, clutching his gym bag.

He felt guilty and sad. He hadn't meant to hurt Carrie. She'd touched Mackenzie's life and his with her generosity of spirit.

Philip cursed himself for the fool he was.

"Go after her," a voice behind him advised.

Irritated, he turned to find Maria and Madame Frederick standing behind him.

"She's a good woman," Maria said, holding a fat calico cat on her arm, stroking its fur. "You won't find another like her."

"You could do worse." Madame Frederick chuckled. "The fact is, you already have."

"Would you two kindly stay out of my affairs?"

Both women looked taken aback by his gruff, cold response to their friendly advice.

"How rude!" the retired schoolteacher exclaimed.

"Never mind, dearie. Some men need more help than we can give them." Madame Frederick's words were pointed.

Disgusted with the two busybodies, and even more so with himself, Philip hurried out of the apartment building, determined that, from here on out, he was taking the stairs. Without exception.

Six

"Did I ever tell you about Randolf?" Madame Frederick asked as she poured Carrie a cup of tea the next Saturday morning. "We met when I was a girl. All right, I was twenty, but a naive twenty. I knew the moment our eyes met that I should fear for my virtue." She paused, her hand holding the lid of the teapot in place, her eyes caught in the loving memory of forty years past. Laughing softly, she continued. "We were married within a week of meeting. We both knew we were meant to be together. It was useless to fight fate."

"He was your husband?" Although Madame Frederick had obviously loved him deeply, she rarely talked about her marriage.

"Yes." She sighed. "The man who stole my heart. We had thirty happy years together. We fought like cats and dogs and we loved each other. Oh, how we loved each other. One look from that man could curl my toes. He could say to me with one glance what would take three hundred pages in a book."

Carrie added sugar to her tea and stirred. Her hand

trembled slightly as her mind drifted back to the kisses she'd shared with Philip in the elevator. She'd taken the stairs ever since. She'd been kissed before, plenty of times, but it had never felt like it had with Philip. What unsettled her was how perfectly she understood what her neighbor was saying about Randolf.

"I didn't remarry after he died," Madame Frederick said as she slipped into the chair next to Carrie. "My heart wouldn't let me." She reached for her teacup. "Not many women are as fortunate as I am to have found a love so great, and at such a tender age."

Carrie sipped her tea and struggled to concentrate on Madame Frederick's words, although her thoughts were on Philip—and his kisses. She wanted to push the memories out of her mind, but they refused to leave.

"I wanted to give you your Christmas present early," Madame Frederick announced and set a small, wrapped package in her lap.

"I have something for you, too, but I was going to wait until Christmas."

"I want you to open yours now."

The older woman watched as Carrie untied the gold ribbon and peeled away the paper. Inside the box was a small glass bowl filled with dried herbs and flowers. Despite the cellophane covering, she could smell the concoction. Potpourri? The scent reminded her a bit of sage.

"It's a fertility potion," Madame Frederick explained.

"Fertility!" Carrie nearly dropped the delicate bowl.

"Brew these leaves as a tea and—"

"Madame Frederick, I have no intention of getting pregnant anytime soon!"

The woman smiled and said nothing.

"I appreciate the gesture, really I do." She didn't

want her friend to think she wasn't grateful, but she had no plans to have a child within the foreseeable future. "I'm sure that at some point down the road I'll be brewing up this potion of yours." She took another drink of her tea and caught sight of the time. "Oh, dear," she said, rising quickly to her feet. "I'm supposed to be somewhere in five minutes." Mackenzie had generously offered to buy her lunch as a Christmas gift. Philip's daughter had written the invitation on a lovely card shaped like a silver bell.

"Thank you again, Madame Frederick," she said, downing the last of the tea. She carefully tucked the unwrapped Christmas gift in her purse and reached for her coat.

"Come and visit me again soon," Madame Frederick said.

"I will," Carrie promised. She enjoyed her time with her neighbor, although she generally didn't understand how Madame chose their topics of conversation. Her reminiscences about her long-dead husband had seemed a bit odd, especially the comment about fearing for her virtue. It was almost as if Madame Frederick knew what she and Philip had been doing in the darkened elevator. Her cheeks went red as she remembered the way she'd responded to him. There was no telling what might have happened had the lights not come on when they did.

Carrie hurried out of the apartment and down the wind-blown street to the deli on the corner. It was lovely of Mackenzie to ask her to lunch and to create such a special invitation.

The deli, a neighborhood favorite, was busy. Inside, she was greeted by a variety of mouthwatering smells. Patrons lined up next to a glass counter that displayed sliced meats, cheeses and tempting salads. The refrigerator case was decorated with a plastic swag of evergreen, dotted with tiny red berries.

"Over here!" Carrie heard Mackenzie's shout and glanced across the room to see the teenager on her feet, waving. The kid had been smart enough to claim a table, otherwise they might've ended up having to wait.

Carrie gestured back and made her way between the tables and chairs to meet her. Not until she reached the back of the room did she realize that Mackenzie wasn't alone.

Philip sat with his daughter. His eyes revealed his shock at seeing Carrie there, as well.

"Oh, good, I was afraid you were going to be late," Mackenzie said, handing her a menu. "Tell me what you want, and I'll get in line and order it."

Briefly Carrie toyed with the idea of canceling, but that would've disappointed Mackenzie, which she didn't want to do. Philip had apparently reached the same conclusion.

"Remember I'm on a limited budget," Mackenzie reminded them, speaking loudly to be heard over the hustle and bustle of the deli. "But you don't have to order peanut butter and jelly, either."

"I'll take a pastrami on whole wheat, hold the pickle, extra mustard."

Carrie set her menu aside. "Make that two."

"You like pastrami, too?" Mackenzie asked, making it sound incredible that two people actually found the same kind of sandwich to their liking.

"You'd better go line up," Philip advised his daughter.

"Okay, I'll be back before you know it." She smiled before she left, expertly weaving between tables.

Carrie unwound the wool scarf from her neck and

removed her jacket. She could be adult about this. While it was true that they hadn't expected to run into each other, she could cope.

The noise around them was almost deafening, but the silence between them seemed louder. When she couldn't stand it any longer, she said, "It's very sweet of Mackenzie to do this."

"Don't be fooled," he returned gruffly. "Mackenzie knew exactly what she was doing."

"And what was that?" Carrie hated to be defensive, but she didn't like his tone or his implication.

"She set this up so you and I would be forced to spend time together."

He made it sound like a fate worse than high taxes. "Come on, Philip, I'm not such a terrible person."

"As far as I'm concerned, that's the problem."

His words lifted her spirits. She took a bread stick from the tall glass in the middle of the table and broke it in half. "Are you suggesting I actually tempt you?" she asked.

"I wouldn't go that far, so don't flatter yourself."

"I'm not." She knew a bluff when she heard one. "If anyone should be flattered it's you. First, I'm at least eight years younger than you, with endless possibilities when it comes to finding myself a man. What makes you think I'd be interested in an ill-tempered, unfriendly, almost middle-aged grump?"

He blinked. "Ouch."

"Two can play *that* game, Philip."

"What game?"

"I almost believed you, you know. You were taking advantage of the dark? Really, you might've been a bit more original."

His eyes narrowed.

"But no one's that good an actor. You're attracted to me, but you're scared to let go of the rein you've got on your emotions. I'm not sure what your problem is, but my guess is that it has to do with your divorce. So be it. If you're content to spend the rest of your days alone, far be it from me to stop you." She took a bite of the bread stick, chomping down hard.

Mackenzie had their order. She carried the tray above her head as she reversed her previous journey among the tables. Her eyes were bright with excitement when she rejoined them.

She handed one thick ceramic plate to Carrie. "Pastrami on whole wheat, no pickle and extra mustard."

"Perfect," Carrie said, taking the plate from her. She was grateful Mackenzie had returned when she did, unsure she could continue her own bluff much longer. As it was, Philip had no opportunity to challenge her statement, which was exactly the way she wanted it.

Mackenzie distributed the rest of the sandwiches, set the tray aside and flopped down in the seat between Carrie and Philip. "Don't you just love the holidays?" she asked before biting into her sandwich.

Philip's eyes locked with Carrie's. "Sure do," he said, but Carrie saw that he was gritting his teeth.

From the way Philip tore into the sandwich, anyone would think he hadn't eaten in a week. It was as though they were taking part in a contest to see who'd finish first.

Philip won. The minute he swallowed the last bite, he stood, thanked his daughter and excused himself.

"He's going back to work," Mackenzie explained sadly as she watched her father leave. "He's *always* going back to the office."

"Inviting us both to lunch was very thoughtful of you,"

Carrie said, "but your father seems to think you asked us to suit your own purposes."

Mackenzie lowered her gaze. "All right, I did, but is that such a bad thing? I like you better than anyone. It's clear that my dad's never going to get married again without my help. My parents have been divorced for three years now and he's never even gone out on a real date."

"Mackenzie, your father needs time."

"Time? He's had more than enough time! He can't keep going through life like this. He's put everything on hold while he tries to forget what my mother did. I want him to marry you."

"Mackenzie!" Carrie exhaled sharply. She couldn't allow the girl to believe that dealing with human emotions was this simple. "I can't marry your father just because you want me to."

"Don't you like him?"

"Yes, I do, very much, but there's so much more to marriage than me liking your father."

"But he cares about you. I know he does, only he's afraid to let it show."

Carrie had already guessed as much, but that could be because she wanted to believe it so badly.

"My mom is really pretty," Mackenzie said, and she lowered her gaze to her hands, which clutched a paper napkin. "I think she might've been disappointed that I look more like my dad's side of the family than hers. She's never said anything, but I had the feeling maybe she would've stayed married to my dad if I'd been prettier."

"I'm sure that isn't true." Carrie's heart ached at the pain she heard in the girl's voice. "I used to feel those kinds of things, too. My dad never wanted anything to do with me. He never wrote or sent me a birthday gift or remembered me at Christmas, and I was convinced it was something I must have done."

Mackenzie raised her eyes. "But you were a little kid when your parents divorced."

"It didn't matter. I felt that somehow I was the one to blame. But it didn't have anything to do with me. And your parents didn't divorce because you took after your father's side of the family. Your parents' problems had nothing to do with you."

Mackenzie didn't say anything for a long moment. "This is why I want you to marry my dad. You make me feel better. In the past couple weeks you've been more of a mom to me than my real mother ever was."

Carrie reached out and silently squeezed Mackenzie's hand.

The girl squeezed back. "I didn't mention it last Saturday, but that was the first time I've ever baked homemade cookies. Dad helped me bake a cake once, but it came in a box."

Carrie had suspected as much.

"I like the way we can sit down and talk. You seem to understand what's in my heart," Mackenzie murmured. "I'm probably the only girl in my school who knows how to crochet, even though all I can do is those snowflakes. You taught me that. The house is going to be finished soon, and Dad and I are going to move away. I'm afraid that if you don't marry my dad, I'll never see you again. Won't you please, please marry my dad?"

"Oh, sweetheart," Carrie whispered and wrapped her arm around the girl's neck. She leaned forward, resting her forehead on Mackenzie's head. "It isn't as simple as that. Couldn't I just be your friend?"

Mackenzie sniffled and nodded. "Will you come visit me when we move?"

"You bet."

"But Madame Frederick says my dad's going to meet someone and—"

Carrie groaned inwardly. "Madame Frederick means well, and she's a dear, dear person, but I'm going to tell you something that's just between you and me."

"Okay." Mackenzie stared at her intently.

"Madame Frederick can't really see anything in that crystal ball of hers."

"But—"

"I know. She says what she thinks *should* happen or what she *hopes* will happen, and in doing so puts the idea in people's minds. If her predictions come true, it's because those people have steered the course of their lives in the direction she pointed."

"But she seems so sure of things."

"Her confidence is all part of the act."

"In other words," Mackenzie said after a thoughtful moment, "I shouldn't believe anything she tells me."

Seven

If Carrie hadn't seen it with her own eyes—and dozens of times at that—she wouldn't have believed any two boys could be so much like their father. Doug and Dillon sat on the sofa next to Jason, watching the Seahawks football game. Three pairs of feet, each clothed in white socks, were braced on the coffee table, crossed at the ankles. Jason had the remote control at his side, a bowl of popcorn in his lap. Each one of his sons held a smaller bowl. So intent were they on the hotly contested play-off game that they gave Carrie little more than a hurried nod of acknowledgment.

The sight of Jason with his sons never ceased to amaze her. The boys were all Manning, too. Smaller versions of their father in both looks and temperament.

Carrie found her mother in the kitchen, whipping up a batch of fudge for the Manning family pre-Christmas get-together. "Carrie, this is a pleasant surprise." Charlotte's face relaxed into a smile when she saw her daughter.

"I came for some motherly advice," Carrie admitted, seeing no need to tiptoe around the reason for her impromptu visit. She'd left Mackenzie less than an hour before and hadn't been able to stop thinking about their conversation, or about Philip's reaction to her being there. It was as though he couldn't escape fast enough.

"What's up?" Charlotte stirred the melted chocolate.

Carrie pulled a padded stool over to the countertop where her mother was working. "I'm afraid I'm falling in love."

"Afraid?"

"Yes." She'd purposely chosen that word. That was exactly the way she felt about it.

"This wouldn't have anything to do with your friend Mackenzie, would it?"

Carrie nodded, surprised her mother even knew about the thirteen-year-old girl. But the boys must have said something. "Do you remember how it was when you first started dating Jason?" she asked.

Her mother paused and a hint of a smile lifted the edges of her mouth. "I'm not likely to forget. I wasn't sure I wanted anything to do with the man, while you were busy inventing excuses to throw us together."

"You really weren't interested in him at first?"

Charlotte chuckled softly. "That's putting it mildly, but gradually he won me over. He was endlessly patient...."

Carrie realized there was a lot more that her mother wasn't telling her. She'd long suspected that in the early days, her mother's relationship with Jason had been anything but smooth.

Charlotte resumed stirring. "As I said, his patience won me over. His patience and his drop-dead kisses," she amended. "If ever a man had a talent for kissing, it's your stepfather." She grinned shyly and looked away.

"Philip has the same gift," Carrie whispered, feeling a bit shy about sharing this aspect of their relationship with her mother.

Charlotte didn't say anything for a long moment. "So you've been seeing Mackenzie's father."

"Not as much as I'd like," she said. "He's been divorced for three years and according to Mackenzie he hasn't gone out on a single date." She assumed that well-meaning friends had tried to set him up. His own daughter had made the effort, too. With Carrie.

"So he comes with a load of emotional trauma. Has he ever talked about what went wrong in his marriage?"

"No." Carrie hated to admit how little time they'd spent together. Feeding Maria's homeless cats was as close as they'd come to an actual date. She wasn't sure how to measure the time in the elevator. Although she'd managed to make him think his callous attitude afterward hadn't fooled her, in truth she didn't know what his reaction had been.

"You're afraid he's coming to mean more to you than is sensible, after so short an acquaintance."

"Exactly. But, Mom, he's constantly on my mind. I go to bed at night, close my eyes and he's there. I get up in the morning and take the bus to the office and all I can think about is him."

"He's attracted to you?"

"I think so.... I don't know anymore. My guess is that he is, but he's fighting it. He doesn't *want* to care for me. He'd rather I lived across the city—or the country—than in the same building with him. We try to avoid each other—we probably wouldn't see each other at all if it wasn't for Mackenzie. The girl's made it her mission in life to make sure we do."

Charlotte dumped the warm fudge into a buttered cookie sheet. "This is beginning to sound familiar."

"In what way?"

Charlotte giggled. "Oh, Carrie, how soon you forget. You're the one who pushed, pulled and shoved me into a relationship with Jason. It would've been horrible if he was a different kind of man. But he was patient and nonthreatening. Like Philip, I came into the relationship with more than my share of emotional trauma. But he was exactly the man I needed. You've always been a sensitive, intuitive child. Out of all the men you might have picked for me, you chose the one man who possessed the qualities I needed most." She reached over and stroked the side of Carrie's face, her expression warm and tender. "In my heart of hearts, I'm confident you've done the same thing for yourself. Philip needs you just as much as I needed Jason. Be patient with him, Carrie. Your heart—and your ego—may take a few jabs before this is finished. Be prepared for that, but don't be afraid to love him. Mackenzie, too. I promise you, it'll be worth the wait."

How wise her mother was, Carrie mused as she left the family home. How wise and wonderful. Not for the first time, Carrie was grateful for a mother she could talk to, a mother she could confide in, a mother who didn't judge, but listened and advised.

"What are you doing here?" Gene Tarkington asked, stepping into Philip's office. He leaned against the doorjamb, striking a relaxed pose. The entire floor was empty. Row upon row of desks stretched across the floor outside his office.

"I thought I'd come in and run these figures one last time," Philip murmured, staring at the computer screen. Although he considered Gene one of his best friends, he'd prefer to be alone just then.

"Hey, buddy, it's almost Christmas. Haven't you got anything better to do than stop by the office?"

"What about you?" Philip challenged. He wasn't the only workaholic in this company.

"I came to get some papers and saw the light on in your office. I thought you were having lunch with Mackenzie this afternoon. A little father-daughter tête-à-tête. That kid's a real sweetheart."

"We had our lunch," Philip muttered, "but it turns out I wasn't the only one Mackenzie invited."

"You mean she brought along that neighbor friend of yours? The woman who works for Microsoft?"

"That's her." Philip frowned anew, remembering how upset he'd been when he discovered what Mackenzie had done. From the way she'd acted, he should've guessed she'd try something like this. What distressed him even more was the way his heart had responded when Carrie walked into the deli. The joy and excitement he'd felt...

But he didn't want to feel these things for her. It'd taken effort to steel himself against those very emotions. He'd been burned once, badly enough to know better than to play with fire. Carrie Weston wasn't some little innocent, either. Every time he was with her, he felt as if he was holding a book of matches.

"Mackenzie's pretty levelheaded. What have you got against this neighbor woman? She's not ugly, is she?"

"No." He recalled what a shock it was when he realized how lovely Carrie was.

"If you want my opinion, I'd say count your blessings. Generally, the divorced guys I know would welcome a woman their daughters like. Remember what happened to Cal? His daughter and second wife hate each other.

Any time they're out together, Cal has to keep them from coming to blows."

"I'm not Cal."

"It seems to me that if your daughter's that keen on this neighbor, you should take the time to find out what she likes so much. I'm no expert on women or romance, but—"

"My thoughts exactly," Philip said pointedly. He'd come to the office to escape Carrie, not to have her name thrown in his face. "I appreciate what you're trying to do."

Gene rubbed the side of his face. "I doubt that. But I hate to see you wasting time in this office when Christmas is only a few days away. If you want to hide, there are better places than here."

Although Gene's tone was friendly enough, the words made Philip's jaw tighten. It was all he could do to keep from blaming his friend for his troubles. Gene owned the apartment complex, and it was because of him that Philip and Mackenzie were living there.

"Well, I've got to get back to the car. Marilyn's waiting. You know how it is the last weekend before Christmas. The malls are a madhouse and naturally my wife thinks this is the perfect time to finish the shopping. She wouldn't dream of going alone. I told her there should be a Husband of the Year award in this for me," he said, and chuckled. "But she promised me another kind of reward." From the contented, anticipatory look on his friend's face, one would think Gene was headed for the final game of the World Series, not a shopping mall.

"See you later," Philip said.

"Later," Gene returned. "Just promise me you won't stay here long."

"I won't."

Gene left, and the office had never seemed emptier.

The place seemed to echo with loneliness, a constant reminder that Philip was by himself. His friend was right; it was almost Christmas, yet he was at the office hiding. While Gene was out fighting the Christmas crowds with his wife, Philip had crept in here, the way he always did whenever life threatened to offer him something he couldn't handle. Even a gift.

Because that was what Gene had more or less told him Carrie was. A woman Mackenzie not only liked, but championed. Like Gene, lots of guys would advise him to count his blessings. But instead of thanking his daughter for lunch, he'd chastised her for using it as an opportunity to get him together with Carrie.

Carrie.

Every time he thought of her, a chill raced through his blood. No, that wasn't it. His blood didn't go *cold*, it heated up. Carrie was charming, generous, delightful, kind—and more of a mother to his daughter than her own had ever been.

Philip rolled his chair away from his desk, stood and walked over to the large picture window. The view of downtown Seattle and Puget Sound was spectacular from his twentieth-story viewpoint. Breathtaking. The waterfront, the ferry dock, Pike Place Market, all alive with activity. Philip couldn't count the number of times he'd stood exactly where he was now and looked out and seen nothing, felt nothing.

He went back to his desk and turned off his computer, feeling more confused than when he'd arrived. It was a sad day, he thought wryly, when he was reduced to accepting his thirteen-year-old daughter's advice, but in this case, Mackenzie was right. She'd told him to get a life. Instead, Philip had dug himself deeper into his rut, fearing that any life he got would include putting the past behind him. It wasn't that the past held any allure for him. The reverse, in fact. He'd married too young, unwisely. He was terrified of repeating the same mistake. Terrified of what that would do to him—and Mackenzie.

Locking up, Philip went back to the apartment building. He parked in the garage across the street and was just walking toward the entrance when he saw Carrie. There was a natural buoyancy to her step, a joy that radiated from inside her. He sometimes wondered what she had to be so happy about. That no longer concerned him, because he wanted whatever it was.

"Carrie!" Unsure what he'd say when he caught up with her, Philip hurried across the street.

Carrie paused midway up the steps and turned around. Some of the happiness left her eyes when she saw him. She waited until he'd reached her before she spoke. "I had no idea Mackenzie had invited us both to lunch," she told him.

"I know that," he said, regretting his angry mood earlier.

"You do?"

Every time he saw her it was a shock to realize how beautiful she was. Her intense blue eyes cut straight through him. "I was wondering… I know it's last-minute and you've probably got other plans, but…" He paused. "Would you go Christmas shopping with me?" He was afraid that if he invited her to dinner or a movie she'd turn him down and he wouldn't blame her. "For Mackenzie," he said, adding incentive. "I could do with a few suggestions."

His invitation had apparently taken her by surprise because she frowned at him before asking, "When?"

"Is now convenient?" he asked hopefully. He was as

crazy as his friend Gene to even consider going shopping today.

"Now," she repeated, then smiled, that soft, sweet smile of hers. "Okay."

Okay. It was crazy how one small word could produce such exhilaration. If this were the theater, he'd break into song about now. A Christmas carol maybe—something like "Joy to the World."

She walked down the three or four steps to join him on the sidewalk. That little bounce of hers was back. The bounce that said she was glad to be alive and glad to be with him.

He was the one who should be grateful, Philip thought. He tucked her arm in his and led her back to the parking garage.

Life was good. It had been a long time since he'd believed that, but he did now.

Eight

A few hours earlier, Carrie had been telling her mother that she barely knew Philip Lark and now she doubted there was any man she knew better. They sat in an Italian restaurant, Christmas packages around their feet, and talked until it seemed there was nothing more to say. Their dinner dishes had long since been removed and Philip poured the last of the red wine into her goblet.

The room swayed gently from side to side, but her light-headedness wasn't due to the pinot noir. Philip was the reason. He'd told her things she'd felt it would take him months if not years to reveal. He'd spoken of his marriage and his feelings about fatherhood. She listened, a lump in her throat, as he heaped the blame for the failure of his marriage on his own shoulders. She doubted very much that he was entirely responsible, but she admired his gallantry.

"You're friends with Laura?" she asked at one point.

"Yes. Beyond anything else, she's Mackenzie's mother. I made mistakes in this marriage, but my daughter wasn't one of them. I'll always be grateful to my ex-wife for Mackenzie."

Tears formed in the corners of Carrie's eyes at the sincerity with which he spoke. How easy it would be for him to blame his ex-wife for all their problems. Carrie was sympathetic to his side, and knew from things Mackenzie had told her that Laura wasn't exactly a loving or attentive mother. Carrie suspected she hadn't been much of a wife, either.

"What are you doing tomorrow?" Philip asked unexpectedly.

"Sunday." Carrie propped her elbows on the white linen tablecloth. "The Mannings are getting together. Mom and I married into this large, wonderful family. Jason has four brothers and sisters. There are so many grandchildren these days it's difficult to keep track of who belongs to whom. Why don't you and Mackenzie come along and meet everyone?" Carrie couldn't believe she'd impulsively tossed out the invitation. While she did want him to attend, there'd certainly be speculation....

"You're sure?"

"Positive. Just... Never mind," she said, stopping herself. Her gaze held his. "It would mean a great deal to me if you'd come."

"Then we will." He reached for her hand with both of his.

Philip had given up the effort of remembering everyone's names. He'd cataloged the first ten or so relatives Carrie had introduced him to, but the others became lost in the maze.

Mackenzie had disappeared almost the minute they arrived. Doug and Dillon had greeted him cheerfully and then quickly vanished with his daughter. Holding a cup of eggnog, Philip found himself a quiet corner.

From this vantage point, he watched Carrie interact with her family. His eyes followed her as she moved across the room, apparently to find her mother so she could introduce her parents to Philip. He couldn't take his eyes off Carrie. Her face was flushed with happiness, her eyes glowing with excitement. She'd married into this family, but it was clear they thought of her as one of their own.

"Do you mind if I join you?" a woman unexpectedly asked him.

"Please do." He stood to offer her his seat.

"No, no. Sit down, please. I can only stay a moment. You're Philip, aren't you?"

"Yes. Philip Lark." The dark-haired beauty had to be Carrie's mother. "You're Charlotte Manning?"

"How perceptive of you. Yes." She held out her hand, which he shook.

He was astonished that he hadn't recognized the resemblance sooner. Charlotte and Carrie had the same intense blue eyes, the same joyous energy and a gentleness of spirit that was unmistakable.

They spoke for a few minutes about unimportant matters. Small talk. Although Philip had the impression he was being checked out, he also had the feeling that he'd passed muster. He liked Charlotte, which made sense, since he definitely liked Carrie.

"So this is Carrie's young man." Charlotte's husband, Jason Manning, joined his wife and slipped his arm around her waist. "Welcome. Where's Carrie? She's left you to fend for yourself?"

"I gather she went in search of you two."

The three of them spoke for a while before Jason glanced over his shoulder and called out, "Paul, come and meet Carrie's friend."

Soon a large group had gathered around Philip, more faces than he could ever remember. He stood and shook hands with Carrie's two uncles. Once again he felt their scrutiny.

Soon a loud, "Ho, ho, ho," could be heard in the background. Jason's father had donned a Santa suit and now paraded into the room, a bag of gifts swung over his shoulder. The children let out cries of glee and crowded around Santa.

Philip was grateful that everyone had begun to watch the scene taking place with Santa Claus. He sat down in his chair again and relaxed, grateful not to be the center of attention. Soon Carrie was with him. She sat on the arm and cast him an apologetic look.

"Sorry, I got sidetracked."

"So I saw." He patted her hand. "I met your stepfather and two uncles."

"Aren't they great?" Her eyes gleamed with pride.

"I need a degree in math to keep track of who's married to whom."

"Don't worry, it'll come. Be thankful not everyone's here."

"You mean there are even more?"

Carrie grinned and nodded. "Taylor and Christy both live in Montana. Between them they have six children."

"My goodness." Adding ten more names to his list would have overwhelmed him. "Mackenzie certainly seems to fit right in."

"Doug and Dillon think she's the best thing since cookie-dough ice cream. Knowing her gives them the edge over their cousins."

While the youngsters gathered around their grandfather in his red suit, Mackenzie made her way toward him and Carrie. Philip understood. At thirteen she was too old to mingle with the kids who believed in Santa Claus, and too young not to be caught up in the excitement, even though Santa wouldn't have a gift for her.

"Are you having fun?" Philip whispered when she sat down on the chair's other arm, across from Carrie.

"This is so great," she whispered. "I didn't know families could get this big. Everyone's so friendly."

Santa dug deep into his bag, produced a package and called out the name. Doug leaped to his feet and raced forward as if he had only a limited amount of time to collect his prize.

Santa reached inside his bag again and removed another gift. "What's this?" he asked, lowering his glasses to read the tag. "This is for someone named Mackenzie Lark. I do hope Mrs. Claus didn't mix up the gifts with those of another family."

"Mackenzie's here!" Dillon shouted. He stood and pointed toward Philip and Carrie.

"Me?" Mackenzie slid off the chair. "There's a gift in there for *me*?"

"If your name's Mackenzie, then I'd say this present is for you."

His daughter didn't need a second invitation. She hurried over to Santa, as eager as Doug had been.

Philip's questioning gaze sought out Carrie's. "I'm sure my mother's responsible for this," she told him.

"I met her," he said. "We talked briefly."

Carrie's eyes widened. "What did she have to say?"

"She was very pleasant. It was your stepfather who put the fear of God into me."

"Jason? Oh, dear. Listen, whatever he said, disregard it. He means well and I love him to death, but half the time he's thinking about sports statistics and he doesn't know what he's saying."

Philip smiled. He'd never seen Carrie more unnerved. Even when they were trapped in the elevator, she'd displayed more composure than this.

"Carrie, good grief, what do you think he said?"

She clamped her mouth shut. "I—I'm not sure, but it would be just like him to suggest you take the plunge and marry me."

"Oh, that, well…"

"Are you telling me he actually—"

Philip had to make an effort not to laugh out loud. "He didn't, so don't worry about it."

Mackenzie had claimed her gift and was walking back, clutching the package in both hands.

"You can open it," Carrie assured her.

"Now?" She tore into the wrapping as though she couldn't wait a second longer. Inside was an elegant vanity mirror with a brush and comb set. "It's perfect," she whispered, holding the brush and comb against her. "I've always wanted one of these sets. It's so…so feminine."

"How'd your family know?" Philip asked. He'd never have thought to buy something like this for his daughter.

"I have one," Carrie whispered. "She's used it a number of times."

"Oh." More and more he felt inadequate when it came to understanding his daughter. She was in that awkward stage, and it was difficult to know exactly where her interests lay. Half the time she talked about wanting a horse and ballet lessons; the rest of the time she listened to music he'd never heard before and gossiped about celebrities who seemed completely irrelevant to him. Part girl, part woman, Mackenzie traveled uneasily from one desire to the next. It wasn't just her interests that confused him, either. One minute she'd be her lighthearted self and the next she'd be in tears over something he considered trivial. He wished Laura had taken more interest in her. Often he felt at a loss in dealing with Mackenzie's frequent mood swings.

Philip had enjoyed himself, but he was exhausted and felt relieved when the party ended. He thanked the elder Mannings for having him and Mackenzie.

"You're welcome anytime," Elizabeth Manning said, clasping his hand between both of her own. In what seemed an impulsive gesture, she leaned forward and kissed his cheek. "You'd be a welcome addition to our family," she whispered in his ear. "Just promise me one thing?"

"What's that?" he asked.

"I want a nice, big wedding," she said, this time loudly enough for half the room to hear.

Philip heard a murmur of approval behind him. "Ah…"

"Thanks again, Grandma," Carrie said, saving him from having to come up with a response.

Carrie hugged the older couple and led the way outside. Jason, Charlotte, Doug and Dillon followed them to the driveway for a second round of hugs and farewells. This had to be one of the most outwardly affectionate families Philip had ever met, but it didn't bother him. The opposite, in fact. He liked everything about them. These were good people, hardworking and family-oriented. He'd never seen himself in that light, although it was what he wanted to be. However, neither he nor Laura had been raised that way.

They sang Christmas carols on the drive home. Carrie's voice blended smoothly with that of his daughter. His own was a bit rough from disuse and slightly off-key, but no one seemed to mind, least of all Mackenzie, whose happiness spilled over like fizz in a soda bottle. He parked in the garage and they walked across the street to the apartment building, still laughing and chattering excitedly.

"I had a wonderful time," his daughter told Carrie, hugging her close as they waited for the elevator.

"I did, too."

"I'm so glad your family get-together was tonight instead of tomorrow. I'll be with my mother, you know."

"I do," Carrie said. "You'll miss the party here, but I'll tell you all about it."

"Do you think Madame Frederick will made a prediction for me, even if I'm not there?"

"I'm sure she will," Carrie answered.

"She'll have to make one for me in absentia, as well," Philip said.

"You aren't coming?" This news appeared to catch Carrie by surprise. She'd asked him about the Christmas party earlier and he'd managed to avoid answering one way or the other.

"No," he said, pushing the button to close the elevator door.

"But I thought… I hoped…" Her disappointment was evident.

Philip didn't want to say anything negative, but as far as he was concerned, the majority of people living in the building complex were oddballs and eccentrics. He didn't have anything against them, but he didn't want to socialize with them, either.

"Talk him into it," Mackenzie said when the elevator stopped on Carrie's floor.

He wished now that he hadn't said anything. "Would you like a cup of coffee?" Carrie asked.

What he'd like was time alone with Carrie.

"Sure he would," Mackenzie answered for him, and shoved him out of the elevator. The doors closed before he could respond.

"I guess I would," he said, chuckling.

Carrie's eyes shyly met his. "I was hoping you would."

She unlocked her door and walked inside, but he stopped her from turning on the light. With his hand at her shoulder, he guided her into his arms. "I've been waiting for this all night," he whispered and claimed her lips.

He meant it to be a soft, gentle kiss. One that would tell her he'd enjoyed her company, enjoyed their evening together. But the minute his mouth settled over hers he experienced a desire so strong it was all he could do to keep it in check. No woman had ever affected him like this. He wove his fingers into her hair and tilted her head to one side in order to deepen their kisses.

She groaned softly. Then again, it could be the sound of his own pleasure that rang in his ears. The hot, breathless kisses went on. And on...

"Why won't you come to the party tomorrow night?" she asked minutes later.

The building's Christmas party was the last thing on Philip's mind. He led her through the darkened living room, sat down and drew her into his lap. "Let's talk about that later, all right?" He didn't give her time to say anything, but directed her lips back to his.

"Why later?" She nibbled the side of his neck, sending delicious shivers down his back.

"I'm not sure I trust Madame Frederick."

She laughed and he felt her breath against his skin. "She's completely harmless."

"So they say." He placed his hands on either side of

her face and brought her lips down to meet his again. The kiss was long and deep, and it left him breathless.

"The people in this building are a bunch of oddballs. Half of them are candidates for the loony bin," he said when he'd recovered sufficiently to speak.

Carrie stiffened in his arms. "You're talking about my friends."

"No offense," he said. But surely she recognized the truth when she heard it.

Carrie squirmed out of his lap and stood in front of him. "I live in this apartment complex. Is that how you think about me?"

"No." He sighed. "If it means so much to you, I'll attend this ridiculous party."

"No, thanks," she muttered. "I wouldn't want you to do me any favors."

From her tone of voice, Philip realized he'd managed to offend her, which he regretted. Yesterday's conversation with Gene had made him understand that she was a blessing in his life. A gift.

A gift he wanted to accept…

"Carrie, I'm sorry. I spoke out of turn."

"Is that what you really think of us, Philip?" she asked, her voice uncertain.

He didn't respond right away, afraid anything more he said would only make things worse.

"That's answer enough. I'm tired…. I'd like you to leave now."

"Carrie, for heaven's sake, be reasonable."

She stalked over to the door and opened it, sending a harsh shaft of light across his face. Philip squinted and did as she asked. "We'll talk about this later, all right?"

"Sure," she said in a sarcastic murmur.

Rather than wait for the elevator, Philip took the stairs to his apartment a floor above Carrie's. He'd discuss this with Mackenzie, get her advice on how to handle it. Ironic that he was turning to his thirteen-year-old daughter for help with the very situation she'd engineered....

The apartment was dark and silent when he entered. He switched on the light and walked down the hall to Mackenzie's bedroom. Her bed was slightly mussed as if she'd sat on it.

"Mackenzie!" he called.

No response.

He checked the other rooms and found a note from her on the kitchen table.

Dad,
Mom left me a message. She said she wouldn't be coming for me, after all, and that I couldn't spend the holidays with her. I guess I should've known she'd be too busy for me. She has time for everything else but me. I need some time alone to think.
                                                          Mackenzie

Nine

Carrie didn't understand why Philip's comment about Madame Frederick and the others had distressed her so much. While it was true they were her friends, she couldn't deny that they *were* all a bit weird. But they were also affectionate, warmhearted people and it hurt to have Philip dismiss them with such carelessness. She was still figuring out her feelings when there was a knock at the door. Whoever it was seemed impatient, because there was another knock immediately afterward.

"Just a moment," she called out.

To her surprise it was Philip. "Have you seen Mackenzie?" he demanded.

"Not since we returned from the party."

He exhaled and rubbed his hand along the back of his neck. "Her mother left a message for her saying she won't be bringing Mackenzie to her place for Christmas after all," he explained.

Carrie saw a muscle beside his jaw jerk with the effort it took to control his anger.

"She was looking forward to spending Christmas

with Laura," he continued. "It was all Mackenzie could talk about."

Carrie knew that. She'd spent time with the girl, discussing her hairstyle and wardrobe for the impending visit. Mackenzie had wanted everything to be perfect for her mother. She'd wanted to impress Laura with how grown-up she was, how stylish. She'd wanted to make herself as attractive as possible, hoping her mother would notice and approve.

"Mackenzie wrote me a note that said she needed time alone." He checked his watch, something Carrie knew he'd probably done every five minutes since discovering the note. "That was an hour ago. Where on earth would she go?"

"I don't know," Carrie whispered. Her heart constricted as she imagined the pain the girl must be suffering. These few days with Laura had meant so much to Mackenzie.

"I thought maybe she'd come to you." He shook his head. "I've tried her cell, but it's off. I've called her girl-friends, but none of them have heard from her. Now I don't know where to look. Think, Carrie."

"She probably doesn't want to be around people just yet," she murmured, trying to clear her head of worry and fear in order to be of help.

Philip nodded. "Do you think she went for a walk? Alone in the dark?" He cringed as he said the words.

"I'll go out with you to look."

His eyes told her he was grateful. Carrie grabbed her coat and purse, and they both rushed out of the building.

Soon after she'd graduated from high school, when Carrie was eighteen, she'd decided to seek out her father. It had been a mistake. He'd seemed to think she wanted something from him, and in retrospect, she knew she had. She'd wanted him to love her, wanted him to tell her how proud he was of the woman she'd become. It had taken her the better part of a year to realize that Tom Weston was selfish and immature and incapable of giving her anything. Even his approval.

In the five years she'd known Jason Manning, at that point, he'd been far more of a father than her biological one would ever know how to be. She hadn't had any contact with Tom Weston since. It had hurt that the man responsible for her birth wanted nothing to do with her, but after a few months she'd accepted his decision. If anything, she appreciated his honesty, hurtful as it'd been at the time.

Not really knowing where they were going, they walked quickly from one spot to another, trying to guess where Mackenzie might have gone. Their fears mounted, but they both struggled to hide them. Instead, they offered each other reassurances neither believed.

"I hate to think of her out in the cold, alone and in pain," Philip finally murmured, his hands in his coat pockets.

"Me, too." The cold air stung her cheeks.

"I could hate Laura for doing this to her," Philip said defiantly, "but I refuse to waste the energy. She can treat me any way she pleases, but not Mackenzie."

Carrie knew it was pointless to remind him that he had no control over his ex-wife. Laura would behave as she chose.

"Perhaps I should've said something to Mackenzie," Philip was saying, "warned her not to count on anything her mother promised. I didn't because, well, because I didn't want Mackenzie to think I'd try to influence how she thinks about her mother."

"I find that admirable. And wise."

"I don't feel either of those things just now." His voice revealed his anger and frustration.

"Mackenzie's smart enough to figure out what her mother's really like. She won't need you or me to tell her," Carrie said.

His eyes met hers under a streetlamp decorated with silver bells. "I hope you're right."

They searched everywhere they could think of, without success. By the time they returned home, it was almost midnight. The building was dark and silent, alarming them even more.

"You don't think she'd do anything stupid, do you?" a worried Philip asked. "Like run away and find her mother on her own?"

"I...don't know."

When they stepped into the lobby, Carrie noticed that the door leading to the basement party room was open. As she came closer, she could hear voices below.

"Let's check it out," Philip suggested.

Carrie followed him down the stairs. As they descended, the sound of voices became more distinct. She recognized Madame Frederick, chatting away with Arnold. Carrie guessed they were putting the finishing touches on the decorations for the Christmas party, which was to take place the following night.

They found Mackenzie busy pinning green and red streamers in the center of the ceiling, fanning them out to the corners. The girl didn't so much as blink when she saw Carrie and Philip.

"Oh, hi, Dad. Hi, Carrie," she said, climbing down from her chair.

"Just where have you been, young lady?" Philip demanded gruffly.

Carrie placed her hand on his arm, pleading with him to display less anger and more compassion. She felt some of the tension leave his muscles and knew it took a great deal of determination not to cross the room and hug the teenager fiercely.

"Sorry, Dad. I forgot to tell you where I was."

"I've been searching for hours! Then Carrie helped me look. We walked through the whole neighborhood."

"Sorry," Mackenzie returned contritely. "I sat in here by myself for a while, then these guys came down to decorate and—" she shrugged "—I decided to pitch in."

"Are you okay?" Carrie asked. "I mean, about not being able to spend the holiday with your mother?"

Mackenzie hesitated and her lower lip trembled slightly. "I'm disappointed, but then as Madame Frederick said, 'Time wounds all heels.'" She laughed and wiped her forearm under her nose. "Mom's got to make her own decisions about what role I'll play in her life. All I can do is give her the freedom to choose. I've got my dad and my friends." Her gaze moved about the room, pausing on each person.

Arnold was there with his spandex shorts and twinkling eyes. Madame Frederick with her crystal ball and her sometimes corny wisdom. Maria with her tenderhearted care for the neighborhood's cats. And, Carrie realized, she was there, too. They were Mackenzie's friends.

The girl wrapped her arms around her father's waist and hid her face in his chest. "I'll be here for the party," she said. "But you don't have to come, Dad. I'll understand."

"I want to come," he said, his eyes on Carrie. He held out his hand to her and their fingers locked together. "It takes moments like this for a man to recognize how fortunate he is to be blessed with good friends."

Mackenzie smiled and glanced over her shoulder at Madame Frederick.

"What did I tell you?" the older woman said, smiling just as broadly. "The crystal ball sees all."

"It didn't help me decide which mutual fund to invest in," Arnold reminded her. "And it didn't help me pick the winning lottery numbers, either. You can take that crystal ball of yours and store it in a pile of cow manure."

"I told you it wouldn't help you for personal gain," Madame Frederick said with more than a hint of defensiveness.

"What good is that silly thing if it doesn't make your friends rich?"

"It serves its purpose," Philip surprised everyone by responding. He slid his arm around his daughter's shoulders. "Now, I'd say we've had enough excitement for one evening, wouldn't you?"

Mackenzie nodded. "Night, everyone."

"Good night," Arnold called.

"Sleep well," Madame Frederick sang out.

"Good night, sweetie. You stop by and visit me tomorrow, you hear?" Maria said.

"I will," Mackenzie promised.

Carrie left with Philip and his daughter. "I'm baking cookies for the party in the morning," she said when the elevator reached her floor.

"Do you need any help?" Mackenzie asked eagerly. "You won't have to worry about eggshells getting in the dough this time."

"I'd love it if you came by."

Content that all was well, Carrie entered her apartment and got ready for bed. As she slipped on her nightgown, the phone rang. It was Philip.

"I know I was with you less than ten minutes ago, but I wanted to thank you."

"For what? I didn't do anything." She'd shared his helplessness in searching for Mackenzie, his frustration and anger.

"You helped me find my daughter—in more ways than one."

"No, your love for her did that."

"I was wrong about your friends."

She'd wondered how long it would take him to admit that.

"They're as terrific as you are." He paused. "Not spending time with her mother was a big blow to Mackenzie. She was devastated when Laura put her off once again. I don't know what Madame Frederick really said, but it was obviously what Mackenzie needed to hear. For all her strangeness, Madame has good instincts about people."

"You're a fast learner."

Philip's amusement echoed over the phone line. "Don't kid yourself. I was with the slow reading group in first grade. I'm not exactly a speed demon when it comes to relationships, either. My marriage is a prime example."

"You'll come to the Christmas party?"

"With bells on." He chuckled. "The thing is, I'll probably fit right in."

Epilogue

Six months later

"This is the most exciting day of my life!" Mackenzie declared, waltzing around the small dressing room in her slender full-length pale green dress. A wreath of spring flowers adorned her head. "You're actually going to be my stepmother, just like Madame Frederick said."

Only Carrie and Mackenzie were still in the room, as Carrie made her final preparations.

"It's an exciting day for me, too." Carrie pressed her hands against her stomach to calm her jittery nerves. The church was full of family and friends, waiting for her to make her appearance. Jason, dressed in a tuxedo, would soon escort her down the aisle. Her step-aunts, Christy and Taylor, were also in her wedding party, and so were her two closest friends from college. Gene was Philip's best man.

"Dad was so cute this morning," Mackenzie said, laughing. "I thought he was going to throw up his breakfast. He's so much in love he can hardly eat."

Carrie closed her eyes. She hadn't even attempted

breakfast, and applauded Philip for making the effort. As for being in love, she was crazy about him and Mackenzie. This day was a dream come true, worthy of the finest fairy tale.

"Madame Frederick, Maria and Arnold are here, and lots of people from the office," Mackenzie said, peering out at the church. "I didn't think that many people knew my dad." Gracefully she waltzed her way around Carrie. "You're going to be the most beautiful bride ever. That's what Dad said, and he's right."

"Thank you, sweetie."

"It's extra-special that you're letting me be in the wedding party. Not everyone would do that. My first wedding," she said, and her eyes held a dreamy, faraway look.

"You're a good friend, Mackenzie."

"You probably wouldn't be marrying my dad if it wasn't for me," Mackenzie reminded her in a low voice. "But then, Madame Frederick's the one who gave me the idea, so I guess I should give her the credit."

"Remember what I told you about Madame Frederick and her crystal ball."

"I remember. It's just that you and Dad really do seem perfect for each other. Madame Frederick couldn't have known that."

"I'm pleased *you* think so."

"If I were to pick someone to be my mother, I'd choose *you*." Her eyes grew dark. "My dad needs you almost as much as I do. You're perfect for both of us. I'd rather spend time with you than anyone, except for Les Williams." She sighed deeply. "But then, Les doesn't know I'm alive."

"Don't be so sure of that."

"Are you two ready?" Jason called from outside the dressing room.

Carrie drew in a breath. "Ready as I'll ever be."

Mackenzie handed her the bouquet and Carrie opened the door. Jason was working his black tie back and forth in an effort to loosen it. He stopped in midaction and his jaw sagged.

"You…you look lovely."

"Don't act so surprised," Carrie teased.

"You look so much like your mother on our wedding day, it's hard to believe. I can't get over it…."

Mackenzie threw her a smile and hurried to join the wedding party for the procession down the aisle.

"Be happy," Jason said, his voice suspiciously low. He tucked her hand in the crook of his arm.

When Carrie glanced his way, she noticed a sheen of tears in his eyes.

"You'll always be my daughter," he murmured, fidgeting with his tie again. "I couldn't be prouder of you than I am right this minute."

"Thanks, Dad," she whispered.

They stood at the back of the church and waited for their cue, which came when Mendelssohn's "Wedding March" began. Carrie took a step forward. Toward Philip. Toward love. Toward their life together.

* * * * *

THE PERFECT HOLIDAY

Sherryl Woods

Dear Friends,

Christmas is one of my very favorite times of the year. Any time I'm asked to write a story about this season of joy and great hope, I'm eager to do it. "The Perfect Holiday" was written a few years ago, and I'm absolutely delighted it's going to find a whole new audience in the company of two of my favorite authors, Debbie Macomber and Robyn Carr.

For many years now I've spent my own holidays in Miami, which doesn't exactly fit the image of an ideal holiday setting. Yes, for you doubters, we do have Christmas here, but it's definitely not the white Christmas of my dreams. So where better to set a Christmas story than an inn in Vermont? Add in the workaholic owner of a toy factory who's never really learned how to play and a single mom struggling to get back on her feet. Then stir in a bit of matchmaking by a doting aunt—from beyond the grave, no less—and you have the makings of a very romantic holiday…the perfect holiday, in fact.

I hope you'll enjoy spending time with Savannah and Trace this holiday season, and that your own holidays will be touched by magic, as well.

Merry Christmas to all!

Sheryl Woods

best she could say about that was that it hadn't

One

"Mom, it's snowing," Hannah shouted from the living room.

Savannah heard the pounding of her daughter's footsteps on the wood floors, then the eight-year-old skidded to a stop in front of her, eyes shining.

"Can I go outside? *Please?*" Hannah begged. "This is so cool. I've never seen snow before."

"I know," Savannah told her, amused despite herself. "We don't get a lot of snow in Florida."

"Wait till my friends back home hear we're going to have a white Christmas. It is *so* awesome. I am *sooo* glad we moved to Vermont."

Though she could understand her daughter's excited reaction to her first snowfall, from Savannah's perspective the snow was anything but a blessing. Since her arrival a couple of days ago, she'd discovered that the furnace at Holiday Retreat wasn't reliable. The wind had a nasty way of sneaking in through all sorts of unexpected cracks in the insulation, and the roof—well, the best she could say about that was that it hadn't fallen in on their heads…yet. With the weight of a foot of damp snow on it, who knew what could happen?

It had been three weeks since the call had come from the attorney informing her that she was a beneficiary of her aunt Mae's estate. The bittersweet news had come the day before Thanksgiving, and for the first time since her divorce the year before, Savannah had thought she finally had something for which to be thankful besides her feisty, incredible daughter. Now that she'd seen the inn, she was beginning to wonder if this wasn't just another of Fate's cruel jokes.

Holiday Retreat had been in the family for generations. Built in the early 1800s as a home for a wealthy ancestor, the huge, gracious house in the heart of Vermont ski country had become an inn when the family had fallen on hard times. Savannah could still remember coming here as a child and thinking it was like a Christmas fantasy, with the lights on the eaves and in the branches of the evergreens outside, a fire blazing in the living room and the aroma of banana-nut bread and cookies drifting from the kitchen. The tree, which they cut down themselves and decorated on Christmas Eve, always scraped the twelve-foot ceiling.

Aunt Mae—Savannah's great-aunt actually—had been in her prime then. A hearty fifty-something, she came from sturdy New England stock. She had bustled through the house making everyone in the family feel welcome, fixing elaborate meals effortlessly and singing carols boisterously, if a bit tunelessly. It was the one time of the year when there were no paying guests at the inn—just aunts and uncles and cousins all gathered for holiday festivities. To an only child like Savannah, the atmosphere had seemed magical.

If the house had been in a state of disrepair then and if

the furniture had been shabby, she hadn't noticed it. Now it promised to be one of the world's worst money pits.

"Mom, did you hear me?" Hannah said again. "I said it's snowing."

"I heard," Savannah said glumly.

Hannah's blue eyes were alight with excitement. "Isn't it great?"

Savannah tried to work up some enthusiasm to match her daughter's, but all she could think about was the probability that too much snow would make the sagging roof plummet down on top of their heads as they slept. Still, she forced a smile.

"There's nothing like a white Christmas," she agreed.

"Can we get a tree and make hot chocolate and sing carols like you used to do when you were a kid?" Hannah pleaded. "Then it won't matter if we don't have any presents."

Savannah cringed at the realistic assessment of their financial plight. The divorce had left her with next to nothing. Her ex-husband hadn't yet been persuaded to send even the paltry child support payments required by the court. As for alimony, she had a hunch hell would freeze over before she saw a penny of that. Since their divorce had hinged on her objections to his workaholic tendencies, Rob clearly saw no reason she should benefit from the income derived from those tendencies.

Last night, after Hannah had gone to bed, Savannah had sat for hours with her checkbook, a pile of final bills from Florida and a list of the repairs needed before the inn could be opened to paying guests in the new year. Her conclusion had left her feeling more despondent than ever. It was going to take more than a glistening snowfall and a few carols to brighten her spirits.

No matter how hard she tried telling herself that they were better off than they had been, she still wasn't totally convinced. Maybe if they'd stayed in Florida, she would have found a better-paying job, something that wouldn't have left them scraping by after making house payments and buying groceries. At least they wouldn't have had to worry about the kind of exorbitant heating bill from last winter that she'd found in a kitchen drawer here. Maybe selling the heavily mortgaged house that had been her home with Rob had been another error in judgment. It had given her barely enough cash to make the trip and to make a start on the repairs the inn needed.

"Mom, what's wrong?" Hannah asked. "Are you afraid we made a mistake?"

Seeing the concern that filled her daughter's eyes and the worried crease in her forehead, Savannah shook off her fears. Hannah deserved better than the hand she'd been dealt up to now. For the first time since the divorce, she was acting like a kid again. Savannah refused to let her own worries steal that from her daughter.

"Absolutely not!" she said emphatically. "I think coming here was exactly the right thing to do. We're going to make it work. How many people get to live in a place that looks like a picture on a Christmas card?"

She gave her daughter a fierce hug. "How about some hot chocolate?"

"Then can we go out in the snow?" Hannah pleaded.

"Tell you what—why don't you bundle up in your new winter jacket and go outside for a few minutes so you can see what it feels like? I'll call you when the hot chocolate's ready."

Hannah shook her head. "No, Mom, I want you to come, too. Please."

Savannah thought of all she had to do, then dismissed it. It was only a few days till Christmas. Most of the contractors she'd spoken to said they couldn't come by till after the first of the year. Until she and Hannah made a trip into the small town at the foot of the mountain, she couldn't strip the old wallpaper or paint. Why not think of this as an unexpected gift of time?

"Okay, kiddo, let's do it," she said, grabbing her coat off a hook by the door. "Only for a few minutes, though. We're going to need some heavy boots, wool scarves and thick gloves before we spend much time outside. We don't want to start the new year with frostbite."

"Whatever," Hannah said, tugging her out the door, seemingly oblivious to the blast of icy air that greeted them and froze their breath.

There was an inch of damp, heavy snow on the ground and clinging to the towering evergreens already, and it was still falling steadily. With no chains or snow tires on the car, they'd be lucky if they got out of the driveway for a couple of days, Savannah concluded, sinking back into gloominess.

Then she caught the awed expression on Hannah's face as she tilted her head up and caught snowflakes on her tongue. She remembered doing the exact same thing the first time she'd visited Aunt Mae and seen snow. She'd been even younger than Hannah, and for several years the Christmas trips to Vermont had been the highlight of her life. She couldn't recall why they'd stopped coming as a family.

She'd come on her own several times after she was grown, but those visits had dwindled off when she'd met, then married, Rob. He was a Florida boy through and through and flatly refused to visit anyplace where the temperature dropped below the midfifties.

Now that Aunt Mae was gone, Savannah deeply regretted not having done more than write an occasional letter enclosing pictures of Hannah. Her aunt had never once judged her, though, and she'd been totally supportive when Savannah had told her about the breakup of her marriage. She'd sent one check explained away as a birthday gift and offered more, but Savannah had turned her down. She'd lied and said they were getting along okay, but she knew now that her aunt had seen through her. She had done in death what Savannah hadn't permitted her to do while she was living.

If other members of her family resented the gesture, Savannah didn't know about it. She'd lost touch with most of them years ago. She'd been estranged from her parents ever since she'd divorced a man of whom they enthusiastically approved. Aunt Mae had tried to broker a peace agreement between Savannah and her father, but he'd remained stubbornly silent and unyielding. He'd been convinced Savannah was a fool for divorcing a man who brought home a steady paycheck.

"Mom, I love it here!" Hannah announced, throwing her arms around Savannah. She was shivering even in her heavy coat. "I want to build a snowman. Can we?"

"I think we'll need a little more snow than this," Savannah told her. "Besides, I'm freezing. How about that hot chocolate?"

"I want to stay out here. I'm not cold," Hannah insisted.

"Then why are your teeth chattering?" Savannah teased. "Come on, baby. Even if you won't admit to freezing, I will. There will be more snow once we've warmed up. I'll teach you how to make snow angels."

"What are snow angels?" Hannah asked, her interest immediately piqued.

"You'll see. Aunt Mae taught me when I was a little girl. Now come inside and get warm."

Far more agreeable lately than she had been for months, Hannah finally acquiesced, following Savannah into the kitchen. Savannah studied her daughter's sparkling eyes, pink cheeks and tousled hair and knew she'd done the right thing, no matter what struggles might lie ahead.

Despite the sad state of the inn, they were going to have the fresh beginning they both deserved, she decided with a surge of determination. And it was going to start with the very best Christmas Hannah had ever had, even if she was going to have to do it on a shoestring. Some of her very best holiday memories had cost nothing.

As for the practicalities—the repairs, the marketing plan she needed to devise—they would just have to wait for the new year.

Mae Holiday had been one of the most eccentric people Trace Franklin had ever known. He had met her when he'd been dragged to Vermont for an idyllic summer getaway by one of the women he'd dated. That had been eight or nine years ago. Twice that number of women had passed through his life since then. Of them all, the one he hadn't dated—Mae—had been the most memorable.

She'd been the grandmother he'd never had, the mentor who tried her best to bring some balance into his life. Until the day she'd died at seventy-eight, it had frustrated her no end that she hadn't managed to convince him that romance was just as important as money.

Trace knew better. His parents had been madly in love, but it hadn't brought either one of them a blasted thing except heartache. Love had kept his mother with a man who never had two nickels to rub together, a man whose big killing was always "just around the corner."

While John Franklin had spun his dreams, his wife had cleaned houses, worked in fast-food chains and, finally, when it was almost too late to matter, gotten a steady job selling toys to families that could afford to give their kids elaborate backyard swing sets and fancy computer games.

When Trace was fifteen, his mom had brought one of those games home to him, but by then he'd been way past playing childish games. He'd been working with single-minded focus on graduating from high school with honors and getting a scholarship to the best college in the state. He didn't want to play with toys. He wanted to own a whole blasted toy company.

And now he did. The irony, which Mae had seen right away, was that he still didn't have time to play. He wasn't even sure he knew how.

He was driving along the snow-covered roads of Vermont right now because of Mae. On his last visit to see her at the end of October, she had made a final request. She had known she was dying, had known it for fully a year before the cancer had finally taken her, but she hadn't said a word to Trace until that last visit when she had detailed her losing battle, reciting the facts with a stoicism and acceptance that had awed him.

"I want you to promise me something," she had said as they'd sat in front of the fire on his last night there. Despite the heat of the blaze, she'd been wrapped in blankets, and still she had shivered.

"Anything," Trace had responded, and meant it. Not only was Mae one of the earliest investors and biggest stockholders in Franklin Toys, she was his friend.

"I want you to spend Christmas here at Holiday Retreat."

It was only a couple of months away and it would require some juggling of his schedule, but there was no question that he would do it. "Of course I will," he said at once. "We'll have a wonderful time."

She had squeezed his hand. "I won't be here, Trace. You know that."

Even now, the memory of that moment brought the sharp sting of tears to his eyes. Her gaze had been unrelenting. From the beginning of her illness, she had refused to sugarcoat the truth to herself. Now that she was revealing it to others, she expected them to face it, as well. The cancer had spread too far and too fast before the doctors had had the first inkling there was anything wrong. She was dying and there was going to be no reprieve.

Trace had returned her unflinching gaze, heartbroken yet unable to face her death with less bravery than she was showing. "Why, Mae? Why would you want me here after you're gone?"

"Just do it for me," she whispered, her voice fading. "Promise."

"I promise," he'd said just as her eyes drifted closed. He'd been willing to do anything that would give her comfort. He owed her that much, and more.

Two weeks later Mae Holiday had died peacefully, a lifelong friend—a man she had loved deeply but never married—by her side. Now Trace was on his way to Vermont to pay his respects…and to keep his promise.

Two

There was smoke curling from the chimney at Holiday Retreat. Lights were blazing from the downstairs windows. Trace sat in his car and stared, trying to make sense of it. He'd expected to spend the Christmas holiday alone here, mourning Mae in private, reliving the happy times they'd spent together over the years they'd known each other.

And, he conceded with a rueful grimace, catching up on the mounds of paperwork he'd brought with him, along with his cell phone, laptop computer and fax machine.

What the dickens was going on? he wondered, thoroughly disgruntled by this turn of events. Mae had said nothing about anyone else being here. Nor had the attorney in the note that had accompanied a key to the inn. The note had merely advised that Mae had seen to having plenty of food and firewood on hand and that she hoped his visit would be a memorable one. If he had any problems, he was to contact Nate Daniels, the man Trace had heard of, but never met, the man who was the shadowy love of Mae's life.

Trace fingered the old-fashioned key in his pocket as he walked through the foot or so of recently accumulated snow. He was halfway to the door when he spotted indentations, a hectic swirl of footsteps and something else. He looked more closely and saw…not one but two snow angels, the sort made by flopping down in new-fallen snow and moving outstretched arms to create wings.

At first the sight brought a smile, reminding him of innocent, long-ago days as a kid before the unpredictability of the family's day-to-day existence had registered with him. Winters back home had been relatively mild, so that rare snowfalls had been regarded with sheer delight. He hadn't owned a sled, but he'd had his share of snowball fights and made more than a few snow angels.

Then the full implication of the snow angels sank in, and pleasant memories gave way to edginess. Judging from the smaller size of one snow angel, there was a kid on the premises and that generally meant noisy chaos, the last thing he'd anticipated when he'd made the commitment to Mae to spend the Christmas holidays here. For a man who made his living by providing expensive hobbies and toys to children, Trace was amazingly uneasy when confronted with an individual child. For him, toys were a multimillion-dollar business, not entertainment. Unless he could persuade himself to use whatever child was around to conduct market research, this whole situation had just gone from bad to worse.

He was about to turn tail and run, but then he heard Mae's voice in his head as she'd extracted that promise from him. He'd never gone back on his word to her, ever. He wasn't about to start now.

Filled with a sense of dread, he made his way to the front door. He stood on the slick porch debating whether to ring the bell, rather than walking in on whomever was here. Then again, he had just as much right to be here as the unknown occupant did. More, perhaps. That remained to be seen.

He stuck the key in the lock, turned it and pushed open the heavy door, noting as he did that it was in serious need of paint. It had once been bright red, as had all the shutters on the house. Now it was faded to a shade only slightly deeper than pink. Maybe he'd take care of that while he was here. It would be a fitting homage to Mae to see the doors and shutters restored to their scarlet holiday brilliance.

He was about to close the door when a girl—just about the size of the snow angel outside, he noted—skidded to a stop in front of him on one of the scooters his company made. It had been the hottest gift of the holiday season two years ago. It was not meant to be used indoors, though he could understand the temptation given the wide expanse of hardwood floors. And it wasn't as if those floors were in particularly great shape. They could do with sanding and a fresh coat of wax. Something else he could do while he was here…in Mae's memory.

First, though, he had to figure out who was this imp of a child regarding him with blatant curiosity, her golden hair scooped through the opening of a baseball cap, her T-shirt half in and half out of her jeans.

"Who are you and what are you doing here?" he demanded in the no-nonsense tone he used on executives who'd failed to deliver on their division's projections.

The kid didn't even flinch. "I'm Hannah and I live here. Who are you? And how come you have a key to my house?"

Trace's head began to throb. What the devil was Mae up to? "Are your parents here?"

"Just my mom. My dad divorced us. He lives in Florida. My mom's baking Christmas cookies." She cast an appealing smile at him. "Don't they smell great?"

Trace automatically sniffed the air. They did smell fantastic, just the way Mae's always had. He'd eaten fancier food than what was served at Holiday Retreat, but he'd never had any that tasted better or was prepared with more love. He wondered if Hannah's mom shared Mae's talents in the kitchen, then sighed. That was hardly the point.

"Want me to get my mom?" Hannah inquired.

"I'll find her," Trace said, heading determinedly toward the kitchen. He'd taken only a step before he turned back. "By the way, that scooter is not an indoor toy."

The kid's smile never faltered. "Maybe not, but it works great in here." And off she went, completely unimpressed by his admonishment.

Trace sighed and went in search of her mother.

He wasn't sure what he expected, but it certainly wasn't the frail wisp of a woman who was bent over in an incredibly provocative pose, her head stuck halfway into the huge, professional-quality stainless-steel oven that had been Mae's pride and joy.

This room was where Mae had splurged, spending her money to design a kitchen that was both welcoming and efficient. Everything in it, from the refrigerator to the granite countertops, was top-of-the-line. When she had shown it to Trace a few years ago, she'd been as excited as a kid on Christmas morning. She told him it was how she'd spent her first dividends from her stock in Franklin Toys.

And now there was an interloper in here, he thought, feeling oddly possessive on Mae's behalf. Unless this woman could prove her right to be on the premises, Trace would have her packed up and out of here before nightfall, even if he had to call on local law enforcement to toss her out on her attractive backside.

Despite his impatience to accomplish that task, and rather than risk scaring her half to death while she was that close to incinerating herself, he waited, barely resisting the desire to haul her out of there immediately and demand an explanation for her presence.

Of course, he was also having some difficulty resisting the urge to smooth his hand over that narrow curve of her denim-clad bottom. That, he concluded, was a very dangerous temptation. He admonished himself to forget it the same way he'd scolded Hannah only moments earlier. He hoped he paid more attention to the warning than she had, since there was likely a lot more at stake than scarred floorboards.

The woman finally retreated, holding a tray almost as big as she was. As she turned to set it on the granite countertop, she spotted him and let go of the tray with a yelp of surprise. Trace caught it in midair, then let out a curse of his own as the hot metal seared his fingers. He dropped the tray with a clatter. Cookies went flying. And the woman regarded him as if he were a living, breathing embodiment of Scrooge and he'd deliberately set out to ruin her Christmas.

"Look what you've done," she said, scowling at him as she bent to pick up the broken remains of sugar cookies decorated with pretty red and green designs. She waved a hatless Santa with half a beard under Trace's nose. "Just look at this."

She didn't seem one bit concerned with the fact that he'd burned himself trying to save her blasted cookies. He stepped past her and stuck his hands under cold running water. That finally got her attention.

"Oh, fudge, you burned yourself, didn't you?" she said. "What was I thinking? I'm sorry. Here, let me see."

She nudged up against him and grabbed his hand. Her touch was anything but soothing. In fact, now Trace was suddenly burning on the inside, too.

"Sit," she ordered before he could unscramble his thoughts. "There's a first-aid kit around here somewhere."

"Cabinet next to the stove," Trace told her, blowing on his fingers.

She stopped and stared. "How do you know that?"

"Mae was always getting distracted and having little accidents in the kitchen. She said it paid to keep the bandages close at hand."

Rather than fetching the first-aid supplies, the woman sank down onto a chair, her eyes promptly filling with unshed tears. "She did say that, didn't she?" she whispered. "I must have heard her say it a hundred times. And even before she remodeled in here, she kept aloe and antiseptic spray and bandages right by the stove."

Trace was startled by the depth of emotion in this stranger's voice. Her love for Mae was written all over her face. That much raw pain was more than he knew how to deal with; his own emotions were shaky enough. He stepped carefully around her and got his own ointment and bandages, using the time to collect himself and try to fill with renewed resolve the tiny chink she'd created in his desire to be rid of her.

When he was finished repairing the damage to his hand, he finally risked another look at her. The color had returned to her cheeks, but there was no mistaking the signs of a woman on the edge. He'd seen that same stressed expression often enough on his mother's face, the same tightness around the mouth, the wariness in her eyes.

"You okay?" he asked at last.

She nodded, still blinking back tears. "Sometimes it just catches me off guard, the fact that she's gone. I hadn't seen her in several years, but I always had such wonderful memories of being here, especially around the holidays."

That must have been a long time ago, Trace thought with a surprising surge of anger on Mae's behalf. He'd been here with Mae every year since that trip when they'd first met. He'd never been entirely sure how she'd cajoled him into coming, but year after year he'd found himself driving north from New York City, looking forward to spending time with the closest thing he had to family now that his folks were both dead.

Oddly, on none of those trips had he ever caught a glimpse of the man in Mae's life. Only at the end had she explained why, that Nate had his own family responsibilities, duties that he had never once shirked through all the years they had loved each other. It had been an unconventional love—an impossible love—she had explained to Trace. The man's wife had suffered a nervous breakdown years before, when his children were little more than toddlers. Nate could never bring himself to divorce her during all the long, lonely years when he'd struggled as a single dad, watching his wife's mind deteriorate degree by degree. He had been the rock that held his family together…and the other half of Mae's soul. If she regretted anything about their long, secret affair, she never once complained of it to Trace. And it had certainly never soured her on the possibilities of romance.

It was little wonder, though, that Mae had sought out Trace's company around the holidays, he had realized as she told him the story. The loneliness at a season meant for sharing with family and friends must have been unbearable. Trace wondered if this woman even knew about that part of Mae's life.

"If you hadn't been here for years, why are you here now?" Trace asked, unable to hide the note of bitterness in his voice. "Did you come to pick over her belongings?"

She seemed startled by the hostility in the question— or maybe by the fact that he thought he had the right to ask it. "I'm here because my aunt left Holiday Retreat to me," she said eventually. "Not that it's any of your business, but I'm Savannah Holiday. Mae was my grandfather's sister. And you are? How did you get in here, anyway?" She sighed. "Hannah, I suppose. I've told her and told her about not opening the door to strangers."

It didn't seem to occur to Savannah Holiday that it had taken her a long time to get around to asking about his identity. In New York, the police would probably have been called the second he appeared in the kitchen doorway and the answers to all those questions could have been sorted out later.

"I'm Trace Franklin," he said. "A friend of Mae's." He retrieved the key from his pocket and plunked it on the table where it glinted in the sunlight. "And I got in with this, though I did see your daughter as I came in."

She stared at the key. "Where did you get that?"

"From your aunt."

"Why would she give you a key to Holiday Retreat?"

"Because she'd invited me here for the holidays." He was only now beginning to grasp just how diabolical that invitation had been. His finding the alluring Savannah Holiday and her daughter underfoot was clearly no accident, but Mae's last-ditch effort at matchmaking. He wondered if Savannah Holiday had figured out what her aunt was up to.

He regarded his unexpected housemate with a wry expression. "Merry Christmas!"

Three

Compared to the man sitting across from her with his cool, flinty gaze and designer wardrobe, Savannah felt like a dowdy waif. She was pretty sure there was flour in her hair and, more than likely, red and green sprinkles on her nose. When it came to baking, she did it with more enthusiasm than tidiness or expertise. The results were equally unpredictable, though she'd been particularly proud of the batch of golden cookies that were currently lying in crumbles around her feet.

She regarded this interloper with caution, in part at least because his presence rattled her. She'd felt a little flicker of awareness the instant he'd entered the kitchen. At first she'd attributed it to surprise, but then she'd realized it was a whole lot more like the sensation she'd experienced the first time she'd met Rob. It was the caught-off-guard, heart-stopping reaction of a woman to a virile, attractive male...or a doe when confronted by a rifle-toting hunter. She was stunned to discover that she was even remotely susceptible to a man after the bitterness of her divorce, especially to a man wearing the clothes of a business executive to a country inn. It was something her uptight ex-husband would have done.

Because her reaction made her uneasy, she focused on the one topic guaranteed to take her mind off it. "You said Mae invited you here. You do know that my aunt died, right?" she asked.

"Yes."

His expression was almost as bleak as the one Savannah saw in the mirror every morning. "But you came anyway," she said, impressed despite the instinct that told her this man was anything but sentimental.

"It's what she wanted," he said simply. "I promised I would."

"And you always keep your promises?"

"I try," he said. "I don't make that many, and the ones I do make mean something."

"What about your family? Won't they miss you over the holidays?"

"In recent years Mae was the closest thing I had to family. What about *your* family?"

"Hannah's here. For all intents and purposes, she's all I have. My husband and I divorced a year ago." She hesitated, then added, "My parents and I aren't on speaking terms at the moment."

"I see."

She was grateful that he didn't bombard her with a lot of questions about that. "How did you know Mae? Forgive me, but you don't look as if you spend a lot of time in the country."

He laughed at that, and it transformed his face. The tight lines around his mouth eased. His dark eyes sparkled. "What gave me away?"

"The clothes, for starters. I'm amazed you stayed

upright walking from the car to the house in those shoes. I don't think snow is kind to Italian leather. And I can't imagine that you'd be able to spend more than a few minutes outdoors before freezing in that shirt. Men around here tend toward flannel."

"But I think the real secret is what they wear under it," he said, barely containing what promised to be a wicked grin.

Savannah's thoughts automatically veered off in a very dangerous direction. She had the oddest desire to strip off his clothes to see if there were practical long johns underneath. She'd never thought that sort of men's underwear to be particularly sexy, but she imagined Trace Franklin could do amazing things for the look.

"You're blushing," he said, regarding her with amusement.

"Well, of course I am! I hardly know you, and here we are discussing underwear."

"It can be a fascinating topic, especially if we move from cotton to satin and lace."

She frowned at him. "You're deliberately trying to rattle me, aren't you?"

"Why would I do that?" he asked, trying for a serious expression. The twinkle in his gray eyes betrayed him.

"I can't imagine, especially when all I was trying to find out was what drew a city man like you to spend time in a country retreat." She studied him thoughtfully, then said, "There must have been a woman involved."

"Bingo. The woman who brought me here years ago was envisioning a quiet, romantic getaway with long hikes through the woods." He shrugged and gave her a beguilingly sheepish look. "Instead I spent the weekend holed up in Mae's study with my computer and fax machine taking care of a business crisis."

Savannah immediately felt a surprising empathy for the woman. "Now, *that* I can imagine. Your friend must have been disappointed."

"Dreadfully."

"What sort of business?"

"I own a company in New York," he said in such a dismissive way that it sparked her curiosity.

"Franklin," Savannah recalled thoughtfully. "Not Franklin Toys, by any chance?"

He seemed startled that she'd grasped it so quickly. "That's the one. How on earth did you figure that out?"

"There were some articles about that company on Mae's desk. Obviously she kept up with it."

"I imagine so," he said, his expression noncommittal.

"Because she knew you from your visits here?" Savannah persisted, sensing there was more.

He shrugged. "That was the start of her interest, I suppose."

She frowned at his evasiveness. "What aren't you saying?"

"What makes you think I'm leaving something out?"

"Instinct."

"Okay, then, here's the whole story in a nutshell. I suppose I owe you that, since I've shown up on your doorstep out of the blue," he said. "Your aunt was the one who encouraged me to start the company. I'd been with another toy manufacturer for a few years. I'd learned all I could, and I had a lot of ideas for ways to do it better. Mae was an early investor in Franklin Toys. Over the years she and I made a lot of money together, but I owe every bit of that success to her initial encouragement."

"I see," Savannah said slowly. "So that first trip here wasn't a waste of your time after all. Did your relationship with the woman last?"

"Only for as long as it took me to get her back to her apartment in New York that Sunday night," he said with no hint of regret. "My friendship with Mae lasted much longer."

"Then you came back here often?" she asked, feeling a vague sense of regret and guilt that he'd spent these last years with her aunt, when she should have been the one spending time here.

"As frequently as I could," he said. "Your aunt was a remarkable woman. I enjoyed my visits with her."

"Even if she did live essentially in the middle of nowhere," Savannah said, needing to remind herself that this man bore way too many resemblances to her ex-husband.

"Funny thing about that," he said, picking up one of the few sugar cookies they'd managed to salvage and breaking off a bite. "I got used to the peace and quiet. And the phone lines, fax and Internet connections work just fine."

"So even though you're here for the holidays, I suppose you brought all of your equipment along," she guessed.

"Of course."

Savannah shook her head. "I hope you watch your cholesterol. Anybody who's as much of a workaholic as you appear to be is clearly a heart attack waiting to happen."

"I'll try not to have one while I'm here," he promised solemnly.

"Thank you for that. I'm afraid I don't have the kind of insurance it would take to cover your medical expenses if you collapse and fall down the stairs."

He grinned. "I do."

"Well, then, I suppose you can stay," she said grudgingly, thinking of the extra work involved in having a guest in a house that was all but falling down around them.

He regarded her with a wry expression. "I had no intention of doing anything else."

"You'll have to pitch in and help," she said, deliberately ignoring his remark. "I'm afraid the inn isn't officially ready for guests again."

"I'm not a guest—not the way you mean, anyway. And I came expecting to take care of myself. The attorney said the refrigerator would be stocked, and I brought along plenty of food from the city."

"Caviar, I imagine," she said, feeling strangely testy at the thought of sharing the house with a man whose tastes, like Rob's, probably ran to the expensive and exotic. "Maybe some imported Stilton cheese? Smoked salmon? The finer things you absolutely couldn't live without?"

His grin spread. "Junk food, if you must know."

Once again, Savannah felt the full effects of that devastating smile. She hoped he wouldn't do it too often. It might make her forget that he was completely unsuitable for a woman who'd already been burned by a man who put his work before his family.

"What exactly do you consider junk food?" she asked.

"Potato chips. Popcorn." He leaned closer and lowered his voice to confide, "I also have a cooler filled with chocolate mocha almond ice cream. I'm addicted to the stuff."

Her eyes widened. Chocolate mocha almond was an indulgence she rarely allowed herself. Aside from the calories, the brand she loved was outrageously expensive. She'd developed a taste for it during her marriage, but had had to forgo it since the divorce. The store brands simply didn't live up to the gourmet ice cream. She had a hunch that cooler of Trace's was stocked with the best.

"Exactly how much ice cream did you bring?" she asked, hoping it sounded like a purely casual inquiry.

"Enough for you and Hannah…if you're good," he teased.

"When it comes to chocolate mocha almond, I can eat a lot," she warned him.

He surveyed her slowly, appreciatively, then shook his head. "Not as much as I can," he said. "And I brought enough for a week. I'll make you a deal. If you let me share in whatever you're fixing for Christmas dinner, I'll provide dessert."

"But that's three days away," Savannah protested.

He winked. "I know. Patience is a virtue."

"Another of Mae's favorite sayings," Savannah recalled as again a wave of nostalgia hit. "Are you sure I can't talk you into sharing sooner?"

He glanced at the piles of cookies on the table and the obvious remnants of hot chocolate in two mugs. "Are you absolutely certain you won't go into some sort of sugar-overload crisis?"

"Absolutely."

"Then I'll bring it in," he said.

"I'll help," Savannah said eagerly, grabbing a jacket off a hook by the door and following him outside.

The instant she spotted his fancy new four-wheel-drive sports utility vehicle out front, she was momentarily distracted from thoughts of ice cream. It could turn out that Trace Franklin was the answer to her prayers.

"I don't suppose you'd be willing to let me borrow your car?" she asked.

"First you want my ice cream, and now you're after my car," he said, shaking his head. "You ask a lot for someone I've barely met."

"I need to get to town to pick up paint and things to start on the work that's needed around here." She glanced toward her own car, a faded six-year-old sedan with questionable tires. "I doubt my car will make it down the mountain, much less back up on these icy roads."

His expression grew thoughtful. "Okay, here's my best offer. I'll trade you breakfast tomorrow for a trip into town."

Apparently the man's obsession with business never quit. "You really do like to negotiate, don't you?"

He shrugged. "Force of habit. I like creating win-win situations. Is it a deal?"

Savannah held out her hand. "Deal." She hesitated. "You could have dinner with Hannah and me this evening, if you like. It won't be fancy. I'm fixing spaghetti."

He seemed startled by the invitation. "It just so happens that I love spaghetti." His gaze narrowed suspiciously. "What do you want in return for that?"

"Ice cream for dessert?" she asked hopefully.

Rather than answering, he reached into the car, then turned back with something in hand and tossed it to her. Savannah caught it instinctively. It was a pint of ice cream. And she'd been right—it was the best.

"It's all yours," he said. "Consider it a gesture of good faith."

He retrieved a huge cooler, which obviously contained the rest. Savannah eyed it enviously. "Is that thing really filled with more of this?"

"Packed solid," he told her. He studied her warily. "Am I going to have to put a lock on the freezer?"

"I would never steal your ice cream," she said with a hint of indignation, then grinned. "That doesn't mean I won't try to talk you out of it."

His gaze locked with hers and anticipation slid over her once again, making her senses come alive.

"This is really, really good ice cream," he said quietly. "It could take more than talk."

Savannah barely resisted the urge to fan herself. She was surprised steam wasn't rising around her. Oh, this man was dangerous, all right. She was obviously going to have to watch her step the whole time he was under-foot. Any man who prided himself on being a shark when it came to business was likely to be equally determined when it came to anything else he wanted.

Well, she'd just have to make sure he didn't decide he wanted her. One glance comparing her flour-streaked jeans to his tailored wool slacks put that notion to rest. They weren't in the same league at all.

She lifted her gaze to his, caught the desire darkening those gray eyes. Uh-oh, she thought. Apparently clothes didn't matter to Trace, because the look in his eyes was anything but neutral.

More worrisome, though, than that discovery was the realization that she wasn't nearly as upset by it as she probably ought to be. In fact, a little *zing* of anticipation had her blood heating up quite nicely. She could probably strip off her sheepskin-lined jacket and be quite comfort-able in the twenty-degree temperature out here.

"You'll want to get all your stuff inside," she said, her tone suddenly brisk. "Who knows how many deals you might have missed while we've been talking?"

"The ones worth making can always wait," he said.

"Still, I'd hate to feel responsible for you missing out on something important. Besides, I promised Hannah that she and I would go cut down a Christmas tree this afternoon."

He regarded her as if she'd just mentioned a plan to cut down the entire forest.

"There's a perfectly good tree lot in town. I passed it on my way out here," he said. "Those trees are already cut. Less work. Less waste."

"Is that an expression of environmental concern?" she inquired. "Because the trees I'm talking about are grown specifically for the holidays. It's how some people make their living."

He looked skeptical. "Still seems like a lot of work."

"But this is a tradition," she countered.

He looked as if she'd used a foreign term.

"Didn't you have any holiday traditions when you were growing up?" she asked.

"Sure," he said at once. "Staying out from underfoot while Mom and Dad argued over how much money was being wasted on presents."

Savannah couldn't imagine a home in which the holidays had meant anything other than a joyful celebration. For all of the problems she and her parents were having now, they had given her years of memories of idyllic Christmases. Very little of that had had anything at all to do with the materialistic things. It had been about family togetherness, laughter…traditions. For some reason, she suddenly wanted to share just a little of that with this man to whom tradition meant so little. She'd never been able to get through to Rob, but maybe Trace Franklin wasn't a lost cause.

"Would you like to help us?" she asked impulsively.

He looked even more disconcerted by that invitation than he had been by her request that he join them for dinner. "I had planned to get some work done this afternoon," he said predictably.

"Surely the company founder can take a break for a couple of hours," she coaxed. "Most people do relax around the holidays. I doubt anyone will be too upset if they don't get a fax today or even tomorrow. Some people might actually be hoping to leave work early to finish their holiday shopping."

A vaguely guilty expression passed across his face, as if he'd already forgotten that Christmas was only a few days away.

"You're right," he said eventually. "The work can wait. In fact, maybe I'll call my secretary and tell her to let everyone leave early."

Savannah grinned at the unexpected evidence that Scrooge had a heart. "That's the spirit," she said. "I'll get my coat and hurry Hannah along. You'd better change into something warmer, too. My hunch is that this could take a long time. Hannah rushes through most things, but she's never made a quick decision about a Christmas tree in her life."

As Savannah left Trace to finish putting his groceries away, she was all too aware that his gaze followed her as she exited from the kitchen. And that she unconsciously put a little extra sway in her hips because of it.

Oh, so what? she thought as a guilty blush crept into her cheeks. If she could grant Hannah's not-so-secret Christmas fantasy of a pair of skis, then surely Fate wouldn't mind granting her the chance to flirt with a handsome man for a couple of days. After the holidays, what were the chances she'd ever see Trace again? Slim to none, more than likely. He was the perfect guy on which to practice a little harmless flirting. She had to get back into the dating game one of these days. Here was her chance to relearn the rules with a man who absolutely, positively was not her type, and better yet, a man who wouldn't be around long enough to break her heart.

Then she recalled that desire she'd read in Trace's eyes only moments before. *Harmless* was not the first word that came to mind. Okay, she concluded, *wicked* would be nice, too.

Four

Trace hauled all of his business equipment into Mae's den, but before he could plug any of it in he was so overcome with emotion that he sank into the chair behind her antique desk and drew in a deep breath. As he did, he was almost certain he could still smell the soft, old-fashioned floral scent she had worn.

The room looked as if she'd just left it moments earlier. A jar of her favorite gourmet jelly beans sat on the desk. He noted with amusement that most of the grape-flavored ones were gone. They had been her favorites, though she had claimed that she continued to buy assorted flavors precisely so she wouldn't get in a rut. She'd never realized that Trace had added a half-pound or so of the grape-flavored jelly beans each and every time he came to visit, secretly stirring them into the mix.

The inn's guest book was still beside the phone with reservations carefully noted. He turned to today's date and saw his own name written in her graceful, flowing script. He saw that Savannah's arrival had been noted for a date only a few days earlier in a script that seemed less steady.

Had she made those final arrangements for her niece's inheritance when she'd known the end was near? Had she cleverly schemed to bring him together with Savannah even as her health was failing? It would have been just like her to plot something for those she loved, something to make them less lonely once she was gone.

Ironically he didn't think Savannah had picked up on the scheme yet. He'd been the subject of so much matchmaking in recent years that he'd seen what Mae was up to the instant he'd realized he wasn't going to be alone at Holiday Retreat over the holidays. It was no accident that he and Savannah were here at the same time. Mae had wanted some of the seasonal magic to rub off on her heart-weary niece and a man she thought was missing out on romance.

So, why hadn't he run? He could have apologized for the intrusion and headed back to New York and the safety of his workaholic routine. It wasn't entirely duty to Mae that had kept him here but—mostly, he had to admit—the sweetly vulnerable Savannah herself. Though she wasn't complaining, it was obvious that her life hadn't been easy lately. Still, she'd maintained an air of determination and her sense of humor. She was too unsophisticated to be his type, but there was something about her—a fragility encased in steel—that drew him just the same. It reminded him of a young man who'd fled Tennessee years ago with little more than a dream and the determination to make it come true. And in many ways it reminded him of his mother, who'd had the strength to endure poverty and hardship. Only in recent years—after spending most of his youth condemning her for the choices she had made—had he come to realize just how strong she had been.

"Trace, are you ready yet?" Savannah asked quietly, startling him. "My goodness, you're not even changed. Is everything okay?"

He met her concerned gaze. "Sorry. I got distracted."

Savannah came closer and perched on the edge of the desk. She regarded him with sympathy. "You feel her presence in here, don't you? I feel it most in the kitchen. It's like she's watching over my shoulder." A grin tugged at the corners of her mouth. "Making sure I don't burn the place down, more than likely."

"She wouldn't have left the inn to you if she didn't trust you to take care of it," he told her, knowing with everything in him that it was true. Mae had been sentimental, but she had also had a practical streak. Her New England heritage, no doubt. "This place meant everything to her. When Franklin Toys started doing really well, I suggested she retire. She had plenty of money to live comfortably for the rest of her life. Know what she told me?"

"That retirement was for people waiting to die," Savannah said. "She told me the same thing. She loved having her company, as she referred to the guests who came here year after year. She said they kept her young. What she missed was having family underfoot for the holidays."

"You and Hannah and I are here this year," Trace said, unable to keep a note of sorrow from his voice.

"Too late," Savannah said, a tear sliding down her cheek.

Trace thought of his suspicions about Mae's reason for bringing them together. Not that he intended to get too carried away trying to see that *all* of her wish came true, but celebrating this Christmas with her niece was the least he could do for the woman who'd believed in him.

"You said yourself that you think she's watching over you," he reminded Savannah. "What makes you think she's not here right this second, gloating over having gotten us up here to celebrate the holiday and her memory at the same time?"

Savannah's expression brightened. "You're absolutely right! Let's not disappoint her. We'll make this the most memorable holiday ever. We'll do everything just the way she used to do it, from the greens in the front hall to the candles on the mantel and in the windows."

"Perfect," he said enthusiastically. "Give me a minute to call my office and change, and I'll meet you and Hannah out front. We'll find the best tree on the tree farm."

"It has to be huge," Savannah warned.

He hesitated, phone receiver in hand. "How huge?"

"Really, really big." She held her arms wide. "And very, very tall."

"How were you and Hannah going to get such a huge tree back here by yourselves?"

"I was counting on help."

"Are you sure you didn't know I was coming?"

"Nope. Mr. Johnson has a truck. He also has a fondness for Mae's sugar cookies."

Trace winced. "The ones on the kitchen floor?"

"Those are the ones."

"Think he'll accept any other sort of bribe?" he asked, knowing that he was going to hate the alternative if Mr. Johnson declined to haul that tree.

"Nope. I think this tree is riding in your pristine, shiny SUV, shedding needles all the way," she said happily.

Trace groaned. "I was afraid of that."

She patted his hand, sending a jolt of awareness through him.

"I'll go get a blanket to lay in the back," she said soothingly. "Now, hurry, or you'll have Hannah to deal with.

Trust me, she's worse than a nagging splinter when she's anxious to get someplace. Right now she's making a family of snow angels on the front lawn, but her enthusiasm for that will wear off shortly."

"I'll hurry," Trace promised, unable to tear his gaze away as she left the room. He sighed, then dialed his office.

Two minutes later, he'd told his stunned secretary to shut the company down until after the new year, changed into warmer clothes and was heading out the front door, only to be greeted by squeals of delight as Hannah upended her mother into a snowbank. Savannah was sputtering and scraping snow out of her mouth. There was a dangerous glint in her eyes as she regarded her traitorous daughter.

Oblivious to her mother's reaction, Hannah spotted Trace. Emboldened by her success with her mother, she raced in his direction. Trace braced for the hit. "Oh, no, you don't," he said, scooping her up when she would have tried to knock him on his backside. He held out a hand and helped Savannah up, even as Hannah tried to squirm free of his grip.

He looked into Savannah's dancing eyes. "What do you think? Should I drop her in that snowdrift over there?"

"No!" Hannah squealed. "Put me down. I'll be good. I promise."

Trace kept his gaze on Savannah's. "Your call."

"Hannah does keep her promises," she began thoughtfully. "Then again, that snow was really, really cold. She needs to know that."

"I know it. I know it," Hannah said. "Really, Mom. I swear."

Before he realized what she intended, Savannah scooped up a handful of snow and rubbed her daughter's face with it, dribbling a fair amount inside the collar of his coat while she was at it. Accident? he wondered. Probably not.

"Mom!" Hannah squealed, laughing.

Savannah clapped her gloved hands together to get rid of the excess snow and regarded Trace with a pleased expression. "I think it's okay to put her down now."

He lowered Hannah to her feet and caught her grin. "I hope you learned a lesson," he said, fighting to keep his own expression somber.

"Oh, yes," she retorted just as seriously. "I learned that my mom is very, very sneaky."

Trace nodded, shivering as the snow melted against his suddenly overheated skin. "I caught that, too. What do you think we should do about it?"

"Hey," Savannah protested, backing up a step. "Don't you two even *think* about ganging up on me."

"Never dream of it," Trace said, winking at Hannah.

She winked back, then giggled. "Never," she agreed.

Savannah looked from one to the other. "I'm going to regret this eventually, aren't I?"

"Could be," Trace said. He took a step closer, reached out and tucked a flyaway strand of hair back behind her ear. "But you'll never see it coming."

Her gaze locked with his, and suddenly the tables were turned. The desire to kiss her, to taste her, slammed through him with enough force to rock him on his heels. He hadn't seen that coming, either.

"We are never in a million years going to get this tree into the house," Trace said, eyeing the giant-size pine that Hannah had picked out. "What about that one over there?" He pointed to a nice, round, five-foot-tall tree. It was cute. It was manageable. Hannah was already shaking her head.

"No," daughter and mother replied in an emphatic chorus.

"I suppose it's also a tradition that the tree has to be too big to fit inside," he grumbled as he began to saw through the trunk. He'd worked for a lawn service one summer and had some skill at sawing down trees and branches, but nothing this size. He should have brought along a chainsaw.

"Exactly," Savannah said, grinning and apparently thoroughly enjoying his struggle with the tree.

"I think my mother had the right idea after all," he said. "A ceramic tree that lit up when she plugged it in."

"Oh, yuck," Hannah said. "That's so sad."

As he breathed in the scent of pine and fresh, crisp air, Trace was forced to agree with her. Despite his grumbling about the endless search for the perfect tree and his protests over the size of their choice, he hadn't felt this alive in years. Something that might have been the faint stirrings of holiday spirit spread through him. He couldn't remember the last time he'd felt like this.

"Stand back, you two. When this thing falls, you don't want to be in the way," he warned as he heard the crack of the wood and felt the tree begin to wobble. One hard shove and it would hit the ground. Before he could touch it, the tree began to topple...straight at him. It knocked him on his back in the deep snow. He found himself staring straight toward the sky through a tangle of fragrant branches.

"Uh-oh," he heard Hannah whisper.

Her mother choked back a giggle and peered through the branches. "Are you okay?"

"What the devil happened?" he asked, frowning up at her.

"I gave the tree a teeny little push to help it along. I guess I pushed the wrong way. You aren't hurt, are you?" The twinkle in her eyes suggested she wasn't all that worried.

Trace bit back his own laughter and scrambled out from beneath the tree. "You are in such trouble," he warned even as she began backing away, her nervous scramble hampered by the deep snow.

"You wouldn't," she said, regarding him warily.

"Oh, but I would," he responded quietly. "Nobody pulls off a sneak attack on me twice in one afternoon and gets away with it."

She tried to escape, but she was no match for his long legs. He caught up with her in a few steps, scooped her up and dropped her into the cushion of snow.

Hannah's laughter mingled with theirs. He whirled on her. "Okay, young lady, you're next. Don't you know better than to injure a man's pride?"

Hannah was quicker to scamper away, but Trace still caught up with her, grabbed a handful of snow and rubbed her face with it. Just then he felt himself being pelted with snowballs from behind. In seconds all three of them were engaged in a full-fledged snowball fight.

"Oh, my," Savannah said a few minutes later, collapsing into the snow. "I haven't laughed that hard in ages."

"Me, either," Trace said, his gaze clashing with hers. In fact, he could barely recall ever laughing that hard.

Or wanting a woman as much as he wanted the virtual stranger lying beside him in the icy snow right this minute. With all the heat crackling between them, he was surprised they hadn't melted the snow right out from under them.

He started to reach out to touch her cheek, but recalling Hannah's presence, he drew back. "Do you know what I'd like to do right now?" he asked, his gaze locked with Savannah's.

She swallowed hard at the question and shook her head.

Trace realized that her thoughts had drifted down the same dangerous path as his own. "Not *that*," he protested, deliberately teasing her.

Her cheeks, already pink from the chill in the air, turned an even brighter shade. Another woman might have called his bluff, but she merely kept her gaze on him, apparently waiting to see just how deep a hole he intended to dig for himself.

"What *I'd* like to do," he said, "is go back to the house, build a nice warm fire in the fireplace, and…" He deliberately let the suspense build. He saw the pulse beating a little more rapidly in her neck. He permitted himself a hint of a smile, then said softly, "Take a nap."

She was still blinking in confusion when Hannah plopped down between them and said, "Grown-ups don't take naps."

"Sure we do," Trace told her. His gaze went back to Savannah. "In fact, sometimes when adults take naps, we have the very best dreams ever."

Savannah shot him a knowing look, then rose gracefully to her feet. "Well, by all means, let's get home so you can get some sleep," she said testily.

She muttered something more, something obviously meant for Trace's ears, not Hannah's. He caught her hand and held her back until they were well out of Hannah's hearing.

"What was that?" he inquired.

She leveled a look straight at him. "I said, I hope you have nightmares."

"No dream with you in it could ever be a nightmare," he said, locking gazes with her once more. "Then again, you could take a nap with me."

"In your dreams," she retorted.

He winked at her. "Exactly."

She stopped in her tracks and scowled up at him. "Is this some sort of game with you?"

There was a hint of anger behind the question that threw Trace completely. "Game? I'm not sure what you mean."

"When you found me at the inn, did you decide I was Aunt Mae's gift to you or something? Because I am here to tell you that hell will freeze over before I fall into bed with you just because it's convenient."

With that, she whirled away and stalked off as gracefully as the deep snow permitted, leaving him to deal with the tree. He considered running after her, trying to explain, but maybe it was better to give her time to cool down.

So he struggled with the monster tree, finally getting a firm grip on the trunk, then dragging it through the snow. The trek took forever. By the time he reached the car, Savannah and Hannah were nowhere to be seen. Since the inn was less than a mile down the road, they'd probably decided to walk.

Trace wrestled with the tree and finally got it half in and half out of the SUV, cursing at the mess it was making of the car's interior. He tied it securely, then climbed into the vehicle and turned the heater up full blast.

He was still stinging from Savannah's tongue-lashing as he drove back to the inn. Granted, he'd only been teasing her, but she didn't know him well enough to understand that. He'd deserved every bit of scorn she'd heaped on him.

As he pulled up in front of the house, he noted that the lights were blazing and that smoke was curling from the chimney. Dusk was falling rapidly, and along with it, the temperature was dropping.

He lugged the tree onto the porch, then left it there to

be dealt with after he warmed up with a cup of coffee or maybe some of that hot chocolate Savannah and her daughter were so fond of.

Inside, he stomped the snow off his boots and tossed his jacket over a chair, then headed for the kitchen where he could hear the low murmur of voices. He found Savannah at the stove stirring a pot of spaghetti sauce. The weathered older man to whom she was talking caught sight of Trace and gave him a wink.

"You must be Trace. Savannah here's been giving me an earful about you," he said. "'Course, it's not exactly the same high praise I was used to hearing from Mae."

Trace saw Savannah's back stiffen, but she didn't turn around. Obviously, the walk had done nothing to cool her temper. She was still royally ticked at him. The apology he owed her would have to wait, though. The man regarding him with such amusement had to be Mae's longtime lover.

"You must be Nate Daniels," Trace guessed at once. "I heard a lot about you over the years, as well, all of it good."

"Only because Mae never had a sharp word to say about anyone," Nate said. "Maybe that's because she brought out the best in people."

"I know she did in me," Trace said solemnly, his gaze on Savannah.

Nate looked from him to Savannah, then stood up and began pulling on his jacket. "Think I'll be going along now."

Savannah whirled around at that. "I thought you might like to stay for dinner."

"Not tonight," Nate said, shooting a commiserating look toward Trace. "I'll be around next time you're interested in having company. Meantime, you two need anything, you give me a call. I'll be happy to do what I can. You both meant a lot to Mae. I know she'd be happy that you're here together for the holidays."

Savannah regarded him with a disappointed expression. "Come by anytime," she said, her voice husky, her eyes shimmering with unshed tears. "I want to hear everything you can tell me about my aunt."

Nate clasped her hand in his. "Come on now, girl. Don't you be crying for your aunt. She's at peace."

"I know. I just wish I'd been here for her."

"She understood why you couldn't be here," Nate assured her. "And I was here. She wasn't alone."

"Thank you for that," Savannah said.

"No need to thank me. My place was by her side," he said simply. "I only wish I'd been able to give her more. Now let me get out from underfoot, so you folks can have your dinner." He regarded Trace with a stern expression. "And a nice long talk."

Trace accepted the admonishment without comment. "I'll walk you out," he offered.

Nate shook his head. "No need. I know the way. Seems to me like you have better things to do," he said, casting a pointed look at Savannah, who'd deliberately turned her back again.

"Yes," Trace agreed.

He waited until he heard the front door close before attempting his apology. "Savannah?"

"What?"

"I'm sorry if I offended you earlier."

"If?" she asked with a hint of disdain. She faced him, eyes flashing heatedly. "You all but propositioned me in front of my daughter!"

"I made sure that Hannah was out of earshot before I said a word," he reminded her, but she didn't seem the least bit pacified. She turned away and began stirring the spaghetti sauce with a vengeance. "Okay, I'm just plain sorry. I never meant to give the impression that I seriously thought you and I ought to be back here tumbling around in bed together."

"Oh, really?" she asked skeptically. "Then exactly what *did* you mean?"

"I was just teasing. Your cheeks get all flushed and your eyes sparkle when you get indignant. That was the only reaction I was going for. I was out of line."

She turned slowly and studied him. "Apology accepted. I probably overreacted, anyway. It's been a long time since I've flirted with a man."

"You'll get the hang of it again." He reached for her hand and tugged lightly until she was standing directly in front of him. "I only think it's fair to warn you, though."

"Warn me? About what?"

"Next time I might not be teasing."

She gulped visibly, then nodded. "I'll keep that in mind."

"Is it all right if I stay here, or would you rather I go?"

She seemed startled—perhaps even dismayed—by his offer to leave. "Aunt Mae invited you here. I'm certainly not going to kick you out."

"I know what Mae wanted," Trace said. "What do you want?"

She drew in a deep, shuddering breath, then stiffened her shoulders as she looked straight into his eyes. "I want you to stay."

The satisfaction that swept through Trace felt a lot like the exhilaration he felt when a difficult business negotiation ended well. "Then that's what I'll do," he told her solemnly.

She muttered something that he couldn't quite make out.

"What was that?" he asked.

A flush crept up the back of her neck. "I said, like I really had a choice."

"Of course you have a choice."

"Not if I want that tree to get put up tonight," she said, facing him with a renewed sparkle in her eyes.

Trace laughed despite himself. "I do love a woman who's always working an angle."

"Of course you do," Savannah said. "Makes you feel more at home, doesn't it? I'll bet you spend most of your time with female boardroom piranha types."

Trace chuckled at the all-too-accurate assessment. "True enough," he admitted. "But something tells me that's about to change."

Five

Savannah sent Trace in search of Hannah, while she got dinner on the table. She also needed the time to compose herself. She knew precisely why she had overreacted to Trace's teasing. It was because she had actually been tempted to take him up on his offer to slip away for a so-called *nap*. Even if they'd actually done no more than crawl into bed together and snuggle, it would have satisfied the yearning that had been building in her ever since he'd arrived earlier in the day.

Of course, she doubted a man like Trace would have settled for simply holding her in his arms. He would have wanted much more, and while she was tempted by that, she didn't want to wind up with her heart broken when he left in a few days. It was better that she'd made her position perfectly clear. If she was lucky, there would be no more temptations.

Next time I might not be teasing.

Trace's words suddenly came back to haunt her. How convenient that she had forgotten the warning.

At the sound of his laughter as he and Hannah came

toward the kitchen, Savannah's pulse raced a little faster. The same wicked yearning that had gripped her earlier teased her senses now. She sighed. Resisting him was going to be a whole lot harder than she'd ever imagined. She'd just have to keep reminding herself that he was cut from the same cloth as her workaholic ex-husband.

"Mom, can we put the Christmas tree up tonight?" Hannah pleaded as they finished up bowls of ice cream after the best spaghetti Trace had eaten in years.

"According to tradition, we never put it up till Christmas Eve," Savannah told her, but she sounded regretful, as if this were one tradition she could be persuaded to change.

"Maybe it's time to start your own tradition," Trace suggested, earning a high-five from Hannah. "Besides, the sooner the tree is in its stand and has some water, the better it will be, right? It'll last much longer, and it will fill the house with the scent of pine. Why not start enjoying it now?"

Hannah studied her mother, clearly trying to gauge her mood. "Please," she begged finally. "I'll go up in the attic and bring down all the decorations you said are up there. Trace will put it up and string up the lights. You won't have to do anything."

"Except keep the carols going on the CD player and the hot chocolate flowing," Trace corrected. "What do you say, Savannah?"

"I say that you two are a formidable team," she said, feigning an air of resignation that was belied by the spark of excitement in her eyes. "Go on. Bring in the tree."

"Do you know where you want it?" Trace asked. "Once it's up, I don't want to be hauling it all over the house."

She frowned at him. "It goes in front of the window in the living room. That's where it's always been."

"And you're happy with that?" he persisted.

"Why wouldn't I be?"

"Since you're starting new traditions and all, I just thought you might want to go for broke and pick a new location."

"I think the old one is just fine," she said. "That way, anyone driving up to the house will be able to see the lights on the tree."

Trace resigned himself to moving the sofa that normally sat in front of that window. "Where should I move the sofa?"

Savannah regarded him blankly. "The sofa?"

"The one in front of that window."

Her eyes suddenly lit with understanding. "So that's why you were so eager to have me put the tree somewhere else. You're going to be stuck moving furniture."

"Hey, I'm not complaining." He glanced at Hannah. "Did you hear me complain?"

"No," she said at once.

"I'll put that sofa just about anywhere you want it except the attic," he insisted.

Savannah regarded him with a wry expression. "I think on the wall facing the fireplace will do."

"Got it. Tree in front of the window. Sofa in front of the fireplace. And the easy chairs currently on that wall? Where should they go?"

A chuckle erupted from deep inside her, lighting up her face. "Maybe Hannah and I can rearrange the furniture while you get the tree in its stand."

"No way," Trace protested. "I'm providing the brawn here. Just give me instructions."

By the time Savannah finished with the instructions,

he was pretty sure that not one single piece of furniture in the living room would be where it had started out. He figured he could live with that, as long as she didn't change her mind a million times.

"That's it?" he questioned. "You're sure?"

"As sure as I can be before I see what it looks like," she said.

Trace sighed. "I'll get started. You might want to hunt for some painkillers and a heating pad in the meantime."

"Very funny."

He leveled a look at her. "Who's joking?" he asked as he headed for the living room to rearrange the furniture.

By the time everything was in its newly designated place, including the tree, the room did have a cozier, more festive air about it. A fire crackled in the fireplace, and the fresh scent of pine filled the air.

Hannah had brought down stacks of boxes of decorations from the attic. They were now scattered over every surface, as she took each one from its tissue and examined it with wide-eyed delight.

"These must be really, really old, huh?" she asked him.

"They certainly look as if they're antiques," Trace said, noting the loving care with which she handled them. It must be nice to have family heirlooms to be brought out year after year, each with its own story. But now with Mae gone, who would share those stories with Hannah?

Savannah came in just then carrying a tray of steaming mugs filled with hot chocolate. Her eyes widened as she saw the decorations.

"Oh, my," she whispered. "I remember these. Mae used to tell us kids about them when she'd take them out of the boxes. We were never allowed to touch them because they were so old and fragile, but we each had our favorites."

She immediately picked up a blown-glass rocking horse, its paint beginning to wear away. "This was mine. This and the angel that goes on the top of the tree. Is that still here?"

"Over here," Hannah said excitedly, picking it up gingerly. "She's beautiful."

Dressed in white satin with red velvet trim, the angel had flaxen hair and golden wings. The delicate porcelain face had been rendered with a serene look totally appropriate for gazing down on the holiday festivities year after year. Even Trace, with his jaded, unsentimental view of the season, could see the beauty of it.

"We always drew straws to see who would get to put it on the top after all the other decorations were on the tree," Savannah said as she held the angel. "My dad or one of my uncles would lift up whoever won so we could reach the very top."

"Can I put it on this year?" Hannah asked. "Trace could lift me high enough."

"Maybe this year your mom ought to do it," Trace suggested, seeing the nostalgia in Savannah's eyes.

"No," Savannah said at once. "It was always one of the kids. Of course Hannah should do it—that's the tradition."

"Well, it'll be morning before we get to it unless we get started," Trace said. "There are a lot of lights here, and there must be hundreds of decorations. You two sit back and relax while I get the lights on. You can tell me when they're in the right place."

"Ah, my favorite job," Savannah teased, settling onto the sofa with Hannah beside her. "Supervisor."

Trace had a devil of a time untangling all the lights, making sure they worked and then getting them on the tree. It was the first time such a task had fallen to him, and he was beginning to see why his father had always grumbled about it. Trace would have settled for three or four strands strategically placed, but Savannah was having none of that.

"At least four more strands," she insisted. "I like a lot of lights."

"I'm not hearing any carols while I work," Trace chided. "What happened to the music? Isn't that your job?"

"Oops. I forgot. What will it be?" She shuffled through a stack of CDs. "Bing Crosby? Nat King Cole? Kenny G? The Mormon Tabernacle Choir? Vince Gill? The Vienna Boys Choir?"

"Your aunt certainly had eclectic taste," Trace commented.

"She loved Christmas music. She used to buy at least one new album every year. Obviously she kept up that tradition. So, what's your pleasure?"

"Surprise me," Trace said.

Despite the suggestion, Savannah didn't surprise him at all when she chose the old standards of Nat King Cole. As the singer's voice filled the room, Trace recalled the way his father had scoffed at the sentimentality of the holiday music. Trace had inadvertently carried that same disdain with him into adulthood. Now, though, with Savannah and Hannah singing along with the music, he began to enjoy the songs.

"Come on," Savannah encouraged. "Sing with us."

"No, thanks, I'd rather listen to you," he said as he wrapped the final strand of lights around the tree.

"But singing helps to get you into the holiday spirit. It doesn't matter if you're off-key," she told him.

"Sorry," he said, his voice a little tight. "I don't know the words."

She stared at him with obvious astonishment. "You never learned the words to all the old standard Christmas carols?"

"They weren't played much at our house. My father objected. He said it was just more crass commercialism. We were lucky he let us put up a tree. After a few years, he carried on so about that, that my mother settled for the little ceramic tree I told you about earlier."

"But you must have heard the carols when you were at your friends' houses," she persisted. "Or on the radio."

"I didn't pay much attention," he said defensively.

"How awful," she said, studying him with sympathy.

"Savannah, I got along okay without knowing the words to a bunch of songs that get played once a year."

She studied him seriously. "Can I ask you something?"

"Sure," he said, despite the wariness creeping over him.

"As a man who doesn't seem to have many happy memories of the holidays, how did you end up running a toy company?"

"Long story," he said.

"It's still early. We have time."

"I don't want to bore Hannah with all this. Besides, we've got a tree to decorate." He deliberately turned to Hannah. "Sweetie, are you ready to start hanging those decorations?" he asked, shutting down the topic of his career.

"Sure," Hannah said eagerly. "Mom, you've got to help."

Savannah cast one last curious look at him, before smiling and picking up several decorations.

By the time they were finally finished and all the boxes were empty, there wasn't a bare spot on the tree's branches.

"Ready for the lights?" Trace asked.

"Wait. Let me turn off the overhead lights," Savannah said. "It's better in the dark."

As soon as the main lights were off, Trace plugged in the tree's. The hundreds of lights shimmered, reflecting off the ornaments and filling the room with dazzling color. Even he was a bit in awe as he stared at it.

"It's beautiful," Hannah whispered.

"The very best tree ever," Savannah agreed.

Suddenly she was slipping her hand into Trace's. "Thank you," she said.

"Just following directions," he said.

"No. It's more than that. I think we all need a touch of magic in our lives this year, and you've made sure we have it."

"All I did—"

She cut off his protest. *"Thank you,"* she repeated emphatically, gazing up at him.

Trace thought he'd never seen anything so lovely in his life as he gazed into her sparkling eyes, which put the lights on the tree to shame. "You're welcome," he said softly, resisting the need to kiss her only because Hannah was in the room.

"I think I'll go to bed," Hannah announced with rare impeccable timing.

"Night, baby," Savannah said, sounding just a little breathless.

"Good night, Trace. Thanks for helping with the tree." Hannah stood on tiptoe to give him a peck on the cheek.

"Good night, angel."

"I'm glad you're here," she murmured sleepily as she headed for the stairs.

Trace looked into Savannah's eyes, aware suddenly that he was caught up in something he couldn't explain with his usual rational practicality. "I'm glad I'm here, too."

* * *

The most amazing sense of contentment stole through Savannah as she settled onto the sofa with Trace beside her. He was careful not to sit too close, but she could still feel the heat radiating from him, and she was drawn to it more than ever.

It had been an incredible evening. Even listening to Trace and Hannah bickering over where to place the ornaments on the tree had been wonderful. Hannah wouldn't have risked such a debate with her father. Things were always done Rob's way. It was a lesson Hannah had learned early, to keep peace in the family.

It was more than that, though. Maybe it was the cozy fire. Maybe it was the hot chocolate and salvaged chunks of sugar cookies.

Or maybe it was simply that for the first time in years, there was no real dissension as the holidays got under way. It had always been a battle to get her husband home from the office in time to help with the preparations. And unlike the bantering between Hannah and Trace, there had been a superior edge to her ex's tone that had always sent Hannah to her room in tears.

"Can I ask you something?" Savannah said, studying Trace intently.

He kept his guarded gaze directed toward the fire, but he nodded.

"Christmas is still a couple of days away. Why did you come up here early?"

"I told you."

"I know. You promised my aunt. But she's been gone for several weeks now. You could have waited till the last second and still fulfilled your promise."

He glanced at her, then looked back at the fire. "You'll think I'm crazy."

Savannah laughed. "I doubt that. Even in the brief time I've known you, I can tell you definitely have all your wits about you."

"Okay, then, here it is. I was planning to wait till Christmas Eve, rush up here, spend the night and rush right back to the city on Christmas Day."

"But you changed your mind. Why?"

"I woke up this morning with this weird feeling that I needed to be up here today." He met her gaze. "Normally I would have dismissed it and kept to my original plan...." His voice trailed off.

"But?" Savannah prodded, intrigued by the distinctly uncomfortable expression on his face. For a man who exuded confidence, it was a rare display of vulnerability.

"You know that cooler of chocolate mocha almond ice cream?"

"Very well. What does that have to do with anything?"

"It was delivered to my apartment this morning with a note that said I should get it up here before it melted."

Savannah stared at him. "Someone sent you that ice cream as a gift?"

His gaze held hers. "Not just *someone*. It was your aunt's handwriting."

"Oh, my," Savannah whispered. "How could that be?"

"I called the store and the delivery service. The arrangements had been made weeks ago." He shrugged ruefully. "I guess Mae was afraid I might not keep my promise without a little nudge from beyond the grave. Needless to say, I packed my bags and hit the road."

She studied him closely. "Are you teasing me?"

"Absolutely not," he said. "I have no sense of humor.

Ask the people who work for me. Heck, it's even in most of the articles about Franklin Toys."

"That's absurd," Savannah said, dismissing the suggestion out of hand. "You've been joking and laughing with Hannah and me since you got here."

"I know," he said, his expression serious. "What do you make of that?"

"We're good for you," she said, her voice suddenly a little breathless. Could it really be that she had something to offer this man who had everything money could buy?

"Which, I suspect, is exactly what your aunt had in mind when she plotted this meeting."

Suddenly it all made sense to Savannah. The inheritance of Holiday Retreat at a time when she desperately needed a change in her life. The unexpected arrival of a handsome stranger on the inn's doorstep. Yes indeed, Aunt Mae had been scheming, all right. The realization horrified her.

"I am so sorry," she told Trace with total sincerity. "She shouldn't have dragged you up here with an ulterior motive. If you want to get back to the city and your friends for Christmas, I will certainly understand."

Her declaration seemed to amuse Trace for some reason. His eyes were glinting humorously when he reached out to caress her cheek. "Are you kicking me out, Savannah?"

"No, of course not. I just wanted you to understand that you're free to go if there's someplace you'd rather be, people you'd rather be spending the holiday with."

As an answer he leaned forward and touched his lips to hers in the lightest, tenderest of kisses. There was a whisper of heat, the promise of fire…and then he was on his feet.

"I'll see you in the morning," he said as he headed for the stairs.

"You're staying?" she asked.

"Of course I'm staying."

"Because it was what Mae wanted?" she asked, determined to clarify the reason.

"No, darlin'. Because it's what *I* want." He winked at
her. "Besides, I promised to take you into town tomorrow."

With that he was gone, leaving Savannah staring after
him. She touched a finger to her lips, where she could still
feel his mouth against hers. "And you always keep your
promises," she whispered to herself. It was such a little
thing, but it meant more than Trace could possibly imagine.

She lifted her gaze to seek out a picture of Aunt Mae
that sat on the mantel. "Thank you."

Just knowing that there was one man left who kept
his promises restored her faith that the future would turn
out all right.

Six

The scent of fresh-brewed coffee drifted upstairs, pulling Trace out of a perfectly fascinating dream. For once it had nothing to do with mergers and acquisitions, but with a woman—Savannah, to be precise.

How could a woman with so little guile, so little sophistication, get under his skin the way she had? That kiss the night before—little more than a friendly peck by most standards—had packed more punch than any kiss he'd experienced in years. He'd left the room, not because he believed in hasty, uncomplicated exits, but because he wanted so much more. If he'd gone after what he'd wanted, more than likely he would have scared her to death. Then she would have kicked him out and he would have spent another lonely holiday season back in New York.

"I hope to hell you knew what you were doing, Mae," he muttered.

When the scent of sizzling bacon joined that of the coffee, Trace quickly showered and dressed in a pair of old jeans, a dress shirt and a heavy pullover sweater. That was about as casual as his attire ever got these days. He reminded himself if he was going to paint the front door and trim and sand the floors, he needed to buy something else to wear.

When he walked into the kitchen, Savannah regarded him with flushed cheeks and wisps of curls teasing her face. "Is that your idea of work clothes?" she asked. "Or do you intend to supervise today, the way I did last night?"

Trace noted that she, too, was wearing jeans, but her University of Florida sweatshirt had seen better days, as had her sneakers. She still looked fabulous. He still wanted her. A part of him had been hoping that last night's desire had been an aberration.

"Did I say I was working?" he inquired as he poured himself a cup of coffee, breathed in its rich scent, then took his first sip. "Good coffee, by the way."

She grinned. "Glad you like it, since it's yours. I figured you wouldn't approve of the instant I had on hand."

Trace shuddered. "Good guess." He met her gaze. "Exactly what sort of work are you planning to do today?"

"I want to pick up paint for the guest rooms, a tarp for the roof and…"

"Whoa! Why a tarp for the roof?"

"Because it's leaking."

"Why not get it fixed?"

"I would if I could get the contractor over here," she explained with exaggerated patience. "He said he can't come till after the first of the year."

"Then call another contractor."

She frowned at him. "Don't you think I thought of that?"

"I'll handle it," he said at once.

"What do you mean, you'll 'handle it'?"

"I'll get someone over here to repair the roof."

"Even if you are a business mogul, I doubt you'll be

any more successful than I've been," she said. "Besides, there's at least a foot of snow up there. They won't even be able to look at it, much less start the repairs."

"Okay, you have a point," he conceded. "Though that would also seem to make the tarp a waste of time, too, unless you're planning to put it over the snow."

She frowned at him. "Okay, then, no tarp."

"What else do you want from the hardware store?"

"The paint and tools to scrape the wallpaper will do it. I don't want to spend any more till I know what the rest of the repairs are going to cost. And I have to set some money aside for new brochures and advertising. I need to start getting paying guests back in here as soon as possible. I've already missed the start of the ski season."

Trace thought he heard a hint of desperation in her voice that she was trying hard to hide. "Savannah, do you have the money to get this place up and running again?"

"I have enough," she said tightly.

"What about a loan? I could—"

"Absolutely not. I won't take money from you."

"Then let me talk to the bank."

"No, I am not going to start off my new life with a pile of debts. Things will get done when I can afford to do them."

Trace admired her pride and her independent streak, but as a practical matter he knew it was better for a business to present its best face from the outset so that word of mouth would spread. She might not take money from him, but she wasn't in a position to turn down a little practical assistance in the form of labor. She could hardly tell him not to pick up his own supplies. He'd just have to be a little sneaky about it. That meant getting in and out of the hardware store without her catching sight of his purchases.

"Fine," he said. "Holiday Retreat is yours."

There was one more thing he could do, too. It would require a few phone calls, routing his attorney away from his new girlfriend for a couple of hours, but he could pull it off by Christmas.

"Is Hannah coming into town with us?" he asked as he ate the scrambled eggs Savannah put in front of him.

"Of course. She's dying to take a look around. We stopped at the grocery store on our way up here, but that's all she's seen. I'll go get her. We can be ready to leave whenever you're finished with breakfast."

"Did you eat?"

"I had a piece of toast," she said.

Trace frowned at her. "I have enough eggs here for three people." He stood up, grabbed a plate from the cupboard, then divided up his eggs, added two slices of bacon and set it on the table. "Sit. You need the protein."

Savannah opened her mouth to protest, but his scowl achieved what his directive had not. She sat down and picked up her fork.

"You know, I have to get used to serving the guests around here without sitting down to eat with each and every one of them," she told him.

"I'm not a guest."

She nibbled thoughtfully on a piece of bacon. "Which means I probably shouldn't have cooked this for you," she said.

"Right. I told you I'd look out for myself."

"I'll remember that tomorrow morning."

He regarded her slyly. "Of course, it wouldn't hurt to get in a little practice in the kitchen. You wouldn't want the first real guests to starve, would you?"

She laughed. "I don't think there's any chance of that.

I may not have had a lot of practice at cooking for a crowd, but Aunt Mae has a whole box filled with recipes she perfected over the years. I can read directions with the best of them."

"I seem to recall some sort of baked French toast Mae used to make," Trace said, his gaze on Savannah. "I don't suppose…"

To his surprise, Savannah's eyes lit up. "I remember that. She always made it Christmas morning."

"Then it's a tradition?" Trace asked hopefully.

"Yes, it's a tradition. And yes, I'll make it. And yes, you can have breakfast with Hannah and me on Christmas morning."

"Before or after we open presents?" Trace asked, only to see her shoulders stiffen slightly.

Hannah arrived in the kitchen just in time to hear the question. "We're not having presents this year, 'cause we're poor," she said with absolutely no hint of self-pity.

"We are *not* poor," Savannah said, obviously embarrassed by her daughter's comment. "It's just that the divorce and the renovations needed on this place have left us temporarily strapped for cash, so we're keeping Christmas simple."

"I see," Trace said slowly.

Simple might be good enough for Savannah, maybe even for Hannah, who seemed resigned to it, but not for him. For the first time in years, he had the desire to splurge on the holidays.

Oh, he always sent truckloads of toys to various homeless shelters in the city, but his personal gift list was small and mostly confined to business associates. He couldn't recall the last time he'd had anyone in his life to whom he'd wanted to offer even a small token of affection.

He made a mental note to make a few more calls the second he had some privacy.

"Why don't you guys grab your coats while I clean up in here?" he suggested. "I'll meet you at the car in a few minutes."

Savannah regarded him curiously, almost as if she suspected something was up because he'd let her description of their financial plight pass without comment.

"Go on. Warm up the car," he encouraged, tossing her the keys. "You cooked. I'll clean up. That's *my* tradition."

"I thought you didn't have any traditions," she replied.

"I'm starting a new one."

To his relief, she seemed to accept that.

"We'll be outside," she said. "Try not to break any dishes."

"Hey," he protested, "I know what I'm doing."

He loaded the dishwasher, turned it on, then grabbed his cell phone. It took less than ten minutes to set things in motion. That was one of the benefits of being rich. Trace rarely threw his weight or his money around. When he did, people were eager enough to do as he asked. He'd always been satisfied in a distant sort of way when he thought of the delight his toys would bring to kids on Christmas morning, but he'd never actually experienced that sense of awe and wonder that was pictured in his commercials. Maybe this year things would be different.

Satisfied that Christmas was under control, he grabbed his coat and joined Savannah and Hannah, who'd already retreated to the slowly warming interior of the car. Hannah shivered dramatically when he opened the door.

"I hate cold weather," she declared.

Trace regarded her in the rearview mirror. "You're

living in the wrong place, then, kiddo. Weren't you the one who was out here half-buried in snowdrifts yesterday?"

"It's colder today," she insisted. "And now I've seen snow. Yesterday I hadn't."

"Does that mean you want to move back to Florida?" Savannah asked.

There was no mistaking the note of trepidation in her voice, Trace thought. He glanced over and saw the tight lines around her mouth.

"No," Hannah said at once. "Even if it is cold, I want to stay here."

Savannah's relief was almost palpable. "Why?" she asked.

"Because since we got here, you've started laughing again," Hannah said quietly. "You never laughed in Florida."

Savannah turned her head away, but not before Trace saw a tear sliding down her cheek. He wanted to reach for her, to hold her...to make her laugh.

Instead he glanced toward Hannah. "How about you and me making a pact?" he said. "The one who makes your mom laugh the most today wins."

Hannah's eyes lit up. "Okay. What's the prize?"

"Hmm," Trace began thoughtfully. "If you win, I make us all hot-fudge sundaes for dessert tonight."

"Good prize," Hannah said enthusiastically. "What if *you* win?"

"Then you make me the biggest, mushiest Christmas card ever, something I can hang on my office wall."

"Deal," Hannah said, slapping his hand in a high five.

He glanced toward Savannah and saw that her lips were twitching. It wasn't a real laugh, but it was at least the beginning of a smile. He pointed it out to Hannah.

"I get the first point," he said.

"That's not a real laugh," Hannah scoffed. She leaned over, slipped her hand down her mother's back and tickled Savannah until she giggled aloud. "*That's* a real laugh," Hannah said triumphantly.

Savannah wriggled away, then scowled at both of them. "What do *I* get if I maintain a totally stoic facade all day long?"

"Never happen," Trace said.

"No way," Hannah agreed.

"Bet I can," Savannah retorted, her eyes twinkling.

"Okay, that does make it more interesting," Trace agreed. "If you win—and that's a really big *if*—you get Hannah's mushy card."

"What about you? What will you give me?"

Trace met her gaze evenly and felt his heart take a leap into overdrive. "Same as last night," he said softly.

He noted the flush that crept into her cheeks as she remembered that fleeting kiss they'd shared.

"You'll have to do better than that," she challenged.

His gazed remained steady. "Oh, I promise you, darlin', it will take your breath away."

The blasted heater in the car must have shot the temperature into the nineties, Savannah thought, barely resisting the urge to fan herself as Trace's words hung in the air.

Unlike the day before, when his seductive teasing had merely irritated her, today she was immediately all hot and bothered and wishing for more…maybe because she knew for a fact exactly what Trace's kiss could do to her. Worse, she wanted another of those kisses so badly, she was going to have to try really, really hard not to laugh for the remainder of the day. Given Hannah's determination to win that bet she'd made with Trace, Savannah was going to have a real struggle on her hands.

She could do it, though. She just had to remember her resolve...and keep a whole lot of distance between herself and those two coconspirators.

The second they reached the hardware store, Hannah begged to take a walk through town.

"Back here in thirty minutes," Savannah instructed, relieved to be rid of one of them. She looked at Trace. "I'll meet you back here in a half hour, too."

"You sure you don't need my help?" he asked, regarding her with a knowing grin.

"Nope. I'm sure someone will help me carry whatever I buy."

"Here's the spare key, then, in case you finish before I get back. You don't mind if I come in and pick up a few things myself, do you?" he asked.

"What sort of things?" she asked suspiciously. Trace didn't strike her as the type who had a lot of fix-it projects back home. Then again, didn't most men get a little giddy around wrenches and screwdrivers and power tools? Maybe he just wanted to soak up the atmosphere.

"This and that," he said vaguely. "I'll know when I see it."

"Fine. It's a big store. I'm sure you won't be in my way," she said.

They parted at the front door. Savannah headed straight for the paint supplies. She'd already thought about the colors she wanted for each of the guest rooms—rich, deep tones, accented by white trim. In no time at all, she'd picked out the appropriate paint chips and had the colors being mixed while she chose brushes, rollers, an edger for trimming and a paint pan.

Just as she headed through the store toward wallpaper-removal materials, she thought she spotted Trace coming around the end of the paint aisle, but then he vanished from sight. She didn't see him again until she was unloading her purchases into the back of his SUV.

"Find everything you were looking for?" he asked, tucking his own mysterious packages beside hers.

"Yes. What about you?" she asked as he lifted something heavy into the car. "What on earth is that? It looks as if it weighs a ton."

"Just a tool," he said, immediately turning his attention to the street. "Any sign of Hannah yet? Maybe we should go meet her. We could grab some lunch while we're in town. There's a little restaurant on Main Street that Mae used to like."

"The Burger Shack," Savannah said at once. "Is it still in business?"

"It was last time I was here. I took Mae a burger, fries and a chocolate shake from there."

"I can almost taste their shakes," Savannah said. "They made 'em the old-fashioned way with milk and ice cream. They were so thick, a straw would stand straight up in them."

When she looked at Trace, his lips were curving into a grin.

"Sounds like that's a yes," he said.

"Absolutely," she said eagerly. "And here comes Hannah."

She noticed that her daughter was carrying a shopping bag and that her eyes were sparkling with excitement. "What did you buy?" Savannah asked.

"Mom, I can't tell. It's almost Christmas, remember?"

Savannah started to question where Hannah had gotten the money to buy a gift, then stopped herself. Rob had probably slipped her a little money before they'd left Florida. Knowing him, that had been his gift to her, and she was turning right around and spending it on Savannah. On Trace, too, more than likely. Her daughter had the most generous heart of anyone Savannah knew, something she clearly hadn't inherited from her father.

"And that's all you need to tell us," Trace said, making room in the back of the car for Hannah's purchases. "Your mom and I were just talking about lunch. You interested?"

"Only if you're talking about that burger place on Main Street. The smell coming out of there is awesome. And I saw lots of kids my age going in. It must be the cool place to go."

Trace grinned. "Then it sounds like it's unanimous."

"Guess what?" Hannah asked excitedly. She went on without waiting for a response. "I met this girl at the store. Her name's Jolie. Isn't that a great name? And she's my age. We'll be in the same class at school. She says the teacher is really great. Her name's Mrs. Peterson. She's been here, like, forever, but everyone loves her because she's so nice."

"Really?" Savannah said, since Hannah didn't seem to expect much of a response. She was already rushing on.

"And guess what else?" she said. "Jolie says there's going to be caroling in town tonight and that everyone will be there, so we should come, too." She regarded Savannah hopefully. "Can we, please?"

Savannah instinctively thought of how uncomfortable Trace had been when she'd asked him to sing carols at the house the night before. She glanced at him.

"I think it sounds like a wonderful idea," he said with apparent sincerity.

Hannah grinned at him. "Jolie says they give out song sheets, so you'll know all the words."

"Then I definitely say we do it," Trace said. "Savannah?"

Being out on a cold, snowy evening two days before Christmas singing carols with her daughter and Trace? Savannah couldn't imagine anything more romantic. That probably meant she ought to say no, but of course she wouldn't. Not if it meant disappointing Hannah.

Sure, as if that were the real reason, she mentally scolded herself. She was going to do it because there was no place on earth she'd rather be tonight.

"Yes," she said, noting the smile that spread across Hannah's face. It was almost as bright as the warmth stealing through her.

Seven

Savannah had the radio blasting as she got into a rhythm of applying paint to the walls of the first guest room. The beautiful deep shade of green brought the color of the evergreens in the surrounding forest inside. When the white trim was added, it would be reminiscent of the way the scenery looked right now with snow clinging to the trees' branches. She envisioned a thick, warm comforter in shades of green and burgundy on the queen-size bed, with aromatic candles to match on the dresser.

Glancing out the window, she caught a glimpse of Hannah building her first snowman and chattering happily, no doubt to Trace, though Savannah couldn't figure out exactly where he was. He'd been up to something, though for the life of her she couldn't figure out what it was. The instant they'd arrived home after lunch, he'd disappeared into Mae's den. She hadn't seen him since.

Despite her declaration that she intended to handle the painting task on her own, a part of her had been counting on his defiance of that. She'd expected him to show up by now, if only to critique her work, maybe try to coax a laugh out of her in his ongoing attempt to win that bet with Hannah. Instead, much as her ex-husband would have done, Trace had retreated to whatever work he considered more important.

Oh, well, this was her job, not his, she thought with a sigh. And a man she barely knew was hardly in a position to disappoint her.

Besides, the painting was going very well, she decided, as she stood back and surveyed the room. There was an elegance and warmth to the result. Once the finishing touches were in place—probably after she could hit the January white sales at the Boston department stores—it would be perfect.

Satisfied, she snapped the lid back on the can of paint and prepared to move on to another room, the one she thought of as the blue room, though at the moment it had faded wallpaper that needed to be stripped. It was already late afternoon, so she probably wouldn't get much of the stripping completed before they left for the caroling in town, but any progress on the messy task was better than none.

She was about to peel off her first chunk of paper when something that sounded a lot like a big-time power tool kicked on downstairs, followed by a muttered curse, then giggles and deep, booming laughter. Savannah went to the top of the stairs and looked down just in time to see Hannah and Trace cast a furtive look in her direction.

"Uh-oh, we're busted," Trace said.

"If she heard you cussing, she'll probably send us to our rooms," Hannah said, looking downcast.

Hands on hips, Savannah scowled at them. "What are you two doing?"

"Nothing bad, Mom. Honest." Hannah's expression was filled with sincerity.

"Trace?"

"She's right. It's just a little surprise," he said.

Savannah remained skeptical. "A surprise, or a shock?"

Hannah giggled. "Mom's not real good with surprises."

"Maybe because I've had so many bad ones," Savannah said. "By the way, I'm not hearing any reassuring explanations. Do I need to come down there?"

"No," they both said at once.

The quick chorus only roused her suspicions further. She started down the steps, only to have Trace take the bottom steps two at a time and meet her when she was less than halfway down. Putting both hands on her shoulders, he gazed into her eyes.

"Do you trust me?" he asked.

Now there was a sixty-four-thousand-dollar question. "I suppose," she said, hedging. Only Mae's faith in him was giving him her current benefit of the doubt.

"Well, you can," he said, clearly disappointed by the less than wholehearted response. "You need to go back to whatever you were doing and let Hannah and me finish up what we're doing."

She returned his gaze without blinking. "I was thinking of quitting for the day, maybe coming downstairs for a snack."

"I'll bring you a snack," he said at once. "Anything you want."

"An entire pint of your ice cream?"

"If that's what you want," he said at once.

"Okay, that's it. Something bad is going on down there, isn't it?" she said, trying to brush past him.

"Mom, please," Hannah wailed. "You'll spoil everything. It's not bad. I promise."

Savannah told herself that it was her daughter's plea,

not the pleading expression in Trace's eyes that won her over. "You can't keep me up here forever, you know."

"Just another couple of hours," he said, looking relieved. "Still want that ice cream?"

"No, that was just a test."

He grinned. "I figured as much."

Savannah sighed. "I'm going back to strip wallpaper."

"Maybe you ought to take a break," he suggested. "Maybe take a long, leisurely bubble bath or something."

"Who has time for that?" Savannah grumbled. "This place isn't going to get fixed up by itself."

He tucked a finger under her chin. "When you start saying things like that, it's exactly the time when you need a break the most."

"This from a workaholic like you?" she scoffed.

"Actually that's something your aunt used to say to me every time I protested that I couldn't get away from the office to come visit. It got me up here every time," he said, an unmistakable hint of nostalgia in his voice. "And she was always right. I always felt better after a few days with her. I even got so I barely cracked open my briefcase the whole time I was here."

"Did she talk you into taking a bubble bath, too?" Savannah teased.

"Nope, but you probably could," he retorted, then added in an undertone, "especially if you were joining me."

Heat and desire shot through Savannah like a bolt of lightning. "Any bubble bath I take, I'll be taking alone," she told him, keeping her own voice muted.

"Too bad."

Before she made the fatal mistake of agreeing with him, she whirled around and went back upstairs. She started toward the room where she'd been about to work, then changed her mind and headed another floor up to her bathroom, where she poured some lavender-scented bubble bath into the tub and turned on the water, knowing that the sound would be enough to keep Trace's imagination stirred up. He wasn't the only one under this roof who had a wicked streak, she thought with satisfaction as she sank into the warm water. Hers had just been on hold for a while.

Unfortunately the memory of his suggestion that he join her and the sensual feel of the water against her skin combined to make the bath far less relaxing than she'd envisioned. In fact, she concluded as she stepped from the tub and wrapped herself in a thick terry-cloth towel, it really was too bad that she wouldn't find Trace waiting for her in her bed. Thank goodness they were going caroling in a couple of hours. It was definitely going to take a blast of icy air to cool off her wayward thoughts.

"Quiet," Trace admonished Hannah when they heard Savannah moving around upstairs. Since they were due to leave for the caroling in less than a half hour, he figured they had five minutes, maybe less, before she started down from the private quarters on the third floor. He squeezed Hannah's hand. "Not a word till she gets all the way down and sees what we've done."

They'd only made a dent in the work that was needed to put Holiday Retreat back into shape for guests, but the outside of the front door and the exterior trim were now a bright red, the brass fixtures glistened and the foyer and living room floors were polished to a mellow sheen. Hannah had even fashioned some greens and ribbon into a decoration that had been hung from the brass knocker. In his opinion, with just a little effort, they had made a vast difference in the appearance of the inn. It looked as it had on his first few visits, before Mae had let some of the maintenance slip.

Beside him, Hannah was practically bursting with excitement as they waited for her mother.

"I should open the door," she whispered. "Otherwise, how will she know about the paint and the decoration?"

Trace grinned at her. "Good point. Why don't you sneak out the back door, run around to the front and open it when I give the word that she's almost down the steps. I'll make sure it's unlocked."

Hannah took off, thundering across the floor in her eagerness.

"Don't forget your coat," Trace called after her just as he heard Savannah's footsteps descending from the third floor to the second.

Since he didn't want Savannah to miss Hannah's grand entrance, he stepped into view as she started down the last flight and blocked her way. She paused halfway down, regarding him warily.

"I am not going back up," she told him.

"Never said you should."

"Then why are you standing in my way?"

"Am I in your way?" he asked, still not budging.

Savannah sighed heavily, just as Trace heard Hannah hit the porch running.

"You look lovely," he said in a voice meant to carry outside.

Her gazed narrowed. "Announcing it to the world?"

"Why not?" he said. "It's worth announcing."

At that instant he heard Hannah turn the doorknob. He stepped aside as the door burst open.

Clearly startled, Savannah looked straight at her

daughter, then caught sight of the freshly painted door. Her eyes lit up.

"Oh, my," she said softly. "It's beautiful." She looked from Hannah to Trace. "Is that what you two were up to?"

"Only part of it, Mom," Hannah said. "Come down the rest of the way and look around some more."

As soon as Savannah stepped off the bottom stair, she glanced around, her expression puzzled.

"Down," Hannah said impatiently.

Savannah's gaze shifted to the floor with its brand-new shine. "What on earth?" There were tears in her eyes when she turned to Trace. "You did this? That's what I heard down here? I couldn't imagine the wood ever looking like this again. It's beautiful."

Hannah beamed at her. "I helped, Mom. Trace and I did it together."

"It's just a start," Trace said. "We only had time to do the foyer and the living room. We'll do the dining room tomorrow."

The tears in Savannah's eyes spilled down her cheeks. "I don't know how to thank you."

"You could start by not crying," Trace said mildly, stepping closer to brush the dampness from her cheeks. "We wanted to do something to help. Hannah made the decoration for the door. She's got a real knack for that sort of thing."

Savannah's gaze shifted to the greens. "Trace is right, sweetie. It's absolutely beautiful. Aunt Mae would be so pleased with all of this."

She turned to Trace. "I know you did it for her, but thank you."

It had started as something he wanted to do for Mae,

but that wasn't how it had ended up. Trace realized he had done it to put that sparkle into Savannah's eyes, the sparkle that shimmered even through her tears.

"It was the least I could do," he said. "Now, do you want to admire our work some more, or shall we head into town for the caroling?"

"Let's go," Hannah said at once. "Mom can look at this forever when we come home."

Savannah laughed. "So much for savoring the moment."

"I made you laugh," Hannah gloated. "That's a whole bunch of points for me and hardly any for Trace. Those sundaes are mine!"

"Ah, well," Trace said with an exaggerated air of res-ignation. "I suppose the art already on my office wall will have to do."

Savannah was quiet on the ride into town. Too quiet, in Trace's opinion. When they'd finally found a parking place a few blocks from the town square and Savannah was exiting the car, he pulled her aside. "Everything okay?"

"Of course," she said brightly, though her smile was as phony as that too-chipper tone.

"Tell me," he persisted.

She sighed. "I was just thinking about all the Christ-mases I missed with Aunt Mae, years when I could have had this, instead of…well, instead of what we had."

"You can't go back and change things," Trace re-minded her. "You can only learn from your mistakes and look ahead."

She regarded him intently. "Are there things about your life that you'd change, mistakes you regret?"

He hesitated over the answer. "I wish things had been easier for my mother," he said slowly. "But I was a boy. I had no control over that. She made her own choice to stay married to a dreamer who was very good at criticizing everything *she* did, but did nothing himself."

A half smile touched Savannah's lips. "You say that, but you sound as if you still believe that you should have fixed it somehow."

"I suppose I do believe that," he admitted. "But by the time I had the money to make a difference in her life, it was too late. She'd already died of pneumonia. She'd let a flu go untreated too long because my father thought she was making too much out of a little cold. Once she got to the hospital, there was nothing they could do. That was the beginning of the end for my dad. He was devastated. I finally saw that in his own way, he had felt my mother was everything to him. He died less than six months later."

"Oh, Trace, I'm so sorry," Savannah said.

He forced aside the guilt that the memory always brought. "Time to take my own advice. I can't change the past. I have to let it go. We all do." He managed a smile. "I think I hear a band warming up. It must be about time for the caroling to begin."

As if on cue, Hannah, who'd been hurrying ahead of them, bolted back. "Hurry up, you guys. The carols are starting. And I see Jolie. Can I go say hi to her?"

"Of course," Savannah said. "But then you come back to join us. Got it?"

"Got it," Hannah said, racing away from them.

Left alone with Savannah, Trace reached for her hand and tucked it through his arm. "This is nice," he said, looking into her shining eyes. "The stars are out. The air is crisp. I can smell the bonfire up ahead. It definitely feels as if Christmas is in the air. And there's a beautiful woman on my arm."

In the glow of the gas lamps on the street, Trace

could see Savannah blush. If a simple compliment rattled her so, it must have been years since she'd heard any. Which made her ex-husband even more of a fool than Trace had imagined.

"You know, as much as I loved growing up in Florida," Savannah said, "this is the only place it's ever really felt like Christmas to me. Just look around. All the stores are decorated along Main Street. There's a tree in the center of the green that's all lit up, and snow underfoot. It's like a Currier and Ives Christmas card. What could be more perfect?"

She looked up into Trace's eyes, and he felt his heart slam to a stop.

"You," he said softly.

"What?"

"You're the only thing I can think of that's more perfect than all of this."

For the second time that evening, she was blinking back tears.

"Hey," he protested. "I didn't mean to make you cry again."

She gave him a watery smile. "It's just that no one's ever said anything so sweet to me before."

"Then you've been spending time with the wrong people," he said emphatically.

Suddenly she stood on tiptoe, and before he realized what she intended, she was pressing a kiss to his cheek. "Thank you. I'm really glad you're spending Christmas with us."

Trace could have let it go at that. It was a tender gesture, not an invitation, but the night was cold and that kiss promised heat. He captured her chin and gazed into her eyes, then slowly lowered his head until his mouth covered hers.

She tasted of mint and felt like satin. Then the anticipated heat began to work its way through his system,
hinting of a simmering passion just waiting to be un-
leashed. He unzipped her jacket and slid his arms inside,
pulling her close until their body heat mingled. She
melted against him. They were a perfect fit, her curves
soft and yielding, his body hard and demanding.

Trace could have been content to stay right here, doing
nothing more than learning the shape and texture and
taste of Savannah's mouth for hours on end, but sanity
finally prevailed. This was a small town. Savannah was
a newcomer. The last thing she needed was him stirring
up gossip. Whatever happened between them—and there
was little doubt that something would—he didn't want
there to be regrets. Not of any kind.

With a sigh, he slowly released her. His gaze clung to
hers as he slid the zipper of her jacket up, then tucked her
scarf more securely around her neck.

"Trace, what…?" She swallowed hard. "What was
that about?"

"New beginnings," he suggested. He drew in a deep
breath of the cold air, then added, "And speaking of that,
I had an idea I thought I'd run by you."

"If it's anything like that last one, the answer's yes,"
she replied, amusement threading through her voice.

"Don't agree until you've heard it," he said. "What about
holding an open house at the inn tomorrow before midnight
church services? The downstairs rooms can be ready by
then, and it would get people talking about the place."

She was staring at him, her expression dazed. "Are you
crazy? I can't be ready for an open house tomorrow night!
Even if we could finish up with the downstairs rooms,
what about food? We'd need wine and eggnog. All of the

good dishes would have to be washed, the table decorated. I can think of a million reasons why it would never work."

He waited through the tirade, then asked, "Is that it? Any other objections?"

"I think those are quite enough."

"Okay, your turn to listen to me. I can have a caterer here first thing in the morning. He's already on standby. He'll bring all the food, the drinks, the table decorations, linens, crystal and china. All you need to do is say yes and stay out of his way." He pulled his cell phone out of his pocket. "What's it going to be?"

She regarded him with obvious astonishment. "You've already done all that?"

"I put it into motion, checked to make sure the caterer I use for our big marketing events was available. I haven't given the go-ahead. That's up to you. I thought it might be the perfect way for you and Hannah to get to know your neighbors, a way to let them know that the inn is back in business."

She looked torn. "It's a wonderful idea, but I can't let you do it."

"Why?"

"Because…" Her voice faltered. She frowned at him. "I don't know why exactly. It's just too much. Besides, how would we let people know?"

He sensed that she was weakening and pressed his advantage. "I think we can count on Hannah and her friend to take care of that. Say the word, and we can send the two of them through this crowd. It'll be faster than an instant-message e-mail."

"What if no one comes?" she asked worriedly. "It is Christmas Eve, after all. People have plans. Then you would've gone to all that expense for nothing."

"I'm not worried about that. I'm sure people are curious. Some are probably anxious to know if you intend to reopen the inn. It's been a historic landmark in the town for years. I think they'll be more than eager to take a little side trip on their way to church." He waited while the wheels turned in her head. He could practically see the pros and cons warring in her brain, as her expression shifted from dismay to hope and back again.

"You're absolutely certain we can pull this off?" she said at last. "It won't be the biggest mistake either of us has ever made?"

"Darlin', when it comes to business, I try really hard never to make mistakes."

"Okay, then," she said decisively. "Make that call. Then let's find Hannah and Jolie and put them to work."

Trace confirmed the plans with the caterer, who was eager to do anything for the bonus Trace had promised him. After that, finding the girls wasn't all that difficult. They were right in front, singing at the top of their lungs. Trace pulled Hannah aside and told her the plan.

"That is so awesome!" she said. "Jolie will help."

She pulled her friend over, introduced her to Trace and Savannah, then told her the plan.

"Sure," Jolie said at once. "I'll tell my mom and dad to spread the word, too. They know everybody. And this will be way better than sitting around at home while my relatives say the same old things they say every year."

"Tell them I'll appreciate whatever they can do to let people know," Savannah told her.

The two girls were about to race off when Jolie turned back. "I was supposed to ask you if it would be okay for Hannah to spend the night at my house tonight. A couple of my other friends are coming over, and my mom said it would be okay. She's right over there, if you want to meet her."

Trace saw the indecision on Savannah's face, but he also saw the anticipation on Hannah's. "Let's go over and say hello," he suggested. "You can discuss it with Jolie's mother."

Five minutes later, Savannah had given her approval for Hannah to spend the night at Jolie's. Donna Jones had been reassuring about the slumber party and enthusiastic about the open house at Holiday Retreat.

"I can't wait to see it," she said. "And I know all my friends are dying to meet you. Mae Holiday was loved and respected, and everyone wants to let you know that. You'll have a huge crowd. An open house on Christmas Eve is a lovely thing to do for the community."

Savannah looked relieved by her genuine excitement. "I'll see you then. What time should I pick Hannah up tomorrow morning?"

"Oh, don't worry about that," Donna said. "You'll have enough to do. I'll bring her by around noon, unless you'd like her there earlier to help out."

"Noon will be perfect," Savannah said, just as the band began to play "Silent Night." She slipped her hand into Trace's and began to sing.

A sensation that felt a whole lot like contentment stole through Trace. Not that he was familiar with the concept. For all of his success, for all of the people who filled his life day in and day out, he'd never experienced a moment quite like this. Maybe there was something magical about the holidays after all.

Or maybe Mae had been even wiser than he'd realized. Maybe she'd known exactly how to grant wishes before they'd even been made.

Eight

The bright red front door closed softly behind Savannah, and she suddenly realized that she was all alone in the house with Trace. Her heart thundered in her chest as she met his gaze and saw the familiar heat slowly begin to stir.

As he had earlier, he reached for the toggle on her jacket zipper and slowly slid it down, his intense gaze never once straying from her face. His knuckles skimmed along the front of her sweater, barely touching it, yet provocative enough to have her breasts swelling, the peaks instantly sensitive.

"Tell me to stop now, if that's what you want," he said quietly.

"I…" Her voice quavered. She swallowed hard and kept her gaze level. "I don't want you to stop."

"Thank God," he murmured, his mouth covering hers.

Savannah hadn't expected the whirlwind of sensations that tore through her at his touch. Trace had kissed her before, each time more amazing than the last, but this was different somehow. Probably because of where it was destined to lead.

It had been so long since any man had wanted her, since she'd been open to feeling this reckless surge of desire. From the moment of her divorce, she had resolved never to let another man take away even one tiny bit of her control over her life or her body. In little more than a couple of days, Trace had made that resolve crumble. She'd wanted him almost from the moment he'd stepped into the kitchen on that first day.

The reaction then had been purely physical. Now it was so much more. She knew the kind of man he was, had seen for herself that the workaholic traits she despised covered a vulnerability spawned years ago. She knew he was kind and generous. Best of all, he'd had Aunt Mae's apparently unwavering faith. That stamp of approval alone would have been enough to convince Savannah that Trace was someone to be respected and admired...maybe even loved.

In one corner of her brain, she wanted to apply reason to all of the feelings he stirred in her, wanted to dissect them with logic, but the rest of her mind was clamoring for something else entirely. Majority wins, she thought, barely containing a giddy desire to laugh with sheer exhilaration.

And then Trace's tongue was teasing her lips, tasting her, and the last rational thought in her head fled. From that instant on, it was all about sensation, about dark, swirling heat and a racing heartbeat, about the brush of his hand over flesh, about the clean male scent of him and the way his eyes seemed to devour her as he gauged the effect of each lingering, provocative caress.

She felt a connection with this near-stranger that she hadn't felt in years with her ex-husband. It was as if Trace could read her mind, as if he knew exactly which part of her was screaming for his touch. Savannah knew he believed that Mae had brought them together with something exactly like this in mind. And maybe that was how it had happened. It hardly mattered, because it felt right. It felt as if she was exactly where she belonged with exactly the right man. Fate or Aunt Mae—it hardly mattered which—had brought them to this moment.

She was breathing hard and barely able to stand when he finally paused to take a breath. "Come upstairs with me," she said, then hesitated, suddenly uncertain. "That is what you want, isn't it?"

"Darlin', I've never wanted any woman more than I want you right this second," he said with flattering sincerity. "Are *you* sure, though? I don't ever want you to regret this."

"I've made mistakes and I have my share of regrets, but this won't be one of them," she said with total conviction.

She held out her hand and Trace took it. Together they walked up the stairs, past the floor of guest rooms and on to the private quarters on the third floor. In recent years Mae had kept a small room for herself on the ground floor, but Savannah had opted for the privacy upstairs for herself and Hannah. She led Trace to her room, which had a panoramic view of the mountains lit by moonlight glistening on the snow.

She walked to the window and stood looking out. "Every time I look at this view, I feel this amazing sense of peace come over me. It's so incredibly beautiful."

She felt Trace come up behind her, his arms circling her waist.

"I think you're more beautiful," he said softly, his breath whispering against her cheek.

His hands slid up to her breasts, cupping them. As if the exquisite sensation weren't enough, the reflection in the window of his hands exploring her so intimately doubled the sweet tug deep inside her.

She was already shivering when his fingers slid beneath her sweater to caress bare skin. Eyes closed, she leaned back against his chest as he made her body come alive. Her breasts were heavy and aching before he undid the zipper on her jeans and repeated the delicious torment between her legs. She shuddered at the deliberate touches, each more intimate than the last, each coming closer to sending her over the edge.

She could feel the press of his arousal against her backside, could feel the heat radiating from him in waves. When she risked another look into the glass, she saw the tension in his shoulders, the hooded look in his eyes as he pleasured her. She'd never known a man could give so much without demanding anything in return.

The complete lack of selfishness inflamed her even beyond the effect of Trace's touch. Savannah turned in his arms, then slipped from his embrace. Her gaze locked with his, she stripped her sweater over her head, then let her already-unhooked bra fall to the floor. She knew the precise instant when he saw the reflection of her actions in the window, when that image merged with the one before him and deepened his desire.

She shimmied out of her jeans and panties, then reached for the hem of his sweater. She slid her hands over his chest, which felt like a furnace in the chilly room.

"One of us has way too many clothes on," he said in a husky growl as he tried to push her hands aside to relieve her of the task of ridding him of his sweater.

"Oh, no, you don't. I get to do this my way," she challenged.

A smile curved his lips. "By all means," he said. "Just hurry it up, will you?"

"Some things should never be rushed."

"And some things can't be stopped," he said, drawing her to him, bending down to circle each throbbing nipple with his tongue in a way that had her gasping.

The gesture pretty much destroyed her intent to torment him. Instead, she began to rush the task that only moments before she'd planned to draw out until he felt the same urgency she felt. Within seconds, they were both naked and moving toward the bed, knees weakened by exploring hands, desire ratcheted up to a height Savannah had never before experienced.

When Trace finally entered her, she was already crying out with the first explosive climax. He stilled while the pulsing sensations slowly died away. Then he began to move deep inside her, stirring her all over again, turning restless need into a demanding urgency that stretched every muscle taut with anticipation, until at last, with one sure, deep stroke, he took them both tumbling into a whirlpool of shuddering sensation.

Finally, still cradled in his arms, she fell into the first dreamless sleep she'd had in months.

Trace's heartbeat was easing, his pulse slowly quieting as he gazed down at Savannah. Such a sweet, innocent face to pack so much heat. If he hadn't been enthralled before, the last few hours would have been a revelation. She had a wicked, wanton streak that could lure a man into the fires of hell. Who would have thought it?

The strength and resilience he'd seen in her from the beginning took on new meaning when it came to making love. She'd all but exhausted him, yet he couldn't seem to stop looking at her—touching her—long enough to fall into desperately needed sleep.

Her porcelain-fine skin was still flushed, her hair

tousled. Her chest rose and fell with each breath she took, drawing attention to breasts so perfect they took his breath away. Amazingly he wanted her again. In fact, he suspected that after tonight there would never come a day when he didn't want her.

Forever? The word he'd always avoided like the plague popped into his head and wouldn't go away. Forever meant commitment. It meant compromising, joining his life with someone else's, putting her needs above his own. Was he capable of such a thing? Or was he his father's son in that regard? His father had certainly never considered for a second what his irresponsible choices meant for the rest of the family. Trace had always made sure that there would be no one in his life to be affected by the choices he made.

Oh, really? This time when he heard the voice in his head, it was Mae's. More than once she'd scolded him for such self-deprecating comments. She'd pointed out that he had hundreds of employees who counted on him for their livelihoods, that he'd never once let them down, that he'd never let *her* down.

He let his gaze linger on Savannah. Was it possible that he could give her everything she needed? Everything she deserved?

And what about Hannah? Being a stepparent wasn't easy. Oh, they got along well enough now, but what if the rules changed? What if he were here all the time? Would she balk at any attempt by him to take the place of her father…in her life or in her mother's?

He chided himself for getting way ahead of himself. Just because he and Savannah were compatible in bed, just because they'd spent a couple of incredible days that felt magical, didn't mean there was a future for the two of them. She might not even want that. Hell, *he* might not want it. If ever there was a time for clear, rational thought, for not looking beyond the moment, this was it.

Just then, Savannah sighed deeply and snuggled more tightly against him. Heat shot through him. Heat and need. The need went beyond sex, he realized. He needed what she represented—steadiness, love, family—things he'd never imagined himself wanting.

It was his turn to sigh then, his turn to tuck his arms more tightly around her. Maybe morning was soon enough for answers. Maybe tonight was simply meant for feeling fresh, new, enticing emotions.

He breathed in her scent—flowers with a hint of musk—then pressed a kiss to her shoulder. In minutes, he was asleep.

Savannah lay perfectly still, her eyes closed against the brilliance of the sun and against whatever she might discover in Trace's expression. It had been so many years since she'd experienced a "morning after" that she had no idea what to expect. Awkwardness topped the list of possibilities, though.

"You're playing possum," Trace teased, his voice low and husky and warm as it whispered against her cheek.

"Am not," she denied, feeling a smile tug the corners of her mouth.

"Come on, Sleeping Beauty, wake up. We have a million things to do today."

"I don't suppose any of them include staying right here in bed?" she asked wistfully.

"Afraid not."

To her relief, he sounded as disappointed about that as she felt. "And once Hannah's back under this roof, I suppose any more nights like this are out of the question, too."

"Your call, but I'd say that's the sensible way to go."

She opened her eyes then and met his gaze. Fighting against the uncertainty spilling over her, she asked, "Then this was a one-night thing?"

His gaze never wavered. "Not if I can help it," he said emphatically. "I think that's something we need to discuss in detail, don't you?"

Actions seemed vastly preferable to words in Savannah's current frame of mind, but he was right. Talking was definitely indicated, someplace and at a time when temptation wasn't inches away.

"I suppose there's enough time for me to do this," he murmured after a quick glance at the clock on the bedside table. "And this."

Kiss followed kiss until Savannah was writhing and crying out for him to slide inside her. The sweet urgency, the rush for one more taste, one more touch, made their joining even better than any they'd shared during the night before.

"Now we really do have to get up," Trace said with obvious regret. "The caterer will be here in an hour, and I've got to polish the dining room floor and be out from underfoot when he gets here."

"I'll fix breakfast," Savannah said. "And clean up the kitchen."

Trace's heated gaze roamed over her. "Or we could take a leisurely shower together, and to heck with breakfast and polishing the floor."

She grinned. "I think breakfast is highly overrated anyway."

"Not a sentiment you should be sharing with prospective guests," Trace advised as he scooped her up and carried her to the shower.

They were still damp and barely dressed when the doorbell rang.

"Nick of time," he said with a wink. "I'll get it. You might want to see if you can tone down that blush before you meet Henri. He's French and considers himself an expert on the nuances of romance. One glimpse of you, and he'll be offering more unsolicited advice than you ever dreamed of."

"Heaven help me," Savannah said wholeheartedly. "I'll be down in a minute…or an hour. However long it takes."

When Trace had gone, she sat down at her dressing table and studied her face in the mirror. He was right. She was flushed in a way that was entirely too revealing. Even so, she couldn't seem to stop the grin that spread across her face.

"Get a grip," she told herself firmly. "Tonight's too important for you to be frittering away time up here."

But no matter how important tonight was, she had a very strong hunch it wouldn't hold a candle to last night, especially if Trace refused to share her bed again.

By eight-thirty, Savannah knew that the open house was going to be a roaring success. Neighbors were crowded into every room, sharing holiday toasts, commenting on the delicious food as Henri basked in their compliments. Again and again, they had paused to welcome her and Hannah and tell them how delighted they were that Holiday Retreat would be reopened.

"My parents honeymooned here," Donna Jones confided when she caught up with Savannah during a quiet moment in the dining room. "My mother claims I was conceived here, since I was born almost nine months to the day after their wedding night."

Savannah grinned. "I'll bet I know which room," she said. "Aunt Mae always referred to it as her honeymoon suite because it's the largest room here. Want to take a peek? The decorating isn't finished, but I painted it yesterday."

"Oh, I'd love to," Donna said, following her upstairs.

At the door of the freshly painted green room with its white antique iron bed, she turned to Savannah with a gleam in her eyes. "It's going to be beautiful." She moved to the window that faced the mountains. "And the view is fabulous. I wonder if I could convince my husband to sneak off here for a weekend sometime."

Savannah heard the wistfulness in her voice and considered it thoughtfully. "You know, it might not be a bad idea to offer an introductory weekend getaway special for locals. People get so used to living in a place like this, they forget that the tourists who come here see it entirely differently."

"And it seems silly to spend money to stay just a few miles from home," Donna said enthusiastically. "But if it were a special promotion, I'll bet you'd be jammed with reservations. There's no better way to build word of mouth. People would start sending all their out-of-town guests here. It could fill in the slack once ski season dies down."

"I'm going to do it," Savannah said, delighted by the whole idea. "And for giving me the idea, your stay will be free."

"Absolutely not," Donna protested. "That's no way to start a business."

"Sure it is. You'll tell everyone you know how fabulous it is, so when I offer the promotion, it will be sold out in minutes."

As they walked back downstairs, Donna regarded

Savannah with open curiosity. "So, what's the story with you and Trace Franklin? I'm sorry if I'm being nosy, but everybody in town remembers his coming to visit Mae. A handsome, single man who owns his own company is bound to stir up comment. Have you known him long?"

Savannah felt a now-familiar flush creep into her cheeks. "Only a few days," she admitted.

"My, my," Donna teased, "you work fast! I know a lot of women who tried to get to know him on his prior visits, and he never gave any of them a second glance. Last night he couldn't take his eyes off you, and, if anything, he's watching you even more intently tonight."

"We're just—"

"If you say you're just friends, I'll lose all respect for you," Donna teased. "Any woman who doesn't grab a man like that ought to have her head examined."

"Talking about me, by any chance?" Trace inquired, stepping up beside Savannah and slipping an arm around her waist.

Savannah felt her face heat another ten degrees. "We were talking about—" she frantically searched her brain for a suitably attractive, sexy bachelor "—Kevin Costner."

Trace regarded her with amusement. "Oh? Is he in town?"

"No, but we do like to dream," she said, as Donna coughed to cover her laughter.

Trace leaned down to whisper in her ear. "Liar," he said softly.

"I think I'll go chat with my husband and tell him about your offer," Donna said. She grinned at Trace. "Nice to see you again. Merry Christmas."

"You, too," he said.

When Donna had gone in search of her husband,

Savannah lifted her gaze to meet Trace's. "I think the party's a success. Thank you for talking me into it."

"It's been fun," he said, as if that surprised him just a little. "Mae's introduced me around before, but this is the first chance I've had to really talk to some of the locals. They're good people, and they really are delighted that you're reopening the inn. Not only has this place been a boon to the economy, its history and charm provide something that the chain hotels can't. I didn't realize that in its heyday, Holiday Retreat employed several full-time people on staff and that the dining room was open to the public for dinner. Is that part of your plan, as well?"

"Eventually," Savannah said. "I'm going to have to take things slowly, so that I don't get overextended financially. Once all the rooms are ready for paying guests, then I can start thinking about whether to offer more than breakfast. I can cope with making eggs or French toast— I'm not so sure I could handle gourmet dinners. And I know I can't afford any help yet."

"Your spaghetti was pretty good," he said.

She frowned at him. "Somehow I doubt that's up to the standard the guests would expect. Remind me and I'll show you some of the old menus. Mae stopped doing the dinners about ten years ago, when it got to be too much for her, but she saved all the records. Since she left the file right where she knew I'd find it first thing, I'm sure she was hoping that I'd open the dining room again in the evenings."

The rest of the party passed in a blur. Soon guests were putting on coats, thanking Savannah for having them over and leaving for the Christmas Eve services planned by the local churches. When the last guest had departed, Hannah found Savannah and Trace standing on the front porch.

"Mom, this was the best. I must have met everybody in my class at school. I can't wait to start after New Year's. And there's going to be an ice-skating party in a couple of days and I'm invited. Isn't that totally awesome?"

"Totally," Savannah agreed.

Trace grinned. "Then you're back to being happy about living in Vermont?"

"Absolutely," Hannah said. "Can we go to church now?"

Trace glanced at Savannah. "What about it? Are you too tired?"

"I'm tired, but exhilarated. Besides, going to Christmas Eve services was always part of the tradition. I'll grab my coat."

Trace drove into town, which was teeming with many of the same families who had just left Holiday Retreat. They were all walking toward the various churches within blocks of the town square. Bells were ringing in the clear, crisp air.

As they entered the same little white chapel Savannah had attended with her family so many years ago, the scent of burning candles, the banks of red poinsettias by the altar, the swell of organ music, all combined to carry her back to another time. A wave of nostalgia washed over her.

How had she let moments like this slip away? As a child, she'd had no choice, but she could have insisted on coming back as an adult, even if she'd had to leave Rob behind to sulk in Florida. His mood had always been sullen around the holidays anyway. What would it have mattered if it got a little worse because she was sharing an experience like this with their daughter?

Ah, well, those days were behind her. She glanced at Hannah and saw the wonder in her eyes as the choir began to sing "O, Holy Night." Trace slipped his hand around hers as the familiar notes soared through the tiny, crowded church.

Savannah's eyes filled with tears at the beauty of the moment. Trace regarded her with such a concerned expression that she forced a watery smile. "Merry Christmas," she murmured.

"Merry Christmas, angel."

Hannah heard the murmured exchange and beamed at both of them. "Merry Christmas, Mom. Merry Christmas, Trace. I don't care if we don't have presents. This is the best holiday ever."

Gazing into Trace's eyes, Savannah couldn't help but agree with her daughter. It was definitely the best one ever.

Nine

Savannah was hearing bells. Convinced it was a dream, she rolled over and burrowed farther under the covers.

"Mom! Mom! You've got to see this! Hurry!" Hannah shouted, shaking Savannah.

Groaning, Savannah cracked one eye to stare at her daughter. "This had better be good." She and Trace had sat up talking until well past midnight, and if she wasn't mistaken, the clock on her bedside table said it was barely seven. Even if it was Christmas morning, she had counted on at least another hour's sleep, especially since Hannah wasn't expecting Santa's arrival.

"It's not just good," Hannah said, clearly undaunted by her testy tone, "it's fantastic. Come on, Mom. Hurry. I'm going to wake up Trace."

"Wait!" Savannah shouted, but it was too late. Hannah was already racing down the stairs screaming for Trace. Savannah heard his groggy reply, which amazingly was far less irritated than her own had been. In fact, he sounded downright cheerful.

Even with all that commotion right downstairs,

Savannah could still hear those bells, louder and more distinct now. She tugged on her robe and went to the window, then stood there, mouth gaping at the sight that greeted her.

There was a huge, horse-drawn sleigh coming through the snow toward the house, the bells on its reins jingling merrily. The back was piled high with sacks and wrapped packages. And the driver was... She blinked in disbelief and looked again. Nope, no mistake. The driver was Santa himself.

Savannah whirled around and headed for the stairs, pausing only long enough to run a brush through her hair and take a swipe at scrubbing her face and teeth. She met Trace at the second-floor landing. Hannah was already downstairs with the front door thrown open to allow in a blast of icy air.

Savannah studied Trace's expression, looking for evidence of guilt. "What do you know about this?"

"Me? I have no idea what you mean."

"Santa? The sleigh piled with gifts? It has your name written all over it."

"Actually I don't think you'll find that's true," he said, giving her a quick kiss. "Stop fussing and go down there. Santa's a busy fellow. I doubt he has all day to hang around here."

"Trace!"

"Go," he said, waiting until she led the way before following along behind.

They arrived downstairs just as Santa trudged up the steps toting two huge sacks. Still filled with suspicion, Savannah stopped him in his tracks. "Are you sure you have the right place?"

"Holiday Retreat?" he said, edging past her. "You're

Savannah Holiday, right? And that young lady out there by the sleigh is Hannah?"

"Yes."

"Then this is definitely the place. Even after such a long and busy night, I try not to make mistakes. Sorry about not squeezing down the chimney the traditional way, but if I go home with this suit all covered with cinders, Mrs. Claus will have my hide."

Savannah barely managed to suppress a chuckle. "I had no idea Mrs. Claus was so tough on you."

The jolly old man with a weathered face and white beard, who looked suspiciously like Nate Daniels, rolled his eyes. "You have no idea. Now, where would you like these gifts?"

"Under the tree, I suppose."

"And that would be?"

"Inside, in the living room on the right."

Santa carried two loads of packages inside, declined Savannah's offer of hot chocolate, then left with a cheery wave and a hearty "ho-ho-ho" that echoed across the still air. Hannah stared after him, still wide-eyed.

"Mom, do you think that was really Santa?" she asked.

Savannah exchanged a look with Trace, trying to gauge from his reaction whether her guess about Nate Daniels was correct. Before she could respond, Trace spoke up.

"Looked exactly like Santa to me," he said. "And you said you weren't going to have presents this Christmas, so who else but Santa would bring them?"

"Oh, I have some theories about that," Savannah muttered under her breath, but she kept her opinion to herself. She might have a few words for Trace later in private, but she was not going to strip that excitement from her daughter's eyes. "How about breakfast before we open gifts?"

"No way!" Hannah protested. "I want to see what's in the boxes, especially that great big one. Santa could hardly get it up the steps."

"You know that Christmas is about more than presents," Savannah felt duty-bound to remind her.

"I know, Mom, but these are here and some of them are for me. I checked the tags."

"Only some? Who are the others for?"

"You, silly. And Trace."

"Me?" Trace said, looking more shocked than he had at any time since this incredible morning had begun.

Savannah studied him intently. His surprise seemed genuine. Was it possible he wasn't behind this? Or at least not all of it? Curious to find out for sure, she acquiesced to Hannah's pleas and followed her into the living room.

"Big box first," Hannah said, rushing over to it. "Okay?"

"Your call," Savannah agreed.

The big box turned out to contain skis and ski boots. Hannah immediately had to try them on. "These are so totally awesome," she said, then wailed, "but I don't know how to ski."

"Maybe Santa thought of that," Trace suggested, his expression innocent.

Hannah's expression brightened at once. She began ripping open her remaining presents in a frenzy, *oohing* and *aahing* over each toy, over a new ski jacket and finally over the certificate for ski lessons that came in a deceptively large box.

Though a part of Savannah wanted to protest the degree of excess, she couldn't bring herself to spoil the moment.

"Your turn now, Mom," Hannah said, bringing her a comparatively small box that seemed to weigh a ton.

"What on earth?" Savannah said when she tried to lift it. She began carefully removing the wrapping paper until Hannah impatiently ripped the rest away, then tugged at the tape on the box. Inside, nestled in packing chips and tissue paper, was a tool kit, painted a ladylike pink but filled with every conceivable practical tool she could ever possibly need.

Her gaze shot to Trace. How had he guessed that she would prefer a gift like this to something totally impractical?

"It's perfect," she said, her gaze locked with his.

"Santa must know you pretty well," he agreed.

"Mom, there's a huge box here for you, too," Hannah said, shoving it across the floor.

This time she discovered a floor polisher, precisely the kind she would need if she was to keep the inn's floors gleaming. For most women, an appliance on Christmas morning would have been cause for weeping, but Savannah's heart swelled with gratitude.

"Wait, Mom. There's something little tucked inside with a note," Hannah said, her expression puzzled as she handed it to Savannah.

At the sight of the jewelry-size package, Savannah's breath caught in her throat. Her gaze shot to Trace, but he looked as puzzled as Hannah had. Then she caught sight of the handwriting on the envelope. It was Aunt Mae's.

Tears stung Savannah's eyes as she opened the note.

My darling girl,
I hope you are happily settled in by now and that
you will love your new home as much as I have
over the years. I've done what I could to be sure
you find joy here.

*Here's something else I hope will bring you hap-
piness. It belonged to your great-great-grandmother.*

*With all my love to you and Hannah. I wish I
could be there with you this morning, but please
know that wherever I am, I will always be looking
out for you.*

Mae

Savannah sighed and blinked back tears. Finding Mae's
present tucked amid all the others made her question everything. She'd been so sure that Trace had sent them, but now?
Recalling Santa's resemblance to Nate made her wonder if
Mae hadn't been behind this whole magical morning.

"Aren't you going to open it?" Hannah asked, leaning
against her and regarding the box with evident fascination.

Savannah slipped off the wrapping paper, then lifted
the lid of the velvet box. Inside, on a delicate gold chain,
was an antique gold cross. The workmanship was exquisite. The gold seemed to glow with a soft light of its own.
She could remember Mae wearing this cross every day
of her life. She had always said it symbolized faith
itself—so fragile yet enduring.

She opened the delicate clasp, slipped on the necklace,
then fastened it. The gold felt warm against her skin, as
if it still held some of Aunt Mae's body heat. Once more,
her eyes turned misty. She felt Trace take her hand and
give it a squeeze.

"Merry Christmas," he said quietly.

"Wait!" Hannah said. "There's another box. It's for
you, Trace."

Once more, he looked completely disconcerted. Hannah gave him the present. He handled it gingerly, studying
the large, flat box with suspicion.

"What does it say on the tag?" Savannah asked, curious herself.

"Just Trace," he said. "No other name."

"Must be from Santa, then," she teased.

He slipped open the paper, then pulled out the box and lifted the lid. The grin that broke over his face was like that of a boy who'd just unexpectedly received his heart's desire.

"What is it?" Savannah asked, trying to peer over his shoulder.

"It's the biggest, mushiest card I could make," Hannah said, grinning. "And Mrs. Jones took me to get it framed so Trace could hang it on his office wall."

Trace stared at her, looking completely mystified. "But I lost the bet."

"I know," Hannah said delightedly. "But I could tell you really, really wanted the card, so I made it anyway." She threw her arms around his neck. "Merry Christmas!"

To Savannah's shock, there was a distinct sheen of tears in Trace's eyes as he hugged her daughter.

"It's the very best present I ever received," he told her with such sincerity that Hannah's whole face lit up.

If this didn't stop, Savannah was going to spend Christmas morning bawling like a baby. She was about to head for the kitchen to start on breakfast, when Trace grabbed her hand and halted her.

"Wait. I think there's one more present for you, Savannah," he said, pointing Hannah toward a flat box beside the chair where he'd been sitting earlier. "Bring that one to your mom."

The box weighed next to nothing, but when Savannah tore off the paper and looked inside, her mouth dropped open. "Stock certificates?" she asked, turning to Trace. "In Franklin Toys? I can't possibly accept such a gift from you."

"It's not from me," he said firmly. "Not directly, anyway. These were Mae's shares of the company. She gave me power of attorney to vote them for her during the last weeks of her illness, but she told me I'd know what to do with the shares after her death." He looked straight into Savannah's eyes. "I think she would want you to have them."

"But she left me the inn," Savannah protested. "And Franklin Toys is your company."

He grinned. "I hope you'll remember that when you vote, but in many ways the company was as much Mae's as it was mine. She'd want you to have the financial independence those shares can give you."

"But I don't know anything about running a corporation."

"You can learn," he said. "Or you can sell the shares back to me, if you'd prefer to have the cash. The choice is yours."

Savannah sat back, still filled with a sense of overwhelming shock and gratitude. And yet... She studied Trace carefully. "Is this really what you want to do? She gave you her power of attorney, not me. I think she wanted you to control these shares."

"She wanted me to do the right thing with them," he corrected. "And I think that's turning them over to you. They're yours, Savannah. My attorney took care of the transfer yesterday."

Once again, Savannah looked at the certificates. She had no idea what each share was worth in today's market, but it had to be a considerable amount. The thought that she would never again have to worry about money was staggering.

This truly was a season of miracles.

Christmas morning had been incredible. It was everything Trace had imagined, from the awe and wonder on Hannah's face to the amazement on Savannah's when she'd realized that her financial future was secure. Trace had given the two of them everything he knew how to give. He'd been deeply touched by their gratitude.

Somehow, though, it wasn't enough. He wanted more, but he had no idea how to ask for it, or even if he had the right to, especially after knowing the two of them for such a short time.

Struggling with too many questions and too few answers, he wandered into the kitchen where Savannah was just putting the turkey into the oven.

She turned at his approach, studied him for a minute, then gave him a hesitant smile. "Everything okay?"

"Sure. Why wouldn't it be?" he asked, feeling defensive.

"I'm not sure. You seem as if you're suddenly a million miles away."

"I've got a lot on my mind. In fact, if you don't need my help right now, I was thinking of taking a walk to try to clear my head."

"Sure," she said at once. "It'll be hours before the turkey's done, and everything else is set to go in the oven once the turkey comes out." She continued to regard him worriedly. "Want some company?"

Trace shook his head. "Not this time. I won't be gone long," he said, turning away before the quick flash of hurt in her eyes made him change his mind. How could he possibly think about what to do about Savannah if she was right by his side tempting him?

He heard her soft sigh as he strode off, but he refused to look back.

Outside, the snow was a glistening blanket of white. The temperature was warmer than it had been, though still below freezing if the bite of wind on his face was anything to go by. He almost regretted the decision to take a lonely walk when he could have been inside in front of a warm fire with Savannah beside him.

He headed for the road, then turned toward town. He'd only gone a hundred yards or so when Nate Daniels appeared at the end of his driveway. He was bundled up warmly, an unlit pipe clamped between his teeth. He paused to light the tobacco, then regarded Trace with a steady, thoughtful look.

"Mind some company?" he asked, already falling into step beside him.

"Did Savannah call you?" Trace asked.

"Nope. Why would she do that?"

"I think she was worried when I took off."

"She called earlier to wish me a merry Christmas, but that was hours ago," Nate said. He regarded Traced curiously. "Funny thing, she seemed to have the idea that I was over there this morning playing Santa. Where would she get a notion like that?"

"Santa did bear a striking resemblance to you," Trace said.

"You didn't tell her, though, did you? You let her go on thinking that Mae was behind all the gifts and that she was the one who conspired with me to bring them."

"Oh, she suspects I had something to do with it, but there were enough surprises to throw her off." He glanced at Nate. "So, if Savannah didn't call, what brings you out into the bitter cold?"

"The truth is, I was all settled down with a new book my son gave me for Christmas when I felt this sudden urge to go for a stroll."

"Really? A sudden urge?" Trace said skeptically.

Nate nodded. "Finding you out here, I'm guessing Mae put the thought in my mind."

Trace kept his opinion about that to himself. Maybe Mae did have her ways even from beyond the grave.

"Something on your mind?" Nate inquired after they'd walked awhile in companionable silence.

Okay, Trace thought, here was his chance to ask someone older and wiser whether there was such a thing as love at first sight, whether a marriage based on such a thing could possibly last.

"Do you think there's such a thing as destiny?" Trace asked.

Nate's lips didn't even twitch at the question. "'Course I do. Only a fool doesn't believe there's a reason we're all put on this earth."

"And that applies to love, too?"

"I imagine you're asking about you and Savannah," Nate said. "Now, granted I've only seen the two of you together once or twice, but looked to me as if there was something special between you. It's not important what I think, though. What do *you* think?"

"I don't know if I even believe in love," Trace said dejectedly.

"Well now, there's a topic with which I'm familiar," Nate said. "You know about Mae and me, I imagine."

Trace nodded.

"You probably don't know so much about me and Janie, my wife. Janie and I met when we were kids barely out of diapers," he said, a nostalgic expression on his face. "By first grade I'd already declared that I wanted to marry her, though at that age I didn't really understand exactly what that meant. Not once in all our years of growing up did I change my mind. Janie was the girl for me. We married as soon as I graduated from college, settled down right here and began raising a family."

He glanced at Trace. "Now that should have been a storybook ending, two people in love their whole lives, married and blessed with kids. But Janie's nerves started giving her problems. The kids upset her. Anytime I was away from the house for more than a few hours, she'd get so distraught, I'd find her in tears when I came home. The doctors checked for a chemical imbalance. They tried her on medicine after medicine, but slowly but surely she slipped away from me."

Tears glistened in his eyes. "The day I had to take her to Country Haven was the worst day of my life. I told her she'd be home again, but I think we both knew that day wouldn't come. She's happy at Country Haven. She feels safe there. But there's not a day that goes by that I don't miss the carefree girl I fell in love with."

"It sounds as though you still love her deeply," Trace said.

"I do," Nate said simply.

"Then what about Mae?"

"After Janie went into the treatment facility, Mae helped out with the kids from time to time. They adored her. They stopped by the inn every day after school, and she always had cookies and milk waiting for them. Soon enough, I took to stopping by, too. Mae was a godsend for all of us during that first year."

He met Trace's gaze. "It's important that you know that nothing improper went on between us. I considered myself a married man and I loved my wife. But I loved Mae, too. Since you're not even sure if love exists, I don't know if you can understand that it's possible for a man to love two women, but I did. If I had thought for a single second that my friendship with Mae would hurt Janie, I would have ended it. But the truth was, there were times when Janie didn't even seem to know who I was, didn't seem to care that I was there to visit. That never kept me from going, but it did make me see that I didn't need to lock my heart away in that place with her. I gave Mae every bit of love I felt free to give her. I also gave her the freedom to choose whether to love me. I admired her too much to do anything less."

He sighed. "Given the way of the world now, a lot of men would have divorced a wife like Janie and moved on. That wasn't my way. I'd made a commitment, and I honored it in the only way I knew how. And whether you believe it or not, I honored my commitment to Mae the same way."

"I'm sorry you were in such a difficult position," Trace said. "It must have been heartbreaking."

"Having Mae in my life was one of the best things that ever happened to me. I can't possibly regret that it couldn't have been more, except for her sake. She deserved better."

"I think you made her very happy," Trace told him.

"I hope so," Nate said, then paused and looked directly into Trace's eyes. "There's a reason I'm telling you this. I always believed that one day Mae and I would be able to be together openly, that we'd marry and spend our remaining years together. Maybe even do a little traveling. We never had that chance."

Trace understood what he was saying. "This is your way of reminding me that life is short and unpredictable."

"Exactly. If you love Savannah, don't waste time counting the days until it seems appropriate to tell her. Don't fritter away precious hours planning for the future. Start living every moment. I've lived a good long life, but I'm here to tell you that it's still a whole lot shorter than I'd like."

They'd circled around and were back at Nate's driveway. "Think about what I said," he told Trace.

"I will," Trace promised. "Would you like to join us for Christmas dinner?"

"I would, but I'll be going out to see Janie in a while. She seems to like it when I come by to read to her."

"Thank you for sharing your story with me," Trace said, genuinely touched that Nate had told him.

"Don't thank me. Take my advice." He grinned. "Otherwise, I have a feeling Mae will find some way to give me grief for failing her. That woman always did know how to nag."

Nate was still chuckling as he walked slowly toward his house. Trace watched to make sure he didn't slip on the icy patches, then walked back to Holiday Retreat, his heart somehow lighter and more certain.

Ten

For the life of her, Savannah couldn't read Trace's expression when he got back from his walk. She thought he looked more at peace with himself, but had no idea what that meant.

She was also still puzzling over his magnanimous decision to give her Aunt Mae's stock. Had that been his way of making her financially independent to ease his own conscience and rid himself of some crazy sense of obligation to look after her? Was that going to make it easier for him to pack his bags in a day or two and walk away? When he left, would he go with no intention of ever looking back on her or Holiday Retreat as anything more than a pleasant memory? If that happened, it would break Hannah's heart.

It would break Savannah's heart, too.

"How's the turkey coming?" Trace inquired, peering over her shoulder to look into the oven. "It certainly smells fantastic."

"Another hour or so," she told him, wishing he would stay right behind her, his body close to hers.

She stood up and turned slowly to face him, relieved that he didn't back away. She reached up and cupped his cheeks. "You're cold. How about some hot chocolate? Or some tea?"

"I'm fine," he said, slipping his arms around her waist. "I'd rather have a kiss. I'm sure it would do a much better job of warming me up."

Savannah tilted her face up for his kiss. His mouth covered hers and brought her blood to a slow simmer. She couldn't be sure if it was working on Trace, but her body temperature had certainly shot up by several degrees. She sighed when he released her.

"Warmer now?" she inquired with forced cheer.

"Definitely," he said, his eyes blazing with desire. "Too bad we can't send Hannah for a ski lesson right this second."

"Are you sure we can't?" Savannah inquired hopefully.

"Nope. They're all booked up at the lodge."

She stared at him, biting back a chuckle. "You actually checked?"

"Of course. I always like to know my options."

"Do we have any?"

"Afraid not."

"Oh, well, once we've eaten, I have it on good authority that the turkey will put us straight to sleep. Maybe when we wake up, we'll have forgotten all about sneaking upstairs to be alone."

"I doubt it," Trace said, his expression wry. "Besides, I promised Hannah we'd all go for a walk after dinner."

"Why on earth would you do that? You just got back from a walk."

"Which taught me the distracting power of exercise," he said. "Besides, maybe we can have another snowball fight, and I can tackle you in the snow."

Savannah laughed. "Now there's something to look forward to."

"Sweetheart, a frustrated man is willing to take any contact he can get."

"Interesting. I would think the chill of the snow would be counterproductive."

"I think I'd have to spend a month outdoors in the Arctic before it would cool the effect you have on me," he said with flattering sincerity. He tipped her chin up to look directly into her eyes. "By the way, let's make a date."

"A date?"

He grinned. "You know, a man and a woman, getting together. A date."

"Out on the town?"

"Or alone in front of a cozy fire."

"Okay," she said with a surge of anticipation. "When do you want to have this date?"

"Tomorrow night?" he suggested.

The level of relief Savannah felt when she realized he intended to stay another day was scary. She had a feeling she wanted way too much from this man. Asking for a date—even making love—was hardly a declaration of undying devotion. She really needed to keep things in perspective and not get ahead of herself.

"Tomorrow would be fine. Maybe I'll see if Hannah can spend the night with Jolie again."

Trace grinned. "Best idea I've heard all day."

Savannah's heart beat a little faster at the promise beneath his words. The memory of the last night they had spent alone in this house brought a flush to her cheeks.

"Then I will definitely make it happen," she vowed. Because she was desperate for another one of those sweet kisses despite the risk of Hannah walking in on them, she backed away from Trace and moved to the stove, opening lids and checking on things that were simmering just fine only moments ago.

"Trace," she said without turning around, "if I ask you something, will you tell me the truth?"

"If I can," he said at once.

"You did make all the arrangements for Santa and the presents, didn't you?"

"Do you really want to know?" he asked, sounding vaguely frustrated. "Wouldn't you prefer to think it was part of the Christmas magic?"

She turned to face him. "Sure," she said honestly. "But I also believe in giving credit where credit's due. I'm not an eight-year-old who still believes in Santa, at least when it suits her. I know the kind of effort and money it takes to make a morning like the one we had happen. The person responsible should be thanked."

He shrugged, looking as if her persistence made him uncomfortable. "Look, it was nothing, okay?"

"It was more than that and you know it. You made Hannah's Christmas, and mine."

"I'm glad," he said. "Can we drop it now?"

"Why do you hate admitting that you did something nice?"

"Because I didn't do that much. I just made a few calls, ordered a few little things. Nate was more than willing to play Santa, especially since he had that gift from Mae for you."

"Which was wonderful of him to do, but you bought me a floor polisher and a professional-quality tool kit, for heaven's sakes."

"A lot of people would say that gift explains why I'm still single," he said.

"And I say it explains why I find you so completely and utterly irresistible," she said.

"Irresistible, huh?" A grin tugged at the corners of his mouth. "Come over here."

"Oh, no, you don't. We agreed that any more fooling around with Hannah underfoot would be a bad idea."

"Did we agree to that?"

"We did," she said emphatically.

"Does one kiss qualify as fooling around?"

"Probably not with a lot of people, but in my experience with you, it has a tendency to make me want a whole lot more."

His grin spread. "Good to know. I'll have to remember that tomorrow night."

Savannah met his gaze, her own expression deliberately solemn. "I certainly hope you do."

Trace woke up in a dark mood on the morning after Christmas. Rather than inflict his foul temper on Savannah or Hannah, he made a cup of coffee, then shut himself away in Mae's den and turned on his computer.

Even though he'd given his staff the week between Christmas and New Year's off, he checked his e-mails, hoping for some lingering piece of business to distract him. Aside from some unsolicited junk mail, there was nothing. Apparently other people were still in holiday mode. He sighed and shut the thing off, then sat back, brooding.

He'd spent the whole night wondering if he hadn't made the biggest blunder of his life the day before by giving Savannah that stock. It wasn't that he thought it was the wrong thing to do or that Mae would have disapproved. In fact, he was certain she'd known all along what he would do with her shares. No, his concern was over whether he'd given Savannah the kind of financial independence that would make her flat-out reject the proposal he planned to make tonight.

He was still brooding over that when the door to the den cracked open and Savannah peeked in.

"Okay to interrupt?" she asked.

"Sure," he said, forcing the surly tone out of his voice. "Come on in."

To his shock, when she walked through the door, she was wearing some sort of feminine, slinky nightgown that promptly shot his heartbeat into overdrive.

"On second thought," he muttered, his throat suddenly dry, "maybe you should change first."

"Why would I do that?" She glanced down. "Don't you like it?"

"Oh, yeah," he said huskily. "I like it. Maybe just a little too much."

Apparently she didn't get the hint, because she kept right on toward him. The next thing he knew, she was in his lap and his body was so hard and aching, it was all he could do to squeeze out a few words.

"What are you up to?" he inquired, staying very still, hoping that his too-obvious response to that wicked gown of hers would magically vanish. "Where's Hannah?"

"Gone," she said, brushing her mouth across his.

"Gone?"

"For the day," she added, peppering kisses down his neck.

"The entire day?" he asked, suddenly feeling more hopeful and a whole lot less restrained.

"She won't be home till five at the very earliest," Savannah confirmed. "I have Donna's firm commitment on that. She couldn't keep her tonight, so we compromised."

"I see," he murmured, sliding his hand over the slick fabric barely covering her breast. The nipple peaked at his touch.

"Sorry my present's a day late," she said as she proceeded to unbutton his shirt and slide it away.

Trace gasped as her mouth touched his chest. "Oh, darlin', something tells me it will be worth the wait."

Savannah had never felt so thoroughly cherished as she did lying on the sofa in Trace's arms, a blanket covering them, as a fire blazed across the room. In a few short days, she had discovered what it meant to be truly loved, even if Trace himself hadn't yet put a label on his feelings. She wondered if he ever would.

She turned slightly and found him studying her with a steady gaze.

"You're amazing, you know that, don't you?"

She shook her head. "I'm just a single mom doing the best I can."

"Maybe that's what I find so amazing," he said. "You remind me of my mother."

"Just what every woman wants to hear when she's naked in a man's arms," Savannah said lightly.

He gave her a chiding look. "Just hear me out. You're strong and resilient. You've had some tough times, but you haven't let them turn you bitter. You've just gotten on with the business of living and making a home for Hannah. When I was a kid, I don't think I gave my mother half enough credit for that. I spent too much time being angry because she didn't tell my dad to take a hike. I realize now that she didn't see him the same way I did. She loved him, flaws and all. It was as simple as that, so she did what she could to make the best of his irresponsible ways."

Trace caressed Savannah's cheek, brushing an errant curl away from her face. "So, here's the bottom line. I meant to do this with a bit more fanfare, but since our date has turned out to be a little unorthodox, this part might as well be, too."

He sounded so serious that Savannah went still. "What's the bottom line?" she asked worriedly.

"Will you marry me? I know we've just met and that you're still recovering from a divorce, but I've fallen in love with you. I talked it over with Nate—"

Savannah stared, sorting through the rush of words and seizing on those that made the least sense. "You what?"

"Now don't go ballistic on me," Trace said, then rushed on. "I ran into him yesterday. He saw that I had a lot on my mind, because I had all these feelings and I thought they were probably crazy, but he put it all in perspective for me. He said life is way too short to waste time looking for rational explanations for everything. I'm not all that experienced with falling in love, but apparently it doesn't follow some sort of precise timetable."

Savannah's lips twitched at his vaguely disgruntled tone. "No," she agreed. "It certainly doesn't."

"Then again, I'm used to making quick decisions. And I do think it's exactly what Mae had in mind when she insisted I come here for Christmas." He met her gaze. "And just so you know, with these quick decisions of mine, I rarely make mistakes."

"Is that so?" Savannah said quietly. "Well, it's certainly true that Aunt Mae was an incredibly wise woman. She hasn't steered me wrong so far."

"Me, either," Trace said, regarding her warily. "So?"

"So what?"

"Bottom line? I've fallen in love with you. Something

tells me that if I don't reach out for what I want with you now, it will be the biggest mistake of my life."

"Then reach," she said softly, her gaze locked with his.

Trace held out his hand. Savannah put hers in it, and for the first time in her life, Savannah felt as if she were truly part of a whole, something real and solid, with a future that was destined to last forever.

"There's something about this place," she said with a sense of wonder. "It must be Aunt Mae." She lowered her mouth to Trace's. "She always did get me the best gifts of all."

* * * * *

UNDER THE CHRISTMAS TREE

Robyn Carr

Dear Reader,

Years ago I decided to hook a rug. Not a bath mat, but a rug about the size of Michigan. Before I got half of Detroit done, I was bored to death. Next I bought an unassembled dollhouse—three stories, twelve rooms and pieces the size of toothpicks. Not such a good idea. Then came my quilting phase, which was limited to collecting boxes and boxes of colorful fabric. I took a whole day off from writing to "piece." When I showed my one-foot square to my neighbor she said, "Don't worry—you'll get the hang of it."

Then one day when my mind went out to play, which lucky for me is my work, it wandered up a mountain road, through some enormous trees, along a wide river in which the fish jumped, and I decided to stay awhile. I began to mentally live in a little town called Virgin River. I got to know the people and began to tell their stories. In no time at all I realized I was hooking together an ongoing story—building and piecing together the fabric of their lives.

Welcome back to Virgin River for another Christmas. And this time what is found "Under the Christmas Tree" not only brings the town together, but works some special magic on a couple of occasional patrons to Jack's Bar. Virgin River has a way of weaving its spell around the hearts of unsuspecting singles who pass through.

Happy holidays to all of you, and most especially to Debbie and Sherry!

Robyn Carr

One

During the Christmas holidays a side trip through Virgin River was a must; the town had recently begun erecting a thirty-foot tree in the center of town, decorated in red, white, blue and gold and topped with a great big powerful star. It dominated the little town, and people came from miles around to see it. The patriotic theme of the decorations set it apart from all other trees. Local bar owner Jack Sheridan joked that he expected to see the three wise men any minute, that star was so bright.

Annie McKenzie didn't pass through Virgin River very often. It was out of her way when driving from Fortuna, where she lived, to her parents' farm near Alder Point. It was a cute little town and she liked it there, especially the bar and grill owned by Jack Sheridan. People there met you once, maybe twice, and from that point on, treated you like an old friend.

She was on her way to her folks' place when, at the last moment, she decided to detour through Virgin River. Since it was the week after Thanksgiving, she hoped they'd started on the tree. It was a calm and sunny

Monday afternoon and very cold, but her heart warmed when she pulled into town and saw that the tree was up and decorated. Jack was up on an A-frame ladder straightening out some trimmings, and standing at the foot of the ladder, looking up, was Christopher, the six-year-old son of Jack's cook, Preacher.

Annie got out of her truck and walked over. "Hey, Jack," she yelled up. "Looking good!"

"Annie! Haven't seen you in a while. How are your folks?"

"They're great. And your family?"

"Good." He looked around. "Uh-oh. David?" he called. Then he looked at Christopher as he climbed down the ladder. "Chris, you were going to help keep an eye on him. Where did he go? David?" he called again.

Then Chris called, "David! David!"

They both walked around the tree, checked the bar porch and the backyard, calling his name. Annie stood there, not sure whether to help or just stay out of their way, when the lowest boughs of the great tree moved and a little tyke about three years old crawled out.

"David?" Annie asked. He was holding something furry in his mittened hands and she got down on her knees. "Whatcha got there, buddy?" she asked. And then she yelled, "Found him, Jack!"

The child was holding a baby animal of some kind, and it looked awfully young and listless. Its fur was black and white, its eyes were closed, and it hung limply in little David's hands. She just hoped the boy hadn't squeezed the life out of it; boys were not known for gentleness. "Let me have a look, honey," she said, taking the creature out of his hands. She held it up and its little head lolled. Unmistakably a puppy. A brand-new puppy.

Jack came running around the tree. "Where was he?"

"Under the tree. And he came out with this," she said, showing him the animal very briefly before stuffing it under her sweater between her T-shirt and her wool sweater, up against the warmth of her body. Then she pulled her down vest around herself to hold him in place. "Poor little thing might be frozen, or almost frozen."

"Aw, David, where'd you find him?"

David just pointed at Annie. "*My* boppie!" he said.

"Yeah, he's right," Annie said. "It's a boppie…er, puppy. But it's not very old. Not old enough to have gotten out of a house or a yard. This little guy should've been in a box with his mom."

"David, hold Chris's hand," Jack ordered.

And David said something in his language that could be translated into *I want my puppy!* But Jack was on his belly on the cold ground, crawling under the tree. And from under there Annie heard a muffled "Aw, crap!" And then he backed out, pulling a box full of black-and-white puppies.

Annie and Jack just stared at each other for a moment. Then Annie said, "Better get 'em inside by the fire. Puppies this young can die in the cold real fast. This could turn out badly."

Jack hefted the box. "Yeah, it's gonna turn out badly! I'm gonna find out who would do something so awful and take him apart!" Then he turned to the boys and said, "Let's go, guys." He carried the box to the bar porch and Annie rushed past him to hold the door open. "I mean, there are animal shelters, for God's sake!"

The fire was ablaze in the hearth and there were a couple of guys dressed like hunters at the bar, sharing a pitcher of beer and playing cribbage. She patted the place by the hearth and Jack put down the box. Annie immediately began checking out the puppies. "I'm gonna need a little help here, Jack. Can you warm up some towels in the clothes dryer? I could use a couple more warm hands. There's not enough wriggling around in this box to give me peace of mind." Then suddenly, she herself began wriggling. She smiled a big smile. "Mine's coming around," she said, patting the lump under her sweater.

Annie kneeled before the box, and David and Chris squeezed in right beside her. She took the wriggling puppy out from under her sweater, put him in the box and picked up another one. At least there was a blanket under them and they had their shared warmth, she thought. She put another one under her sweater.

"Whatcha got there?" someone asked.

She looked over her shoulder. The hunters from the bar had wandered over to the hearth, peering into the box. "Someone left a box of newborn puppies under the Christmas tree. They're half-frozen." She picked up two more, made sure they were moving and handed them over. "Here, put these two inside your shirt, warm 'em up, see if they come around." She picked up two more, checked them and handed them to the other man. The men did exactly as she told them, and she stuffed one more under her sweater.

Then she picked up a puppy that went limp in her palm. "Uh-oh," she muttered. She jostled him a little, but he didn't move. She covered his tiny mouth and nose with her mouth and pushed a gentle breath into him. She massaged his little chest gently. Rubbed his extremities, breathed into him again and he curled up in her palm. "Better," she murmured, stuffing him under her shirt.

"Did you just resuscitate that puppy?" one of the hunters asked.

"Maybe," she said. "I did that to an orphaned kitten once and it worked, so what the heck, huh? Man, there are eight of these little guys," she said. "Big litter. At least they have fur, but they are so *young*. Couple of weeks, I bet. And puppies are so vulnerable to the cold. They have to be kept warm."

"Boppie!" David cried, trying to get his little hands into the box.

"Yup, you found a box full of boppies, David," Annie said. She picked up the last puppy—the first one she'd warmed—and held it up to the hunters. "Can anyone fit one more in a warm place?"

One of the men took the puppy and put it under his arm. "You a vet or something?"

She laughed. "I'm a farm girl. I grew up not too far from here. Every once in a while we'd have a litter or a foal or a calf the mother couldn't or wouldn't take care of. Rare, but it happens. Usually you better not get between a mother and her babies, but sometimes… Well, the first thing is body temperature, and at least these guys have some good fur. The next thing is food." She stuck her hand into the box and felt the blanket they'd been snuggled on. "Hmm, it's dry. No urine or scat—which is not so good. Besides being really cold, they're probably starving by now. Maybe getting dehydrated. Puppies nurse a lot and they were obviously taken from the mother's whelp box."

Jack reappeared, Preacher close on his heels. Preacher was tall enough that he was looking over Jack's shoulder into the empty box. "What's up?" Preacher asked.

"Dad! David found a box full of puppies under the tree! They're freezing cold! They could be *dying!*" Christopher informed him desperately.

"We're warming 'em up," Annie said, indicating her and the hunters' lumpy shirts. "About half of them are wriggling and we'll know about the other half in a little bit. Meanwhile, we need to get some fluids and nourishment into them. They shouldn't be off the tit this young. Infant formula and cereal would be ideal, but we can make due with some warm milk and watered-down oatmeal."

"Formula?" Jack asked. "I bet I can manage that. You remember my wife, Mel. She's the midwife. She'll have some infant formula on hand."

"That's perfect. And if she has a little rice cereal or baby oatmeal, better still."

"Do we need bottles?" he asked.

"Nah," Annie said. "A couple of shallow bowls will work. They're young, but I bet they're awful hungry. They'll catch on real quick."

"Whoa," one of the hunters said. "Got me a wiggler!"

"Me, too!" the other one said.

"Keep 'em next to your body for a while," Annie ordered. "At least until we get those warm towels in the box."

Because of a box full of cold, hungry, barely moving puppies, Annie had all but forgotten the reason she'd ended up in Virgin River. It was three weeks till Christmas and her three older brothers, their wives and their kids would descend on her parents' farm for the holiday. Today was one of her two days off a week from the beauty shop. Yesterday, Sunday, she'd baked with her mom all day and today she'd gotten up early to make a couple of big casseroles her mom could freeze for the holiday company. Today, she'd planned to cook with her mom, maybe take one of her two horses out for a ride and say hello to Erasmus, her blue-ribbon bull. Erasmus was very old now and every hello could be the last. Then she'd planned to stay for dinner with her folks, something she did at least once a week. Being the youngest and only unmarried one of the McKenzie kids and also the only one who lived nearby, the task of looking in on Mom and Dad fell to her.

But here she was, hearthside, managing a box of newborn puppies. Jack rustled up the formula and cereal and a couple of warm towels from the dryer. Preacher provided the shallow bowls and mixed up the formula. She and Chris fed a couple of puppies at a time, coaxing them to lap up the food. She requisitioned an eyedropper from the medical clinic across the street for the pups who didn't catch on to lapping up dinner.

Jack put in a call to a fellow he knew who was a veterinarian, and it turned out Annie knew him, too. Old Doc Jensen had put in regular appearances out at the farm since before she was born. Back in her dad's younger days, he'd kept a thriving but small dairy farm. Lots of cows, a few horses, dogs and cats, goats and one ornery old bull. Jensen was a large-animal vet, but he'd be able to at least check out these puppies.

Annie asked Jack to also give her mom a call and explain what was holding her up. Her mom would laugh, knowing her daughter so well. Nothing would pry Annie away from a box of needy newborn puppies.

As the dinner hour approached, she couldn't help but notice that the puppies were drawing a crowd. People stopped by where she sat at the hearth, asked for the story, reached into the box to ruffle the soft fur or even pick up a puppy. Annie wasn't sure so much handling was a good idea, but as long as she could keep the little kids, particularly David, from mishandling them, she felt she'd at least won the battle if not the war.

"This bar has needed mascots for a long time," someone said.

"Eight of 'em. Donner, Prancer, Comet, Vixen, and... whoever."

"Which one is Comet?" Chris asked. "Dad? Can I have Comet?"

"No. We operate an eating-and-drinking establishment," Preacher said.

"Awww, Dad! Dad, come on. *Please,* Dad. I'll do *everything.* I'll sleep with him. I'll make sure he's nice. *Please.*"

"Christopher..."

"*Please.* Please? I never asked for anything before."

"You ask for everything, as a matter of fact," Preacher corrected him. "And get most of it."

"Boy shouldn't grow up without a dog," someone said.

"Teaches responsibility and discipline," was another comment.

"It's not like he'd be in the kitchen all the time."

"I run a ranch. Little hair in the potatoes never put me off." Laughter sounded all around.

Four of the eight pups were doing real well; they were wriggling around with renewed strength and had lapped up some of the formula thickened with cereal. Two were trying to recover from what was certainly hunger and hypothermia; Annie managed to get a little food into them with an eyedropper. Two others were breathing, their hearts beating, but not only were they small, they were weak and listless. She dripped a little food into their tiny mouths and then tucked them under her shirt to keep them warm, hoping they might mistake her for their mother for now, all the time wondering if old Doc Jensen would ever show.

When yet another gust of wind blew in the opened front door, Annie momentarily forgot all about the puppies. Some of the best male eye candy she'd chanced upon in a long while had just walked into Jack's bar. He looked vaguely familiar, too. She wondered if maybe she'd seen him in a movie or on TV or something. He walked right up to the bar, and Jack greeted him enthusiastically.

"Hey, Nate! How's it going? You get those plane tickets yet?"

"I took care of that a long time ago." He laughed. "I've been looking forward to this forever. Before too long I'm going to be lying on a Nassau beach in the middle of a hundred string bikinis. I dream about it."

"One of those Club Med things?" Jack asked.

"Nah." He laughed again. "A few people from school. I haven't seen most of them in years. We hardly keep in touch, but one of them put this holiday together and, since I was available, it sounded like an excellent idea. The guy who made the arrangements got one of those all-inclusive hotel deals—food, drinks, everything included except activities like deep-sea fishing or scuba diving— for when I'm not just lying on the sand, looking around at beautiful women in tiny bathing suits."

"Good for you," Jack said. "Beer?"

"Don't mind if I do," Nate replied. And then, like the answer to a prayer she didn't even know she'd uttered, he carried his beer right over to where she sat with the box of puppies. "Hello," he said.

She swallowed, looking up. It was hard to tell how tall he was from her sitting position, but certainly over six feet. Annie noticed things like that because she was tall. His hair was dark brown; his eyes were an even darker brown and surrounded with loads of thick black lashes.

Her mother called eyes like that "bedroom eyes." He lifted his brows as he looked down at her. Then he smiled and revealed a dimple in one cheek.

"I said hello," he repeated.

She coughed herself out of her stupor. "Hi."

He frowned slightly. "Hey, I think you cut my hair once."

"Possible. That's what I do for a living."

"Yeah, you did," he said. "I remember now."

"What was the problem with the haircut?" she asked.

He shook his head. "Don't know that there was a problem," he replied.

"Then why didn't you come back?"

He chuckled. "Okay, we argued about the stuff you wanted to put in it. I didn't want it, you told me I did. You won and I went out of there looking all spiky. When I touched my head, it was like I had meringue in my hair."

"Product," she explained. "We call it product. It's in style."

"Yeah? I'm not, I guess," he said, sitting down on the raised hearth on the other side of the box. He reached in and picked up a puppy. "I don't like *product* in my hair."

"Your hands clean?" she asked him.

He gave her a startled look. Then his eyes slowly wandered from her face to her chest and he smiled slightly. "Um, I think you're moving," he said. "Or maybe you're just very excited to meet me." And then he grinned playfully.

"Oh, you're funny," Annie replied, reaching under her sweater to pull out a tiny squirming animal. "You make up that line all by your little self?"

He tilted his head and took the puppy out of her hands. "I'd say at least part border collie. Looks like mostly border collie, but they can take on other characteristics as they get older. Cute," he observed. "Plenty of pastoral breeds around here."

"Those two are the weakest of the bunch, so please be careful. I'm waiting for the vet."

He balanced two little puppies in one big hand and pulled a pair of glasses out of the pocket of his suede jacket. "I'm the vet." He slipped on his glasses and, holding both pups upside down, looked at their eyes, mouth, ears and pushed on their bellies with a finger.

She was speechless for a minute. "You're not old Doc Jensen."

"Nathaniel Junior," he said. "Nate. You know my father?" he asked, still concentrating on the puppies. He put them in the box and picked up two more, repeating the process.

"He…ah… My folks have a farm down by Alder Point. Hey! I grew up there! Not all that far from Doc's clinic and stable. Shouldn't I know you?"

He looked over the tops of his glasses. "I don't know. How old are you?"

"Twenty-eight."

"Well, there you go. I'm thirty-two. Got a few years on you. Where'd you go to school?"

"Fortuna. You?"

"Valley." He laughed. "I guess you can call me old Doc Jensen now." And there was that grin again. No way he could have grown up within fifty miles of her farm without her knowing him. He was too delicious-looking.

"I have older brothers," she said. "Beau, Brad and Jim McKenzie. All older than you."

At first he was startled at this news, then he broke into a wide smile. Then he laughed. "Are you that skinny, fuzzy-haired, freckle-faced, tin-mouthed pain in the neck who always followed Beau and Brad around?"

Her eyes narrowed and she glared at him.

"No," he said, laughing. "That must have been some-one else. Your hair isn't pumpkin orange. And you're not all that…" He paused for a second, then said, "Got your braces off, I see." By her frown, he realized he hadn't scored with that comment.

"Where is your father? I want a second opinion!"

"Okay, you're not so skinny anymore, either." He smiled, proud of himself.

"Very, very old joke, sparky," she said.

"Well, you're out of luck, *cupcake*. My mom and dad finally realized a dream come true and moved to Arizona where they could have horses and be warm and pay lower taxes. One of my older sisters lives there with her family. I've got another sister in Southern California and another one in Nevada. I'm the new old Doc Jensen."

Now it was coming back to her—Doc Jensen had kids, all older than she was. Too much older for her to have known them in school. But she did vaguely remember the son who came with him to the farm on rare occasions. One corner of her mouth quirked up in a half grin. "Are you that little, pimply, tin-mouthed runt with the squeaky voice who came out to the farm with your dad sometimes?"

He frowned and made a sound. "I was a late bloomer," he said.

"I'll say." She laughed.

Nate was now checking out his third set of puppies.

"Why don't I remember you better?" she mused aloud.

"I went to Catholic school down in Oakland my junior and senior year. I wasn't going to get into a good college without some serious academic help, and those Jesuits live to get their hands on a challenge like me. They turned me around. And I grew five inches my first year of college." He put down the puppies he'd been holding and picked up the first one. He became serious. She noticed a definite kindness, a softness, in his expression. "Annie, isn't it? Or do you go by Anne now?"

"Annie. McKenzie."

"Well, Annie, this little guy is real weak. I don't know if he'll make it."

A very sad look came into her eyes as she took the puppy from him and tucked him under her sweater again.

Nodding at her, Nate said, "As much incentive as that is to live, I don't know if it'll do. How long were these guys outside before someone found them?"

"No one knows. Probably since before sunrise. Jack was in and out all day, fussing with the tree, and he never saw anyone. His little boy crawled under the tree and came out holding a puppy. That's how we found them."

"And what's the plan now?"

"I don't know," she said, shaking her head.

"Want me to drop them off at a shelter for you? Then you don't have to witness the bad news if one or two don't make it."

"No!" she exclaimed. "I mean, that's probably a bad idea. Some of the shelters over on the Coast are excellent, but you know what it's like this time of year. All those people adopting cute puppies for Christmas presents and then returning them in January. And returning them is the *good* scenario. All too often they're neglected or abused. Wouldn't it be better to take care of them until reliable homes can be found?"

"Who, Annie?" he asked. "Who's going to take care of them?"

She shrugged. "I have a small house in Fortuna and I work all day."

"What about the farm?" he asked.

She was shaking her head before he finished. "I don't think so. My dad's arthritis is bad enough that he slowly sold off the stock and my mom runs around like a crazy woman taking care of all the things that wear him out."

"Your dad's Hank McKenzie, right? He gets around pretty good for someone with bad arthritis."

"Yeah, he's proud. He doesn't let on. But it would fall to my mom and I can't ask her to take on eight puppies. And the whole family is coming home to the farm for Christmas. All thirteen of 'em."

"Well, Annie, I can't think of many options here," he said. "I know a few vets in the towns around here and I don't know one that would take this on. They'd put 'em in a no-kill shelter."

"Can't you help? You and your wife?"

He smiled at her. "No wife, Annie McKenzie. I have a real nice vet tech who's going to keep an eye on the stable while I'm out of town over Christmas, but that's the only help I have out there, and she doesn't have time to add eight puppies to her roster."

"Jack!" Annie called. She stood up. "Can you come here?"

Jack ambled over, wiping his hands on a towel.

"We have a situation, Jack," Annie said. "Dr. Jensen can't take the puppies and get them through this rough patch. He offered to drop them off at a shelter, but really, that's not a great idea." A couple of people had wandered over to listen in to the conversation, eavesdropping and making no bones about it. "I've volunteered at some of those shelters and they're awesome, but they're really, really busy at Christmastime. A lot of animals get adopted for presents, especially the really young, cute ones like these. You have no idea how many people think they want a fluffy pet for little Susie or Billie—until the first time the dog thinks the carpet is grass."

"Yeah?" Jack said, confused. A couple more people had wandered over from the bar to listen in to the conference.

Annie took a breath. "It's bad enough animals get returned. The worst case is they're not taken care of properly, get neglected or abused or get sick and aren't taken to the vet because the vet costs money. Sometimes people are embarrassed to return them and admit it was a mistake. Then they just take them to animal control, where they're on death row for three days before…" She stopped. "It can be a bad situation."

"Well, what are you gonna do?" Jack said. "Better odds than freezing to death under a Christmas tree."

"We could take care of them here, Jack," she said.

"We?" he mimicked, lifting a brow. "I see you about four times a year, Annie."

"I'll drive up after work every day. They're kind of labor-intensive right now, but I'll tell you exactly what to do and you can get—"

"Whoa, Annie, whoa. I can't keep dogs in the bar!"

An old woman put a hand on Jack's arm. "We already named 'em, Jack," she said. "After Santa's reindeer. At least the ones we could remember. Little Christopher already asked Preacher if he could have Comet. 'Course no one knows who Comet is yet, but—"

"There's no mother to clean up after them," Nate pointed out. "That means puppy excrement. Times eight."

"Aw, that's just great," Jack said.

"Don't panic," Annie said. "Here's what you do. Get a nice, big wooden box or big plastic laundry basket. You

could even put a wooden border around a plastic pad
from an old playpen, then toss an old blanket or a couple
of towels over it. Pull the blanket back to feed 'em the
formula and cereal every few hours. Or feed a couple or
three at a time outside the box so you can wipe up the
floor. Trade the dirty towels for clean ones, wash one set
while you use the other, and vice versa. Oh, and at least
two of these little guys need a lot of encouragement to
eat—the eyedropper gets 'em going. I could take the
littlest, weakest ones to a vet but, Jack, they're better off
with their litter mates."

"Aw, f'chrissake, Annie," Jack moaned.

"You can just grab someone at the bar and ask them
to take a couple of minutes to coax some food into a sick
puppy," she said hopefully.

"Sure," the old woman said as she pushed her glasses
up on her nose. "I'll commit to a puppy or two a day."

"Annie, I can't wash towels with puppy shit on 'em in
the same washer we use for napkins for the bar."

"Well, we did at the farm. My mom sterilized a lot,"
she said. "Bet you washed shitty baby clothes in the
same… Never mind. If you just get the towels, bag 'em
up in a big plastic bag, I'll do it. I'll come out after work
and spell you a little, take home your dirty laundry, bring
back fresh every day."

"I don't know, Annie," he said, shaking his head.

"Are you kidding?" Annie returned. "People will love
it, keeping an eye on 'em, watching 'em plump up. By
Christmas, all of them will be spoken for, and by people
who know what to do with animals. These little guys will
probably turn into some outstanding herders around here."

"Nathaniel, did you put her up to this?" Jack asked.

Nate put up his hands and shook his head. He didn't

say so, but she did have a point. Adopted by a town, these puppies would get looked after.

"I can't say yes or no without Preacher," Jack said, going off to the kitchen.

Annie smiled crookedly as she listened to the people who had followed Jack to the hearth, muttering to each other that, sure, this plan could work. They wouldn't mind holding a puppy every now and then, maybe donating a blanket, getting a puppy to eat, wiping up the floor here and there.

When Preacher trailed Jack back to the box of puppies, his six-year-old son was close on his heels. Jack tried to speak very softly about what all this would entail, but Christopher didn't miss a syllable. He tugged at Preacher's sleeve and in a very small voice he said, "Please, Dad, please. I'll help every day. I'll feed and hold and clean up and I won't miss anything."

Preacher pulled his heavy black brows together in a fierce scowl. Then, letting out an exasperated sigh, he crouched to get to eye level with the boy. "Chris, there can never be a dog in the kitchen. You hear me, son? And we have to start looking for homes right away, because some may be ready to leave the litter sooner than others. This has to be real temporary. We prepare food here."

"Okay," Chris said. "Except Comet. Comet's going to stay."

"I'm still thinking about that. And I'll have to look up on the computer how you take care of a bunch of orphaned pups like these guys," Preacher added.

Annie let a small laugh escape as she plucked the smallest, weakest puppy from under her sweater and put him back in the box. "Well, my work here is done," she said with humor in her voice. "I'll try to cut my day as short as I can at the shop, Jack. I'll see you tomorrow."

"Annie, they're not your responsibility," Jack said. "You've already been a huge help. I don't really expect you to—"

"I'm not going to turn my back on them now," she said. "You might panic and take them to the pound." She grinned. "I'll see you tomorrow."

Two

The puppies were found on Monday and Nate managed to stay away from the bar on Tuesday, but by Wednesday he was back there right about dinnertime. He told himself he had a vested interest—they might be about a hundredth the size of his usual patients, but he had more or less treated them. At least he'd looked at them and judged the care Annie recommended to be acceptable. In which case he didn't really need to check on them. But Jack's was a decent place to get a beer at the end of the day, and that fire was nice and cozy after a long day of tromping around farms and ranches, rendering treatment for horses, cows, goats, sheep, bulls and whatever other livestock was ailing.

But then there was Annie.

She was no longer a skinny, flat-chested, fuzzy-haired metal-mouth. Something he'd been reminding himself of for more than twenty-four hours. The jury was still out on whether she was a pain in the butt. He suspected she was.

She was tall for a woman—at least five-ten in her stocking feet—with very long legs. That carrot top was no longer bright orange—maybe the miracle of Miss Clairol had done the trick. In any case, her hair was a dark auburn she wore in a simple but elegant cut that framed her face. It was sleek and silky and swayed when her head moved. Her eyes were almost exotic—dark brown irises framed by black lashes and slanting shapely brows. And there was a smattering of youthful freckles sprinkled over her nose and cheeks, just enough to make her cute. But that mouth, that full, pink, soft mouth—that was gonna kill him. He hadn't seen a mouth like that on a woman in a long time. It was spectacular.

She was a little bossy, but he liked that in a woman. He wondered if he should seek therapy for that. But no— he thrived on the challenge of it. Growing up with three older sisters, he'd been fighting for his life against determined females his entire life. Meek and docile women had never appealed to him and he blamed Patricia, Susan and Christina for that.

The very first thing Nate noticed when he walked into the bar on Wednesday was that Annie was not there. He smiled with superiority. Hah! He should have known. She talked Jack and Preacher into keeping eight tiny puppies—a labor-intensive job—promising to help, and was a no-show. He went over to the box and counted them. Seven. Then he went up to the bar.

"Hey, Jack," he said. "Lose one?"

"Huh?" Jack said, giving the counter a wipe. "Oh, no." He laughed and shook his head. "Annie took one back to Preacher's laundry room for a little fluff and buff. He mussed his diaper, if you get my drift. It's the littlest, weakest one."

"Oh," Nate responded, almost embarrassed by his assumption. "He hanging in there?"

"Oh, yeah. And wouldn't you know—Christopher has decided that that one is *his*. Comet. Annie tried to talk him into falling in love with a stronger, heartier pup, but the boy's drawn to the one most likely not to make it."

Nate just laughed. "It was that way for me," he said. "I was older, though. We had the most beautiful Australian Kelpie—chocolate brown, silky coat, sweet face, ran herd on everything. My dad had her bred and promised me a pup. Out of her litter of six, I picked the runt and practically had to hand-feed him for weeks. The other pups kept pushing him off the tit. I was fifteen and, probably not coincidentally, also small for my age. I named him Dingo. He was big and tough by the time I was through with him, and he lived a long life for a hardworking Kelpie. We lost him just a few years ago. He lived to be fifteen. 'Course, he spent his last four years lying by the fire."

"You'd think a boy would pick the strongest in the pack."

"Nah." Nate snorted. "We don't feel that strong, so we empathize. Can I trouble you for a beer?"

"Sorry, Nate—I wasn't thinking. Fact is, I've been sitting on our nest on and off all day. I have a whole new appreciation for what you do."

"Have they been a lot of trouble?"

"Well, not really, just time-consuming," Jack said. "They eat every three hours or so, then their bedding has to be changed, then they nap, then they eat. And so on. Kind of like regular babies. Except there are eight of them and half of them need encouragement to eat. Plus, every so often, you have to check that they're not too warm or too cold. I don't want to freeze 'em or cook 'em. And the bar's getting lots more company during the day—visitors to the litter. Since they're here, they decide to eat and drink—more serving, cooking and cleanup than usual. Other than that, piece of cake. And if I ever find the SOB that left 'em under the tree, I'm going to string him up by his—"

"Well, hey, Doc Jensen," a female voice sang out.

Nate turned to see Annie come out the back of the bar, Christopher trailing so closely that if she stopped suddenly, he'd have crashed into her. She carried a furry ball of black and white that fit perfectly into her palm. Looking at her, he realized he hadn't remembered her quite accurately. Or rather, quite *enough*. Tall, curvaceous, high cheekbones, soft dark auburn hair swinging along her jaw, long delicate fingers... She was beautiful. And her figure in a pair of snug jeans and turquoise hoodie with a deep V-neck just knocked him out. Where the heck had this girl been hiding?

And why was he, a man who could appreciate cleavage and tiny bikinis, suddenly seeing the merits in jeans, boots and *hoodies?*

Then he remembered she'd been hiding in a little hair salon in Fortuna, under a pink smock.

He picked up his beer and wandered over to the hearth. Christopher and Annie sat on opposite sides of the box, which left no place for him, so he stood there in the middle.

Annie passed Chris the puppy. "Hold him for just a minute, then snuggle him back in with his brothers and sisters," she said. "It's good for him to be part of his family. They give him more comfort than we can right now."

"A little maintenance?" Nate asked.

Annie looked up at him and smiled. "This is the part that gets to be a bother—without a mother dog to change their diapers and keep them clean, by the end of the day they're looking a little worse for wear. Some of them actually needed washing up. My dad always used to say a little poop never hurt a puppy, but you let that go long enough and it will. Gets them all ugly and matted and sick."

"You bathed him?"

"Four of them, without dunking them," she said. "Can't let them get cold. Preacher's wife loaned her blow-dryer to the cause. Okay, Chris, he's been away from home long enough now." She reached into the box and pushed some puppies aside to make room, and Chris gently put his puppy into the pile. "They'll be ready to eat again in about an hour. Why don't you get back to your homework, or dinner, or chores, or whatever your folks have in mind."

"Okay, Annie," he said.

And Nate fought a smile as Chris vacated his place on the hearth. But before he sat down he asked Annie, "Can I buy you a beer? Or something else?"

She tilted her head and smiled at him. "I wouldn't mind a beer, thanks." He was back with a cold one for her in just moments and sat down opposite her. "I think they're doing okay here," she said to him.

He wasn't a hardhearted guy, but he only pretended interest in the pups, picking one up and then another, looking at their little faces. He'd rather be looking at her, but didn't want to seem obvious. "Were you here yesterday?" he asked, studying a puppy, rather than her.

"Uh-huh," she said, sipping her beer. "Ah, that's very nice. Thanks."

"You planning to come every day?" he asked.

"If I can swing it," she said. "I kind of made a deal— if they wouldn't hand them over to some shelter, I'd do my part. These little guys are just too cute and vulnerable. They could turn into impetuous Christmas presents, no matter how carefully the shelter volunteers screen the potential owners. And look at their markings—I'd say Australian-shepherd-and-border-collie mix. Outstanding herders. They should find good homes around here, and they'll be glad to work for a living."

Nate lifted his eyebrows. "Good guess," he said. "You get off work before five?" he found himself asking.

"Not usually. I have a small shop in Fortuna—six chairs. It's a franchise—my franchise. So I'm responsible, plus I have a large client list and it's Christmastime. But I'm moving appointments around the best I can—a few of my clients will take another stylist in a pinch. And I've been training an assistant manager, so she's getting thrown into the deep end of the pool because of these puppies. And I'm doing my puppy laundry and paperwork at midnight."

"What kind of paperwork?" he asked.

"The kind you have with a small business—receipts, receivables, bills, payroll. Jack and Preacher are managing real well during the day when it's sort of quiet around here, but when it gets busy at the dinner hour, they need a hand. And you heard Jack—he's not washing puppy sheets with his napkins." She smiled and sipped her beer. "We should all take comfort in that, I guess."

"I guess." He smiled. "How'd you end up with a beauty shop?"

"Oh, that's not interesting. I'd rather hear about what you do. I grew up around animals and being a vet is my fantasy life. You're living my dream."

"Then why didn't you pursue it?" he asked.

"Well, for starters, I had exactly two years of college and my GPA was above average, but we both know it takes way more than that to get into veterinary college. Isn't it harder to get into veterinary college than medical school?"

"So I hear," he said. "So, after two years of college…?"

She laughed and sipped her beer. "One of my part-time jobs was grooming dogs. I loved it. *Loved* it. The only thing I didn't love was going home a grimy, filthy mess and not exactly getting rich. But I saw the potential and needed to make a living. I couldn't focus on a course of study in college, so I went to beauty school, worked a few years, hit my folks up for a loan to buy a little shop, and there you have it. I do hair on two-legged clients now. And it's working just fine."

"And your love of animals?"

"I stop by this little bar every evening and babysit a bunch of orphaned puppies for a few hours," she said with a laugh. "I still have a couple of horses at the farm. My dad got rid of the livestock years ago except for Erasmus, a very old, very lazy, very ill-tempered bull who my dad says will outlive us all. They're down to two dogs, my mom keeps some chickens and their summer garden is just amazing. But it was once a thriving dairy farm, plus he grew alfalfa and silage for feed."

"Why isn't it still a thriving farm?" he asked.

"No one to run it."

"Your brothers don't want the farm life?"

"Nope," she said. "One's a high-school teacher and coach, one's a physical therapist in sports medicine and one's a CPA. All married with kids and working wives. All moved to bigger towns. And the closest one lives a few hours away."

"What about you?" he asked.

"Me?"

"Yeah, you. You sound like you love the farm. You love animals. You still have a couple of horses at your parents' farm…."

She smiled. "I'd be real happy to take on the farm, but that's not a good idea. Not the best place for me."

"Why not? If you like it."

She cocked her head and smirked. "Single, twenty-eight-year-old woman, living with Mom and Dad on the farm, building up the herd and plowing the fields. Picture it."

"Well, there's always help," he said. "Hired hands for the rough stuff."

She laughed. "Rough stuff doesn't scare me, but I can't think of a better way to guarantee I'll turn into an old maid. My social life is dull enough, thanks."

"There are ways around that," he pointed out. "Trips. Vacations. Visitors. That sort of thing. Something to break up the isolation a little."

"That's right—that's what I heard. Before I knew who you were, I heard Jack ask you if you had your plane tickets yet and you said something about Nassau, a Club Med vacation and lots of string bikinis. Right?"

For some reason he couldn't explain, that embarrassed him slightly. "No, no. I don't know anything about that Club Med stuff. A buddy of mine, Jerry from vet school, set up a get-together over Christmas with our old study group. We've only been in touch by e-mail and haven't been together since graduation. The Nassau part is fact, the string-bikinis part is fantasy. I'm planning to do some scuba diving, snorkeling, some fishing. I haven't been away in a while." He laughed. "Frankly, I haven't been warm in a while."

"You don't get together with your family over the holidays?" she asked.

"Oh, they were gracious enough to invite me to join them all on a cruise. *All* of them," he stressed. "My folks, three sisters and brothers-in-law, four nephews and two nieces. It's going to be hell to give up all that shuffle-board, but I'll manage somehow."

"Do they ever come back here?" she asked. "You know—to the old homestead? Where you all grew up?"

"Frequently. They move in, take over, and I move out to the stable and take up residence in the vet tech's quarters."

"You and the tech must be on very good terms."

He grinned at her. "She's married and lives in Clear River, but we keep quarters for her for those times we have cases that are going to need attention through the night. She was my dad's assistant before he retired. She's like a member of the family." Then he studied her face. Was that relief? "The family was all home for Thanks-giving," he went on to explain. "It was great to see them all, and boy was I glad when they left. It's madness. I have really good brothers-in-law, though. At least my sisters did that much for me."

She sipped her beer. "You must be looking forward to your vacation. When do you leave?"

"The twenty-third. Till the second of January. I plan to come home tanned and rested." And with any luck, he thought, sexually relaxed. Then he instantly felt his face grow hot and thought, *Why the hell did I think that?* He wasn't typically casual about sex. He was actually very serious about it.

Annie peered at him strangely. "Dr. Jensen, are you blushing?"

He cleared his throat. "You don't have to be so formal, Annie. Nate is fine. Is it a little warm by this fire?"

"I hadn't noticed, but—"

"Have you eaten?" he asked.

"No. I hadn't even thought about it."

"Let's grab that table, right there close by, before

anyone else gets it. I'm going to tell Jack we want dinner. How about that?"

"Fine," she said. "That sounds fine. By the time we're finished, Chris will be back, ready to feed his puppy."

Through the rest of that first week the puppies seemed to do just fine. Thrived in fact. So did Annie, and she hoped it didn't show all over her face. There was no particular reason for Nate to show up day after day; the pups weren't sick, didn't need medical care and he hadn't made the commitment to help that she had. Yet he returned on Thursday, Friday and Saturday. She'd love to believe he was there to see her, but it seemed such a far-fetched idea. So highly unlikely that she could interest a man like him through this odd doggie-day-care-in-a-bar that she wouldn't allow herself to even think about it.

But he was there by six every day, right about the time she finished her puppy chores. He always bought her a beer, then Jack provided dinner, which they ate together at a table near the hearth. They talked and laughed while catching up on their families and all the locals they knew, getting to know each other in general. Although she knew this friendship would probably fade and disappear by the time the puppies were adopted, and even though traipsing out to that bar every day was wearing her out, she was enjoying his company more than she could admit even to herself.

"Did you always plan to come back here? To take over your father's practice?" Annie asked him one evening.

"Nope," he said. "Wasn't part of my plan at all. First of all, I prefer Thoroughbreds to cows. I wanted to treat them, breed them, show them, race them. I did a couple of years' residency in equine orthopedics, worked in a big practice in Kentucky, then in a real lucrative practice outside Los Angeles. Then my dad wanted to retire. He'd put in his time—he's seventy-five now. Years back, he and my mom bought a horse property in a nice section of southern Arizona, but they wanted to keep the house and stable, not to mention the vet practice, in the family. You have any idea how hard it is to build a practice with these tough old farmers and ranchers?" He chuckled. "The name Nathaniel Jensen goes a long way around here, even though I am the upstart."

"So here you are…back at the family practice?" she asked. But she was thinking that he'd been rubbing elbows with big-money horse people. Society people, whom she'd seen at a distance at certain competitions and fairs, but knew none of. She'd been riding since she could walk, took lessons and competed in dressage, and so was more than a little familiar with the kind of wealth associated with breeding, racing and showing Thoroughbreds. The well-to-do could send their daughters to Europe for lessons, fly their horses to Churchill Downs in private planes and invest millions in their horse farms. Humboldt County farm girls couldn't compete with that. She swallowed, feeling not a little out of her league.

"I said I'd give it a chance. My plan was to put in a year or two, save some money, maybe break in a new guy with an interest in the stable and practice. But I haven't gotten around to that and it's been two years."

"I see," she said. "You're still planning to leave?"

"I don't have to tell you what's great about this place." He smiled. "And I think I don't have to tell you what's missing. It's kind of a quiet life for a bachelor. Remember that dull social life you mentioned?"

"How could I forget?" she threw back at him.

"You seeing someone?" he asked suddenly, surprising her.

"Hmm? No. No, not at the moment. You?"

"No. Date much?" he asked.

Startled, she just shook her head. "Not much. Now and then." She thought for a moment and then said, "Ah. The vacation. Getting away to see if you can jump-start your social life a little bit?"

He just smiled. "Couldn't hurt. And it'll be nice to catch up with friends. We were real tight in vet school. We got each other through a lot of exams."

"How many of you are going?" she asked.

"Five men, including me, two of them married and bringing wives. Two women vets."

"Women vets? Married?"

"One's still single and one's divorced."

"Gotcha," she said. "I bet one's an old girlfriend."

"Nah," he said.

"Come on—didn't you ever date one?"

"I think I dated both of them. Briefly. We worked out better as study partners than...well, than anything else." He took a drink. "Really, I want to fish."

She took a last bite of her dinner. "Fishing is real good around here," she said.

"I fish the rivers here. A little deep-sea fishing sounded like a good idea. Some sun would be acceptable. I have golf clubs," he said with a laugh. "I used to play a lot of golf in L.A. Yeah," he mused, "a little sunshine won't hurt."

After a moment she reminded him with a smile, "And soon you'll be lying on a beach in the middle of a hundred string bikinis."

"Maybe you're right," he said with a grin. "Maybe I should do more fishing around here if I want to catch the big one."

By the time Sunday rolled around, Annie was back at the farm. She went early in the day so she could drop by the bar later that afternoon. Today, so close to Christmas, she was baking with her mother all day—breads, pastries, cookies to be frozen for the barrage of company—but she would have her dinner at the bar. Because of the puppies, of course.

"You're very quiet, Annie," her mother said. "I think you're letting this adventure with the puppies wear you out. You've always had such a tender heart."

"I am tired," she admitted, rolling out cookie dough. "I'm getting up extra early, starting at the shop earlier so I can leave earlier, staying up late to finish work. And you know I won't leave my house alone—I'm decorating for Christmas. I've been doing a little here and there, before and after work."

"Then you shouldn't be out here two days a week," Rose McKenzie said. "Really, I appreciate the help, but I'm not too old to do the holiday baking."

"I count on our baking as gifts," Annie said. "So I'm glad to help.

"I didn't realize we had a new and improved Doc Jensen," she went on, changing the subject. "I thought it was still old Doc Jensen who came for the horses and Erasmus when you needed a vet. But when he stopped to look at the puppies, he explained he was Nathaniel Junior. You never mentioned."

"Oh, sure we did, honey. His coming home was good gossip there for a while. He had some woman living with him, but she took off like a scalded cat. I don't think we talked about anything else for months."

"A woman? When was that?"

"A couple years ago. Some fancy young Hollywood girl," Rose said with an indulgent laugh. "We ran into them a few times—at the fair, the farmers' market, here and there." Her mother was kneading dough as she chattered. "You know, you don't run into people that often around here. They could've been here a year before anyone met her, but Nathaniel had her out and about. Probably trying to help her get acquainted. But it didn't work too well, I guess."

"I'm sure I would have remembered, Mom. I don't think you ever mentioned it."

Rose looked skyward briefly, trying to remember. "That might've been about the time you were preoccupied with other things. Like buying the Clip and Curl shop. And then there was Ed, and that ordeal with Ed. You might've had other things on your mind."

Ed. Yes, Ed. She hadn't exactly been engaged, thank God, but they'd been an item for about a year and she'd expected to be engaged. They *had* talked about marriage. She laughed humorlessly. "That could have distracted me a little," Annie agreed.

"The bum," Rose McKenzie muttered, punching dough more aggressively than necessary. "He's a pig and a fool and a liar and a…a bum!"

Loving it, Annie laughed. "He's really not a bum. He works hard and earns a good living, which it turned out he needed for all the women he had on a string. But I concede to pig, liar and fool, and I'm certainly not missing him. The louse," she added. "I can't remember now—why was it we didn't let the boys shoot him in the head?"

"I can't remember exactly, either," Rose said. "I knew all along he wasn't right for you."

"No, you didn't," Annie argued. "You had me trying on your wedding dress about once a month, asking me constantly if we'd talked about a date. You expected him to give me a ring."

"I just thought *if…*"

Ed was in farm-equipment sales and had a very broad territory in northern California, a job that had him on the road most of the week. Then she learned that for the entire time they'd dated, Ed was involved with another woman in Arcata. About six months ago he'd decided it was time to make a choice, and he chose the other woman.

Ouch.

Annie's pride was hurt, but worse than hurt pride was her embarrassment. How had this been going on without her getting so much as a whiff of it? When she hadn't seen him, she had talked to him every single day. He never betrayed the slightest hint that she was not the only female in his life. And it made her furious to think he'd been with another woman while he was with her. She even drove to Arcata to sneak a look at her, but she couldn't figure out, based on looks, just what it was that won her the great prize that was Ed.

Before she could ponder that for long, that Arcata woman found *her,* looked her up, informed her they weren't the only two. Ed, as it happened, was quite the dabbler. He had at least one other steady girlfriend to spend the nights with.

Her tears had turned to fumes. She threw out everything that reminded her of him. She bought all new bedding and towels. Went to the doctor and got a clean bill of health. But at the end of the day when she grieved, it wasn't so much for Ed as for the *idea* of Ed; she had invested a year in a man she thought would give her the stability of marriage and family, a settled life. The dependence of love. Security. When she thought about Ed, she wanted to dismember him. She wanted her brothers to go after him and beat him senseless. But not only would she never take him back, she'd cross the street to avoid him. So maybe Rose was right—maybe they both really knew all along he just wasn't the one.

But neither was anyone else. She hadn't been out on five dates since the breakup a little more than six months ago, and the number of boyfriends she'd had before Ed had come along were too few to count. She went out with her girlfriends regularly, but the best part of her life was spending a couple of days on the farm, riding, cooking or baking or putting up preserves with her mom.

The farmhouse had a wide porch that stretched the length of the house, and from that porch you could watch the seasons come and go. The brightness of spring, the lushness of summer, the burnt color of fall, the white of winter. She watched the year pass from that porch, as she had since she was a little girl. But lately it seemed as though the years were passing way too quickly and she wondered if she'd ever find the right partner to sit there with rather than alone.

A Hollywood woman? A fancy Hollywood woman? That would explain things like Caribbean vacations. Nate was drawn to flashy, sexy women. Or maybe the kind of women found in the private boxes at races or horse shows; Annie had seen enough of those televised events to know the type—model gorgeous, decked out in designer clothes, hand-stitched boots, lots of fringe and bling. Or the type seen at the fund-raisers and society events attended by the wives, daughters and sisters of Thoroughbred breeders, the kind of women whose horses were entered in the Preakness. Or perhaps he preferred medically educated women, like another vet who could appreciate his professional interests—the kind of women who also rubbed elbows with the well-to-do because of their profession.

But probably ordinary, sensible-shoes farm girls didn't do anything special for a man like Nate.

Annie's thoughts were broken when her father walked into the kitchen and refilled his coffee cup. He put a hand on the small of his back and stretched, leaning back, rolling his shoulders.

"Are you limping, Dad?"

"Nah," he said. "Got a little hitch in my giddy-up is all."

"As soon as I'm through with this puppy project, I'll make it a point to get out here more often to help."

"The doctor says the best thing is for him to keep moving," Rose said. "You do enough to help already."

"You don't remember that fancy Hollywood woman?" Hank asked, going back to the conversation he had over-heard. Without waiting for an answer, he added, "Breeze woulda blown her away. Skinny thing. Could see her bones. Not at all right for Nathaniel." He took a sip of coffee and lifted his bushy brows, looking at her over the rim of his mug. "You'da been more his speed, I think. Yeah, better Nathaniel than that son of a so-and-so you got yourself mixed up with."

"I didn't even know Nate Jensen was here until a few days ago, remember?" Annie pointed out. "And before that, I was with the so-and-so, and Nate was taken."

"Yeah, you'da had to kill that skinny thing, but she looked near death, anyhow." Then he grinned at her and left the kitchen.

"Will Nathaniel have his family for Christmas?" Rose asked.

"Actually, he said his parents, sisters and their families are going on a cruise. I gathered, from the way he said it, he'd throw himself off the boat if he were along. He said something sarcastic, like it would be hell to give up all that shuffleboard, but he'd manage."

"Oh, you must invite him to join us for the holiday dinners, Annie. As I recall, he was friendly with one of your brothers when they were kids."

"Mom, he's not hanging around. He's going on some highfalutin Caribbean vacation, meeting up with some old classmates from veterinary college, hoping to get lost in a sea of very tiny bikinis on the beach. Apparently his taste in women hasn't changed much."

"Really?" Rose asked. "Now to me, that sounds dull."

"Not if you're a single guy in your thirties, Mom."

"Oh. Well, then take him some of these cookies."

"I'm sure he couldn't care less about home-baked cookies." *Not if what he prefers is some fancy, skinny, rich girl,* she thought.

"Nonsense. I don't know the man who doesn't like home-baked cookies. Reminds them of their mothers."

"Just the image I'd most like to aspire to," Annie said.

Three

Rose McKenzie insisted that Annie take a plate of Christmas cookies to Dr. Jensen, but it made Annie feel silly, farm girlish, so she left them in the car when she went into Jack's bar later that afternoon.

She gasped in pleasure when she walked in—the place had been decorated for Christmas. A tree stood in the corner opposite the hearth, garlands were strung along the bar and walls, small evergreen centerpieces sat on the tables, and the buck over the door wore a wreath on his antlers. It was festive and homey, and the fresh pine scent mingled with wood smoke and good cooking from the kitchen to complete the holiday mood.

It took her less than two seconds to see that Nate wasn't there, which made her doubly glad she hadn't trotted in her plate of baked goods. Maybe this was the day he wasn't going to show. It wasn't as though he had any obligation here. In fact, besides giving the puppies a cursory look and asking Annie if there was anything wrong with any of them, he didn't do anything at all.

She gave Jack a wave and went directly to the puppies,

which, in the past week, had gotten surprisingly big. Boy, if those weren't all border collies, she was no judge of canines. Out of the eight, two were solid black with maybe a little silver or gray or perhaps a mere touch of white—the only indication another breed might've been involved. But they had grown so much! And they were doing so beautifully—plump and fluffy and adorable. Just like everyone else who passed by that box, she couldn't resist immediately picking a puppy up and cuddling it against her chin.

Jack came over to the hearth and she grinned at him. "The bar looks wonderful, Jack. All ready for Santa."

"Yeah, the women got it ready for their hen party. Cookie exchange tomorrow at noon—you should come."

"Nuts, I'll be at work. But tell them the decorations are beautiful."

"Sure," he said. "Annie, we've got a situation. We're going to have to come up with another plan here."

Instinctively she picked up Comet to judge his size and strength; he wriggled nicely. "Why's that, Jack?" she asked.

He was shaking his head. "This isn't going to work much longer. I can go another day, two at the most, while you figure something out, but the puppies have to find a new home. They're getting bigger, more energetic, and giving off the kind of odor reminiscent of a box full of puppy shit. This is an eating-and-drinking establishment, Annie."

"Are people complaining?" she asked.

"Just the opposite," he said, shaking his head. "We're drawing a nice crowd on account of the big tree and the cute little puppies. But you know puppies, Annie. They're wetting on a lot of laps while they're being held and snuggled. This is going to go from cute and fun to a big problem real soon."

"Oh," she said, helpless. "Oh." Well, it wasn't as though she had trouble understanding. It was different when the litter was in your downstairs bathroom or under the laundry sink in a home, or when there was a mother dog around tending the nursery. You just didn't realize how hard that mother dog worked unless you had to care for the puppies yourself. Even when there were eight of them, as long as they were nursing, good old Mom licked them from head to toe, keeping them clean and dry. The second you started giving them solid food, Mom stopped cleaning up after them and it took no time at all for them to get a little stinky and messy. But under normal circumstances, that came at about six weeks, right about the time they were ready to leave the nursery anyway.

In this case, there'd been no mom, and the formula and cereal that went in one end came out the other. Their bedding couldn't be changed fast enough or their cute little bottoms washed often enough to avoid a smell.

"What am I going to do?" she asked herself.

"We've got homes for some of them figured out," Jack said. "I'm not sure any of them are ready to be out of the box yet, but we've got a few adoptions worked out. There's Christopher, of course. He's not letting Comet get away."

"Comet's not ready to be the responsibility of a six-year-old. He needs a couple more weeks. And good as Chris is with him, he'll have to be supervised," Annie said.

"I know. And I'm sunk," Jack said. "David keeps babbling about his 'boppie.' I've been thinking about getting a dog, anyway, something to clean up the spills around my place. But…"

"And, Jack, you can't turn a puppy this size over to a three-year-old boy any more than you can put him in charge of eggs and ripe tomatoes."

"Yeah, yeah, when it's time, we'll be careful. And Buck Anderson, sheep rancher, says it's about time to get a couple of new herders ready. He's got a little child of his own and seven grandchildren. He can speak for two—his sons can help get 'em grown before they turn them over to the other dogs and the sheep. He'd like them to be Christmas dogs, though. Now, I know you don't trust people looking for puppies as Christmas gifts, but you can count on Buck. He knows the score." Jack took a breath. "I don't like their chances if they won't herd sheep, however."

"Okay, that's four taken care of," she said.

"Couple of other people have been thinking about it, but that's the progress so far. Did you realize everyone in town has named them after the reindeer?"

"Yeah, cute, huh? Jack, I don't have a place for them. I guess I could take them to my house and run home between haircuts to make sure they're fed and watered, but to tell the truth, I don't have that kind of time. At Christmastime, everyone wants to be beautiful. And I try to spend as much time at the farm as I can—the whole family's coming."

"Maybe we need to rethink that shelter idea. Couldn't they just look after them for a couple of weeks? Then we'll take at least a few off their hands...."

Just then Nathaniel blew in with a gust of wind. He pulled off his gloves and slapped them in his palm. He looked around the recently decorated bar and whistled approvingly. "Hey," he said to Annie and Jack. "How's everything?" Silence answered him. "Something wrong?"

Annie stepped toward him. "Jack can't keep the puppies here anymore, Nate. They're starting to smell like dogs. It is a restaurant, after all."

Nate laughed. "I think you've hung in there pretty well, Jack. Lasted longer than I predicted."

"Sorry, Nate. If Annie hadn't been so convincing, these guys would have gone to a shelter right off the bat. Or someplace way worse. At least we've figured out homes for a few—when they're old enough and strong enough to leave the litter."

"Yeah, I understand," Nate said good-naturedly. "Well, if Annie promises not to bail on me, I'll take 'em home. I'm pretty busy most days, but I have a vet tech at the clinic to help. And they don't need quite as much hands-on care as they did a week ago—at least they can all lap up their meals without an eyedropper now. I can put 'em in the laundry room and close the door so they don't keep me up all night."

"Will they be warm enough?" Annie asked. "Are they strong enough?"

"They'll be fine, Annie. Jack—what's for dinner?"

"Chili. Corn bread. Really? You'll take them out of here?"

Nate laughed. "Can we mooch one more meal before we cart them away? I'm a bachelor—there's hardly ever any food in the house." He draped an arm around Annie's shoulders. "This one is spoiled now—she's used to getting fed for her efforts. And two beers."

"Yeah," Jack said, lifting a curious eyebrow. "Coming right up."

"After we eat, you can follow me home," he said to Annie, as if the matter was settled.

Annie knew approximately where the Jensen clinic, stable and house were, but she couldn't remember ever going there. You might take your poodle or spaniel to the small-animal vet, but the large-animal vet came to you, unless you had a big animal in need of surgery or with some condition that required long-term and frequent care. His stable also provided occasional short-term boarding for horses. And he had breeding facilities, but that also was most often done at the farm or ranch by the farmers and ranchers. Some owners of very valuable horses preferred to leave their prefoaling mares with the vet.

Nate transported the puppy box in the covered bed of his truck. They were bundled up with extra blankets and wouldn't get too cold on the short ride. Annie followed in her own truck. They made a left off the main road at the sign that said Jensen Stables, Dr. Nathaniel Jensen, DVM. The road was paved, which was high cotton in this part of the world. It was tree-lined and the snow-covered brush was cut back from the edge. The road had to be at least half a mile long. Then it opened into a well-lit compound. The stable was on the left of a large open area, with a corral surrounding it on the side and back. The clinic itself was attached to the stable. There were Christmas lights twinkling in one of the windows. On the right was a sprawling, modern one-story house with a brick sidewalk that led up to double front doors of dark wood set with beveled-glass windows. Not a single Christmas light or ornament on the house at all. Annie wondered if the vet tech had decorated the clinic.

Between the house and stable were two horse trailers. One could hold six horses, the other two, and both were so fancy they probably came with a bar and cabin attendants.

The garage door at one end of the house opened automatically, and Nate pulled in. Annie parked outside and walked through the garage. She carried the formula and baby cereal while he carried the box, managing to open the door into the house and flick on lights with his elbow as he walked through the kitchen and then disappeared.

The kitchen was the kind Annie's mother would have died for—large new appliances, six-burner stove, double oven, work island with a sink. It was gorgeous. It looked newly remodeled.

Annie moved more slowly, peering past a long breakfast bar into a spacious family room with big, comfy-looking furniture and a beautiful fireplace. On each side of the fireplace were floor-to-ceiling bookcases filled with leather-bound volumes.

"Annie? Where are you?"

She stopped gawking and followed the voice. She passed a very long, old oak table in a large breakfast nook inside bay windows that looked out on the back of the property. A sharp left and down a short hall took her past a bathroom, a bedroom and into a laundry room. In addition to cabinets, there was a stainless-steel washer and dryer, along with a deep sink. This was not an old farmhouse, that was for sure.

"I'll use linens from the clinic to line their box," Nate said. "They'll be fine in here. Listen, I know you signed on for this duty, but I don't want you to feel like you have to rearrange your schedule to get out here the first minute you can escape work every day. Virginia, my tech, can help during the day and I get called out sometimes, but this time of year, no one's breeding or birthing, so it's not usually too hectic. But—"

"Okay," she said. "I won't come. I'll leave a number. If you need me."

"Well, could you still come sometimes?" he asked with a laugh. "If you give me a hand feeding and cleaning up, I'll thaw a hunk of meat to throw in the broiler or something. Nothing like Preacher's, but edible. Just let me know when you can be here."

"You have your tech…."

"I don't like to ask Virginia to stay after five unless we have special patients—she wants to get home, have dinner with her husband. I'll fix you up with a key, in case I'm tied up on a case and you beat me home."

"Sure. Tell me exactly what you want," she said.

He put his hands on his hips. "I want to know what's wrong. Why are you frowning like that? You've been frowning since I walked into Jack's."

Mentally, she tried to smooth out her eyebrows, but she could still feel the wrinkle. She'd been trying to picture him with a trophy girl on his arm, that was what. Or with an equestrienne from a high-muck-a-muck ranch who raced or showed horses all over the world. Or maybe a mature and attractive woman his age who was as smart and successful as he was. And he was so damn handsome it wasn't hard to imagine all this. But she said, "You're downright chipper. This is *exactly* what you didn't want, but you're almost thrilled about having the puppies here. What's up with that?"

He laughed. "Nah. I knew it was going to come to this. I'm glad Jack and Preacher handled them for that first week for two reasons—they had to be fed, dried and checked frequently, and I enjoyed stopping by the bar on the way home every day. Don't know when I've eaten so well," he added, rubbing a flat belly. "Now that it's apparent they're all going to make it, they only have to be checked and fed every few hours, something Virginia and I can handle during the day. I agree with you about the shelter. They'd probably be just fine—those folks are devoted, and they interview and screen efficiently before they let a tiny, orphaned animal out of there. But why take chances? If we have to use the shelter, we'll just do so after Christmas."

"That's it? You knew all along you'd get stuck with them?"

He just laughed. "Come on, I'll show you the house I grew up in, we'll put on some coffee, feed the pups and put 'em down for the night. How about that?"

"You don't have to show me the house. I'm not going to be poking around in here."

He grabbed her hand. "I'm not worried about you poking around. Come on," he said again, pulling her back through the kitchen. He took her through a spacious great room, where he said, "Many fights between my sisters happened here. When I grew up, there was old, floral, ratty furniture in here, but once everyone got educated and off Mom and Dad's payroll, new things began to appear around the house. Things got updated and remodeled." He pulled her down the hall, showed her where the master bedroom and three others were located. "I got the bed-and-bath on the other side of the kitchen. Kept me away from the girls." Then he took a right turn off the great room. "Formal living room, used only on family holidays like Christmas, and dining room, used for overflow at big family dinners." And then they were back in the huge kitchen.

"It's enormous," she said breathlessly. "It's very beautiful. What must it have been like to grow up in a house so large?"

"I probably took it for granted, like any kid would," he said with a shrug. "It's still my parents' house, though I doubt they'll ever move back here. Come on, I'll put on coffee."

"You don't have to entertain me, Nate."

"Maybe I'm entertaining myself. I don't have much company out here."

The moment they had the coffee poured Annie remembered. "Damn," she said. "Don't move. I have some-thing for you." She dashed out the garage door to her car, retrieved the cookies and brought them in. In typical country fashion, they were arranged on a clear, plastic plate with plastic wrap covering them. "For you," she said. "They should be warm, but now they're nearly frozen. My mother insisted."

"She baked them for me?" he asked, surprised, as he peeled off the wrap and helped himself.

"Well, kind of."

"Kind of?"

"We baked together today. All day. We do that for the holidays. Stuff for the freezer, gifts for neighbors and for my girls at the shop. We bake on my days off for weeks right up to Christmas."

"You bake?" he asked, looking mesmerized, maybe shocked.

She smirked. "All farm girls bake. I also know how to quilt, garden, put up preserves and chop the head off a chicken. I couldn't butcher a cow by myself, but I know how it's done and I've helped."

"Wow."

She was not flattered by his response. She'd hardly led a glamorous life and she'd much rather have told him she'd gone to boarding school in Switzerland and dres-sage training in England. "I bet I remind you of your mother, huh?"

He chuckled. "Not exactly. Do you fish? Hunt?"

"I've been fishing and hunting, but I prefer the farm. Well, I shot a mountain lion once, but that was a long time ago and I wasn't hunting. The little bastard was after my mother's chickens, and the boys had already moved away, so I—"

"How old were you?" he asked.

She shrugged. "I don't know—thirteen or fourteen. But I'm not crazy about hunting. I like to ride. I miss the cows. I loved the calving. Ice cream made from fresh cream. Warm eggs, right out from under the chicken. I have more 4-H ribbons than anyone in my family. Erasmus, that mean old bull? He's mine. Blue ribbon—state fair. I was fifteen when he came along—he's an old guy now, and the father of hundreds. I have a green thumb like my mother—I can stick anything in the ground and it grows. I once grew a rock bush." He threw her a shocked expression and she rolled her eyes. He recovered. "Just one of those plain old farm girls. Size-ten boot and taller than all the boys till I was a senior in high school. My dad calls me solid. Steady. Not the kind of girl men are drawn to. I attract…*puppies*. That's what."

He smiled hugely, showing her his bright white teeth and that maddening dimple. "Is that a fact?"

"Not *your* type, certainly. I've never had a string bikini. I wouldn't know what to do with one. Floss your teeth? Is that what you do?"

He laughed. "There are sexier things than string bikinis," he said.

"Really?" she asked. "The minute I heard you describe being lost in the middle of a hundred string bikinis, I got a picture in my mind that I haven't been able to get rid of. It's like having a bad song stuck in your head."

"Oh, Jesus, don't you just have a giant bug up your ass," he said, amused.

"I have no idea what you mean," she said, though she knew *exactly*. She was a terrible liar. "I didn't even know you weren't your father, you know. I had no idea you were the vet until you showed up at Jack's. And today while we were baking, my folks told me that when you came up here to take over the practice, they'd talked about nothing else for months. I guess you brought your girl-friend with you. A beautiful, fancy, Hollywood woman."

Shock widened his mouth and eyes. "Get outta here," he said. Then he erupted into laughter. "Is that what they're saying?"

A little embarrassed, she shrugged. "I don't know that anyone's saying anything anymore, and I don't know who besides my folks saw it that way."

He laughed for a long time, finally getting himself under control. "Okay, look. She was my fiancée, okay? But it was my mistake, bringing her up here, because she was far too young. I must have been out of my mind. She wasn't ready to get married. Thank God. And she wasn't a Hollywood woman, although she really wanted to be. Maybe she is by now, for all I know. Susanna was from Van Nuys. The only thing she knew about horses was that they have four legs and big teeth. She was twenty-four to my twenty-nine, had never lived in a small town and really didn't want to."

"And thin," Annie added. "Very thin."

He put his hands in his pockets, rocked back on his heels, lifted expressive dark brows and with a grin he said, "Well, not all over."

"Oh, that's disgusting," she returned, disapproval sounding loud.

"Well, it's not nice to talk meanly about past girlfriends."

"I bet she looked great in a string bikini," Annie said with a snort.

"Just unbelievable," he said, clearly taunting her. "Now, why would you be so jealous? You don't even know poor, thin Susanna. For all you know, she's a sweet, caring, genuine person and I was horrible to her." And he said all this with a sly smile.

"I am certainly not jealous! Curious, but not jealous!"

"Green as a bullfrog," he accused.

"Oh, bloody hell. Listen, I'm shot. Long day. Gotta go." She grabbed her purse and jacket and whirled out of the kitchen. And got lost. She found herself in the wide hall that led to the bedrooms. She found her way back to the great room, then to the kitchen. "Where the hell is the door?"

He swept an arm wide toward the door that led to the garage, still wearing that superior smile. What an egomaniac, she thought, heading for the door.

When she got to her car, she thought, well, that was perfectly awful. What's more, he saw right through her. She was attracted to him, and because she knew there had probably been many beautiful women in his past, she'd let it goad her into some grotesque and envious remarks about the only one she knew of, Susanna. The child-woman who obviously had a little butt and nice rack. Why in the world would she do that? What did she care?

It probably had something to do with touring a four-thousand-square-foot custom home, beautifully furnished, across the compound from a spacious stable with a couple of horse trailers her dad would have killed for. Well, what was one to expect from a veterinary practice that served so many, over such a wide area? And not a new practice, either, but a mature one—probably forty years old. Established. Lucrative.

She'd grown up in a three-bedroom, hundred-year-old farmhouse. Her three brothers shared a bedroom and never let her forget it for a second. They *all* shared one very small bathroom. But she loved the way she'd grown up and had never been jealous a day in her life—why would she be now? Could it be that in addition to all that, she'd never gone to special, private schools, never worn custom-tailored riding gear, never could afford the best riding lessons or most prestigious competitions? Also, she had wide hips, big feet and a less-than-memorable bustline. "Oh, for God's sake, Annie," she said to herself. "Since when have you even thought about those things!"

How long had she been sitting here in her car? Long enough to get cold, that was how long. Well, it was time to suck it up. She'd go back in there and just tell him she was cranky, that being one of those "sturdy" farm girls who owns exactly one pair of high heels she can barely walk in, it just rubbed her the wrong way hearing about the kind of woman who could get the attention of one of the county's few bachelors. Not that *she* wanted his attention, but just the same... She'd apologize and promise never to act that way again. She wasn't usually emotional. Or irrational.

She walked back into the still-open garage, up to the back door and gave a short tap. It flew open. He reached out and grabbed her wrist, pulled her roughly into the house, put his arms around her, pressed her up against the kitchen wall just inside the door, and *kissed* her! His mouth came down on hers so fiercely, with such dominance and confidence, her eyes flew open in shock. Then he began to move over her mouth while he held her against the wall with his wide, hard chest, his big hands running up and down her rib cage, over her hips.

She couldn't move. She couldn't raise her arms or let her eyes drift closed or even kiss back. She held her breath. What the hell...?

He finally lifted his lips off hers and said, "You like me. I knew it."

"I don't like you that much. Never do that again," she said.

"You want me," he said, smiling. "And I'm going to let you have me."

"You're conceited. I do not want you."

He kissed her again, and again her eyes flew open. This time she worked her arms free and pushed against his chest.

"Well, hell, just kiss me back and see if I start to grow on you," he said.

"No. Because you think this is funny. I came back in here to apologize for being crabby. I don't care about that skinny woman. Girl. I'm just a little tired."

"You don't have to apologize, Annie. I think it's kind of cute. But you don't have to be jealous of Susanna. She's long gone and I hardly even missed her. We weren't right for each other. At all."

"That's what my dad said."

"Hank said that?"

She nodded.

"What did he say? Exactly?" Nate wanted to know.

She shouldn't. But she did. "He said I'd be more your type, but I'd have had to kill the skinny blonde first. He said she looked near death, anyway."

Nate thought that was hilarious. He laughed for a long time, but he didn't let go of her. "Good thing she left, then. She couldn't hold her own in any kind of fight. She cried if she broke a nail."

"I bet she was just one of many."

He withdrew a little, but the amusement stayed in his eyes. "You think I'm a player."

"How could you not be? It's not like I don't know about those rich horse people. And you're the *doctor!* Of course you've had a million girlfriends."

The smile finally vanished. "No," he said. "I'm not that guy, Annie. Just 'cause I've been around those folks doesn't mean I'm that kind of guy."

"Well, there are the girl vets you're going to the islands with," she reminded him.

"Tina and Cindy," he said with a laugh. "Shew. I hate to brag, but I'm thirty-two, Annie, and there have been a couple of women in my past. But I bet there are a couple of guys in yours, too. Tina and Cindy are just friends of mine."

"Uh-huh. I'm sure. Old friends and a hundred string bikinis."

"Come back in and finish your coffee," he said with a tolerant chuckle.

"I have to go. I have to get home to Ahab."

"Who's that?" Nate asked.

"My cat. Ahab. Tripod. He has a lot of names. He's three-legged."

"What happened?" Nate asked.

"I don't know. I adopted him from the shelter when it was clear no one else would ever take him. He's got a bad attitude, but he loves me. He's very independent, but he does like to eat. I have to go."

"Are you coming back tomorrow after work?"

"Are you going to be a gentleman?" she asked.

He lifted one of those handsome brows. "You want me to?"

No. "Absolutely. Or I'm leaving the puppies all to you without helping."

"Just come tomorrow after work. Swing by home and feed your cat first so you don't have to be in a hurry to leave." He gave her a very polite kiss on the cheek that just oozed with suggestiveness. "I'll see you then."

Four

Christmastime in a beauty shop was always frantic and the Clip and Curl was no exception. There were less than two weeks till Christmas and Annie's clientele, the clientele of the whole shop, wanted to look their best for parties, open houses, family visits, neighborhood gatherings. Appointments were one after the other. There was a lot of gossip, a lot of excited chatter. Annie was pretty quiet the next day, but there was plenty of talk in the place to cover the void.

Pam, who was older than Annie by a few years and had been married for ten, was training to be the assistant manager. While Annie was applying foil to strips of hair for highlighting, Pam approached with the appointment book in her hands. "We have three choices. We can turn away some of our best regular customers, stay open till nine a couple of nights or open up the next two Mondays to fit them in."

"Why don't people schedule ahead of time?" Annie asked.

"As you taught me, they expect to be accommodated and we can either do that or lose them to another shop."

"Staying late is hard for me and you have a family. I don't want to stick you with that duty," Annie said. Then after thinking about it, she said, "Maybe I should work nights. That would settle that."

"Settle what?" Pam asked, holding the large appointment book in her crossed arms, against her chest.

"Oh, that guy. The vet. You know."

"Know what?"

"The guy at the bar, Jack, he said they couldn't keep the litter of puppies there anymore. The dogs are doing very well, growing, which means they'll soon be up to their eyeballs in puppy poop. Not a real appetizing prospect for a restaurant. So Jack said that's it, they have to go. Dr. Jensen took them to his house, which is part of the whole stable-and-vet-clinic operation. And since I made a commitment to help…he's counting on me coming over after work."

"To his house?"

"Yeah. He said if I'd help, he'd thaw something for us to eat. We've been having a beer and dinner at that bar."

"Listen, it's up to you, Annie. It's your shop. My husband's on board to get the kids from school and take care of their dinner and homework. You know I need whatever hours…"

"Then *you* make the decision," Annie said.

Pam lowered the appointment book and held it against her thigh. "Annie, I don't need you to stay if the shop is open till nine or open Mondays for a couple of weeks. Two of the girls are willing to work a little extra to help pay for Christmas. But you have to feel comfortable about leaving me in charge. And I don't want to push you to do that before you're ready. You've run a pretty tight, one-woman show here."

"Have I?"

Pam nodded. "But I don't blame you, Annie. This is your shop, your investment, your responsibility. Whenever you think I'm ready, I'm glad to help."

"Thing is, he kissed me."

It became very quiet in the shop. Pam's mouth dropped open.

"Nuts," Annie said. There were no ears gifted with supersonic hearing like those found in a beauty shop, despite the noise of dryers and running water. She looked around the small shop. It was tiny—three chairs on each side of the room. Two dryers and two deep sinks in back. Behind that was their break room and Annie's little office.

In the salon now were women in various stages of beautifying, rods, rollers, foils or backcombed tresses blooming from their heads. Beauticians with blow-dryers, curling irons, combs and brushes in their hands, poised over those heads. All silent. All waiting. "Talk among yourselves," Annie instructed.

"Lotsa luck," Pam said. "Is this guy, this vet, in any way appealing?"

Annie's cheeks got a little rosy.

"Is he cute?" Pam asked.

Annie leaned toward Pam and whispered, "You'd wet yourself."

And Pam's cheeks got a little pink. "Whew."

"Well, tell us about him," someone said.

"Yeah, what kind of guy is he?"

"Should you call the police or wear something with a real low neckline?"

"How old is he? How many times has he been married? Because that's key. Believe me!"

"Listen, I can't talk about this," Annie said. "I've

known the man barely a week! And only because of these puppies! Honestly, if it weren't for these puppies, we wouldn't even know *about* each other. He's a large-animal vet. He was just doing the bartender, Jack, a favor by looking at the orphaned litter."

"Um, Annie, don't *you* have large animals? Who's your vet?"

"Well, *he* is, but I didn't *know* that. I mean, my folks keep an eye on the horses and Erasmus. My bull," she clarified for those confused stares in the room. "When they said they called Doc Jensen to the farm, I thanked them and paid the bill. I mean, it hardly ever happens that the horses or the bull needs something. I thought he was the same Doc Jensen who'd been looking after our animals since I was in diapers. But it turned out to be his son. Doc Jensen Junior." She cleared her throat. "He's thirty-two. And never been married."

"Whoa," someone said. Another woman whistled.

"He's had girlfriends," Annie said. "Not from around here. But when he came up here to take over his dad's practice a couple of years ago, he brought a young buxom blond fiancée with him and it didn't work out, but—"

"Low neckline," someone advised.

"Tight jeans. Snug, anyway. I mean this in the nicest way, but if you could think about a little extra makeup, like eyeliner and lip liner," someone said.

"You don't need that," Pam said quietly.

"I was thinking that maybe being unavailable would be a good—"

"No!" three women said at once.

"Why would you do that?" Pam asked.

"He's just too damn sure of himself," Annie answered.

"Well, how about this," Pam said. "Maybe you could try being sure of *your*self?"

Annie thought about that for a second. "See, that's the hard part."

Usually Annie was very confident. She knew she was intelligent; she was a small-business owner and it was going well. She was independent and doubted that would ever change, even once she partnered up. And as for her modest upbringing, she had not yet met the person she'd trade places with. Life on the farm was rich in many ways. She might've had a moment of shallow jealousy over the skinny, fancy, city girl who could attract not only Nathaniel's attention, but acquire a big engagement rock, as well, but all that had passed pretty quickly.

There was one area in her life where her confidence was a little shaky, however. She'd barely recovered from Ed. She'd put a lot of faith and trust in a man who'd clearly been using her. If this new guy, the big-shot vet, was really interested in her, he'd have some proving to do. She wasn't going to be played for a fool. And she certainly wasn't going to be the only available two-legged female he'd run across lately.

Later that day after work, she fed Ahab, dug around in her refrigerator and fluffed up a nice green salad, fixed a plate of frosted brownies and headed for Nate's place.

When she pulled up to his house, a woman was just leaving the clinic, locking the door behind her. She was a tiny thing with salt-and-pepper hair cut supershort, and when she might have headed for the only car parked outside the clinic, she stopped and waited for Annie with a smile on her lips.

Annie approached her. "You must be Virginia," she said.

"And you would be Annie McKenzie," the older woman said. "Nice to meet you. I met your parents some years ago, but I think all you kids were either at school or had maybe already left home. Nate's not home yet, but you have a key, right?"

"I do," she said. "Thanks for helping with those puppies. These are for you," she added on a whim, passing Virginia the plate of brownies.

"You shouldn't have, but I'm glad you did. Annie, tell Nathaniel to give you both the clinic and my home phone numbers and to leave your phone number for me. If we run into a situation when he's stuck out at a farm or ranch, we can work together to cover for him. I live in Clear River and he tells me you're in Fortuna. It's about the same distance for both of us to get here."

"Sure. And I'll tell him to call me first. I don't have a husband to irritate by running off somewhere to take care of puppies."

Virginia tilted her head, regarding her. "He doesn't talk about women, you know," she said.

"Your husband?" Annie answered, confused.

Virginia laughed. "Nathaniel. Can't get a word out of him about his love life. And I've known him since he was this high," she said, her hand measuring about midthigh.

"Maybe it's not much of a—"

"But he's talked about you for a week now. Annie this, and Annie that."

Annie's eyes grew round and maybe a little panicked. "This and that *what?*" she asked.

"I think he finds you delightful. Maybe amazing. You knew exactly what to do with the puppies because, raised by Hank and Rose, you were trained to know. And you're tall. For years he's been asking me if I've always been this short. I think he likes tall women. When you were little, he said, you had a big batch of curly, carrot-orange hair, but you obviously outgrew it. You shot a mountain lion, butchered a cow, raised a blue-ribbon bull. Oh, and you're beautiful. But a little crabby, which he finds humorous." Virginia shook her head. "Nathaniel likes to try to find his way around a difficult woman," she said with a grin. "Being the youngest of four with three bossy older sisters, he can't help it, so don't let down your guard."

Annie laughed. No problem there—her guard was up.

"It's nice that you two have renewed your friendship," Virginia added.

"But, Virginia, we were never friends," Annie said. "We barely recall each other from childhood. He knew my older brothers, but not that well. We all went to different schools and might've run into each other at fairs, 4-H stuff, that sort of thing. Really—a long time ago. A couple of decades ago."

But the woman only flashed her friendly grin. "Isn't it great when you renew an acquaintance with someone you have that kind of history with?"

That kind of history? Annie wondered. That wasn't much history. "But we don't know each other as adults. Not at all."

Virginia laughed. "Bet that'll be the fun part. Now you call me if you need me," she said, moving toward her car. "And thanks for the brownies! My husband will be as thrilled as I am!"

"Sure," Annie said. "Of course."

Virginia paused at her car door. "Annie, if you need anything other than puppy care, don't hesitate to call on me."

"Thanks," she said.

* * *

It wasn't long after Annie had spoken to Virginia and let herself into Nate's house that he came home. She heard his truck enter the garage, and when he walked in the door to the kitchen, his face lit up. "Hey," he said. "I thought I'd beat you here."

"Just got here," she said. "And something smells good."

"I just hope it also tastes good. I admit, Virginia gave me a hand."

"No shame in that, Nate." Then she smiled at him. Standing in the kitchen like that, waiting as he walked in the door after work, felt very nice. And then she told herself not to fantasize. Just one day at a time.

They fed the puppies and while a roast simmered in the Crock-Pot, complete with potatoes, carrots, onions and whole mushrooms, they let the puppies loose in the family room. They sat on the floor with them, a roll of paper towels handy, and laughed themselves stupid trying to keep track of the little animals, which escaped under the sofa, down the hall, behind furniture. They kept grabbing the puppies, counting, losing count, temporarily misplacing one. Nate estimated they were just over four weeks old because they were starting to bark, and every time one did, he or she fell over. It was better than television for entertainment.

After the puppies were put away again, dinner eaten, dishes cleaned up, Annie made noises about leaving, and Nate talked her into sitting down in the family room. "It's early," he said. "Let's just turn on the TV for a while."

She plopped onto the couch. "Oh God," she said weakly. "Don't let me get comfortable. I really have to go home. You have no idea how early I start my day."

"Oh, really?" he asked. "Do you have eight whiny,

hungry puppies in your laundry room? I start pretty early myself. Besides, I want you comfortable. This is such a great make-out couch."

"How do you know that?" she asked.

He shrugged like it was a stupid question. "I've made out on it."

"You said you'd be a gentleman!"

"Annie, you just have to try me out—I'm going to be very gentlemanly about it. Come on, don't make me beg."

She grinned at him. "Beg," she said. "I think that's what it's going to take."

He got an evil look in his eye and said, "Come here." He snaked his fingers under her belt and tugged, pulling her down into the soft sofa cushions. "Let's put a little flush on your cheeks."

The next night Annie took eight lengths of ribbon in eight different colors to Nate's house. They tied the ribbons around the puppies' necks, so they could be iden-tifiable. They weighed them, made a chart, had dinner—and Nathaniel was more than happy to put a flush on her cheeks again.

Night after night, she fed Ahab right after work so she'd be free to—ahem—help with the puppies. And talk and play and kiss. The kissing quickly became her favorite part. Greedy for that, she trusted Pam to hold the shop open two nights a week and a half day on Monday. In exchange for that, Annie insisted Pam take a little comp time to get her own Christmas baking and shopping done; she came in late a few days to compensate.

There was more contributing to that flush of happi-ness on Annie's cheeks than just the kissing. Minor though it might seem, getting to know him when he had his shirt pulled out of his jeans and his boots off seemed so much more than casual. Of course her boots were off, also, and while they necked, their feet intertwined and they wiggled their toes. They wiggled against each other, too. It was delicious.

When they were feeding or cleaning up after puppies, preparing a meal together, they were also getting to know each other. Annie had never really thought about it before, but that was what courtship was all about—figuring out if you had enough in common after the spark of desire to sustain a real relationship.

Nathaniel had wanted to work with Thoroughbreds since he was a kid. He owned a couple of retired racehorses, good for riding. "One good stud can set you up for a great side business," he said. The initial investment, however, could be major. "In the next year or two, I'm going to invest. See what I can do."

"Why not show horses?" she asked.

"That's good, too, but I like the races."

"I love horses," she said. "You knew that. But did you know this? I've competed in dressage events all over the state. When I was younger, of course. Eventually it became too expensive for me. The best training was never in my neighborhood and the biggest competitions, including for the Olympics, were out of my reach. But if I could ever do anything, I would teach beginner dressage. Maybe even intermediate."

She told him she had thought about inviting him out to the farm to meet her parents and horses, but realized he already knew them. He knew them before he knew her, in fact. So she invited him to see her little Fortuna house and she made him dinner there. "I don't have a great make-out couch, however," she warned him.

"Doesn't matter anymore," he said. "I needed that couch to get you going, but now that you're all warmed up, we can do it anywhere. The floor, the chair, against the wall, the car…"

"I was so right about you. You're just arrogant."

He was also sentimental. Nathaniel was charmed by her two-bedroom house with a detached garage. The decorating was not prissy like a little dollhouse, but dominated by strong colors and leather furniture. The best part was, she had it completely decorated for Christmas, a garland over the hearth, lights up on the outside eaves. She had drizzled glitter on her huge poinsettia, had a Christmas cactus as big as a hydrangea bush, lots of what his mother had always called gewgaws. Ribbons, candles, potpourris, a Santa collection and, of course, a tree. A real tree, decorated to match the house—in burgundy, green, cream and gold. "And you're not even spending Christmas at home," he said.

"But I live here," she reminded him.

"It just doesn't make sense for me to put up decorations," he said. "Mother left a ton of them in the garage cabinets, but I'm leaving before Christmas. And I didn't think anyone would be around to see them."

"I do it for myself," she said. "I'm having holidays, too. I'll spend nights here since it gets so crowded at the farm. In years past, I've been known to loan the house to one of the brothers and sisters-in-law and kids and just take the couch. Brad brings an RV, which the teenage boys pretty much commandeer. During summer visits, the kids stake out the barn and front porch."

"Sounds like fun. I think I would have liked that, growing up," he said. "When they all get here, will you let me meet them? Or re-meet them? I haven't seen the boys since junior high."

"Sure, but you have to be prepared."

"For what?"

"They're going to treat you like you're my boyfriend."

He smiled and pulled her against him. "What makes you think I'd have a problem with that?"

"I don't think we're in that place," she informed him. "I think we just eat, talk, take care of puppies and kiss."

"Annie," he said as if disappointed. "What do you think a boyfriend is?"

"Um, I never really…"

"Tomorrow is Sunday, your day at the farm with your folks," he said. "Get done with whatever it is you do by early afternoon. Come for a ride with me. Let me show you my spread—it's so peaceful in the snow. Bring a change of clothes so you can freshen up before we have dinner."

"I can do that," she said. "I'd like that."

Annie had seen herself as plain and sturdy, until she'd been under the lips and hands of Nathaniel Jensen, because he was so much more than she'd ever reckoned with. Handsome, smart, funny, compassionate, independent, strong, sexy—the list was endless. And he made her feel like so much more than a solid, dependable farm girl. When he kissed her, dared to touch her a bit more intimately than she invited, pulled his hands back when she said *not yet,* she felt sexy and pretty and adored. This was a man she looked forward to exploring, and she was taking him in slowly, with such pleasure.

So she told Rose she had a date to go riding with the vet and was, of course, excitedly excused from Sunday baking and dinner at the farm. "Please don't get all worked up," Annie told her mother. "This isn't anything special. We've become friends on account of those puppies."

"Right," Rose said. "Still, could you wear a little color to bring out your hair and eyes?"

"I said, take it easy," Annie stressed. "And don't mention it to anyone. I don't want to be the talk of the county the way that skinny Hollywood woman was."

But Annie wasn't taking it lightly—she was almost sizzling with pleasure. And she tried dressing up a little more. For riding, she wore her best jeans, newest boots and oldest denim jacket over a red turtleneck sweater. She added a black scarf. She brought along attractive slacks and high-heeled boots with a silk blouse and her best suede blazer to wear for dinner afterward. They talked about horses while they rode two of Nate's favorite mounts, a couple of valuable, albeit retired, Thoroughbreds, disciplined and with just the right amount of spirit. The conversation about breeding, training, racing and showing horses was so stimulating she could almost forget for a while that she was trying not to fall in love with him.

"I'm not around horse people enough anymore," she said. "When I was riding in competition as a girl, that was enough to keep me occupied twenty-four hours a day. No wonder I didn't have fun in college—I wasn't riding."

"You're good on a horse," he said. "You should ride every day. So should I—it's the best part of what I do."

They rode into the foothills behind Nate's stables along a trail that, although covered by a layer of snow, had been well used. The trees rose high above them and the sun was lowering in the afternoon sky. They talked about growing up as the youngest in their families, and the only one of their gender. While Annie's brothers treated her like a football, Nathaniel's older sisters played with him as if he were a baby doll they could dress up at will. "It's amazing I'm not weirder than I am," he said. "The next oldest is Patricia, who's thirty-seven. Then Susan, and the oldest is Christina—one every two years. My parents had decided to quit while they were ahead and then, bingo." He grinned. "Me. I upset the balance in a big way."

"I think a similar thing happened at the farm," she said. "The boys are thirty-three, thirty-four and thirty-seven. Then I came along and upset the bedroom situation. My parents decided I had to have my own, which left one for the boys. And then I raised a bull—did I mention he won a blue ribbon?"

"Several times, I believe."

"We actually needed him. We had a couple of old bulls who just couldn't step up to the plate anymore, y'know? But Erasmus was Ready Freddy. I'm real proud of that old bull." She smiled. "My brothers had their shot at raising animals and they did all right, but Erasmus was the blue-ribbon baby. I blew my brothers out of the 4-H water with that guy." She sighed wistfully. "I think having a daughter was harder on my dad and brothers than being the only girl was on me. And being the only girl wasn't easy. They were ruthless."

"Yet protective?" he asked.

"It's an uncomfortable place sometimes, to be tossed around like a beanbag and hovered over like a china doll."

"Did they make it hard on your boyfriends?" he asked.

"There weren't very many boyfriends," she said.

"I don't believe you," he replied with a grin. "You're lying to make me feel better."

So she told him about Ed. She hadn't planned to, but this was a perfect segue to explaining that she might have an issue or two with trust. Not only had the man in the only really serious relationship of her adult life cheated on her, horribly, but she had never had a clue. That bothered her. After it was over, it was so obvious, but while it was going on, she was oblivious. Not good.

They were headed back toward the stables when she told him. She expected him to be sympathetic and sweet. Instead, he was fascinated. "Are you *serious?* He had about three women going at once? Scattered around? Telling each one he was in love with only her? Really?"

"Really," she said, annoyed.

"How in the world did he manage that?" Nate asked.

"Well, a lot of phone calls while he was working. He talked to each one of us every day, sometimes several times a day. But with very few exceptions, we were assigned certain nights. We thought those were the days he didn't have to leave town. I should have known where I stood in the line. I was getting Mondays and Tuesdays. The woman he decided was the real one in his life was getting the weekends—Saturdays and Sundays. She dumped him, of course, when she discovered Ms. Wednesdays, Thursdays and Fridays. Three days a week must be the trump, huh?"

"Holy cow," Nate said. "He didn't even need a house or apartment! He had all his nights covered!"

"You know, I'm not impressed by his ability to pull it off."

"Of course you're not," Nate said. "But if you just think about it, he had quite a scam going. Did he take you lots of places? Buy you nice things?"

"He couldn't do either," she explained. "First of all, he couldn't risk being seen out and about with a woman, since one of the other women or their friends might run into him. So he said he was so tired, and after a week of being on the road and eating in restaurants, he enjoyed staying home."

"Where you could cook for him," Nate stated.

She pursed her lips, narrowed her eyes and nodded. "He did buy me a hot-water heater when mine went out," she admitted. "He might've needed that hot shower," she muttered.

"The man's a genius," Nate said. Then upon studying her face, he said, "Oh he's a bastard, but you have to give him some credit for all the planning and subterfuge that—"

"I give him no credit," she said harshly.

He grabbed her hand then, pulled her closer and said, "Of course not. No credit. He should be killed. But I'm glad he didn't choose you. What if he'd chosen you? Can you imagine? We'd never meet and fall in love!"

She was so stunned that she pulled back on the reins and stopped her horse. "Are we in love?" she asked.

"I don't know about you, but I'm just getting started here—there's lots of potential. And he doesn't deserve you. I, however, deserve you. And will take you anywhere you want. And I'm going to hold your hand the whole time. I'll feed you cookies and kiss your neck in public."

"People will think I'm your girlfriend."

"That's what I want people to think. I'm going to start right away. We're going to go out. We'll drive into town to look at Christmas decorations, go to Virgin River to check out the tree and have some of Preacher's dinner, and then I'm going to take you to a nice restaurant on the weekend. And anything else you feel like doing."

"Why?" she asked.

"I want everyone to know you're with me. I want everyone to know you're not Sundays and Mondays—you're every day."

Again she pulled back on the reins and stopped her horse. "What's sexier than a string bikini, Nathaniel?"

"Are you kidding me?" He reined in beside her. His voice grew quiet and serious. He rubbed a knuckle down her cheek, over her jaw, gazing into her dark eyes. "Denim turns me on. Long legs in jeans and boots astride a big horse, making him dance to subtle commands. A rough workshirt under a down vest, feeding a newborn foal with a bottle because the mare isn't responding." He threaded his fingers into her hair and said, "Silk, instead of cotton candy. A fire on a cold, snowy night. A woman in my arms, soft and content, happy with the same things that make me happy. Help making homemade pizza— that turns me on. A woman who knows how to deliver a calf when there's trouble—that blows my horn. A woman who can muck out a stall and then fall into the fresh hay and let me fall right on top of her. I'd like to try that real soon."

Her eyes clouded a bit. "Are you just leading me on? Because when Ed pulled his trick, my brothers wanted to kill him, but I wouldn't let them. You? If you're lying, I'm going to let them. You'll suffer before you die."

"I'm not lying, Annie. And you know it."

"Well, okay, then answer this—if you like me, why haven't you liked someone before me? Because these hills are full of girls just like me—sturdy farm girls who have pulled their share of foals from the dams, fed them and kept them warm and—"

"No, there aren't," he said. "I've been looking. Just like you, I haven't had a whole lot of dates because there really wasn't anyone like you. You're one of a kind, Annie McKenzie. I'm sorry you don't seem to know that. But now that I've found you, we need to date…and a whole lot more."

"Be warned," she said. "I'm not casual about this stuff."

"Me, neither," he said.

* * *

After they put up the horses' tack and brushed them down, when it was time to change for dinner, he suggested they share a shower.

"I don't think so, Nate. Not yet," she said. "Does my door lock?" And he laughed at her.

On the way to Arcata they enjoyed the multicolored Christmas lights all along the coastal towns and up into the mountains. The Arcata square was decorated with lights, lit-up trees and a life-size nativity scene. Many of the shop windows were also decorated and filled with Christmas ornaments, gaily dressed mannequins and animated toys. Just as he'd promised, he held her hand everywhere they went. He had chosen an Italian restaurant on the square, and as it happened, it was one of her favorites. It boasted homemade pasta, robust red wine and excellent tiramisu.

"When are your brothers and their families arriving?" he asked over dinner.

"Tomorrow," she said. "By the way, you're invited to dinner. Please be cool around my brothers and don't give anything away. They haven't grown up at all since you knew them, despite the fact they have sons of their own."

"I'll be cool, all right," he promised. "Don't you worry." And then he grinned.

Five

It was a successful date, proved by the way they were in each other's arms, kissing deeply, before they were even in his house. It was still early enough to get in a good, long session of kissing on that soft, deep, inviting couch, and they fell on it together, taking turns helping each other out of boots and jackets without hardly breaking the kiss. Within moments they were in their favorite position on that great sofa, lined up against each other, exploring the inner softness of their mouths. Her body grew predictably supple and soft while his grew more urgent and hard.

Nathaniel whispered, "Annie. Come to my bed."

And she said, "No."

"No?" he answered weakly. "Annie, you don't mean that."

"I do mean it. No."

"But you kiss me like you're ready. Why not?"

She pushed herself up on the couch just slightly so she could look at his eyes. "We've only known each other three weeks, for starters."

"I've kind of known you my whole life, even if I

haven't known you since you got your braces off. But I've known you *intensely* for three weeks."

"We knew each other superficially for one week and intensely for the next two weeks. I might require a little more than that."

"Why?"

"Because I just broke up with Ed. Six months ago. It isn't that long."

"It's forever," he said. "I should have made you forget he ever existed by now."

"I think in another couple of weeks, I will have forgotten. And I'd kind of like to know how you feel after you've had your chance to lie on the beach surrounded by beautiful bodies in very small bathing suits."

"Oh, that. Listen, that's not even part of the equation," he said. "Really. That trip has nothing to do with how I feel."

"It has to do with how *I* feel," she said.

"Annie, if I hadn't made arrangements for this vacation long before I met you, I sure wouldn't plan it now. And it was a lot more than wanting to be lost in bikinis, believe me. It was a very convenient, very convincing plan, so I wouldn't find myself held hostage on a cruise ship with all my sisters and their kids. I explained—my brothers-in-law are great, but when their wives are around…"

"They have to act like husbands and fathers?"

"As opposed to regular guys," he clarified with a nod. "We've been on a couple of fishing trips together and I'm telling you, these guys are the best. They *are* my brothers. But when my sisters and the kids are around…"

"Husbands and fathers," she said helpfully again.

"But I'm not," he said. "I'm bored out of my mind. The

only reprieve I get is a brandy and cigar with my dad and a conversation about veterinary medicine. Come on, don't you feel sorry for me? It's murder."

"So, you're not looking forward to seeing all your old buds?" she asked.

"That? Sure, that'll be great. We used to study together several nights a week. And then after graduation, we went off in all directions. This was a great idea Jerry had, but I can think of things I'd rather do." He lifted one eyebrow and grinned lasciviously.

She laughed at him. "Still, I'm not ready. Not till after your Club Med vacation."

"It's not Club Med, I told you. Are you waiting for me to say I love you, because if you're waiting for that, I—"

She put a finger to his lips and shushed him. "Don't go out on a limb here, Nathaniel."

"I'll call the travel agent in the morning and get you a ticket," he said. "Come with me."

She laughed, actually pleased by the offer. "My goodness, you'll go to a lot of trouble and expense for sex."

"For *you*," he clarified. "Not just for sex, for *you*."

"I am kind of impressed, but no thank you."

"Why not?"

"Ordinarily, if it were another time of year, I would, but not this time. Plus, I don't get to be with the whole family that often. The boys have it worked out that they do either Thanksgiving or Christmas with our side, the other holiday with their wives' side. So it's been a couple of years since we've all done Christmas together and I love that. My mom and I knock ourselves out to make it great."

He kissed her deeply. He pressed her down into the sofa with his body and held her hands at her sides, entwining his fingers with hers. "How about if I decide not to go on that vacation?"

"That you've paid for? To see your old best friends from school? Don't be ridiculous."

"Then come with me."

"No."

"Then I won't go," he said.

"You have to go. This is important, Nathaniel. You should get away, broaden your horizons. You've probably forgotten how much you miss your friends, how much you'd like to see a hundred tiny bikinis on perfect women. You have to go. I'm kind of interested in what you'll be like when you come back."

He thought about this for a few seconds. "Okay, then," he whispered. "A compromise."

"Hmm?"

"I'll go to the stupid beach without you, my virtuous girlfriend, you'll have Christmas with your family, and tonight you come to my bed."

She laughed. "No. Not till you've passed your time with the bikinis. And the women vets you used to date. Are they pretty?"

"Tina and Cindy? Oh, yeah, very pretty, but like I said, we were better as study partners. Honey, I've completely lost interest in bikinis. Unless you want to put one on for me just for fun."

"I don't know that that will ever happen."

"Annie, I'm not interested in bikinis. Not now. I'm only interested in you. Hey! This doesn't have anything to do with skinny Susanna, does it? Because I'm not all weirded out by Ed, who's really much stranger than Susanna."

She shook her head. "The only thing about Susanna that I still have to get over is that she was beautiful, feminine, small—except for her apparently exceptional boobs—and fancy, while I'm flat-footed and can cut the head off a chicken. But I'm working on that."

"They weren't real," he said. "She bought herself a pair for her twenty-first birthday. I'd much rather touch smaller real ones."

She kissed him, a short one on the lips. "Well, Nathaniel, if this works out, I like your chances." Then she grinned at him.

He was quiet for a moment and his eyes were serious, burning into hers. "You know, if I hadn't already paid for the whole damn thing, I'd cancel that trip. It's not what I want right now."

"Hey, I want you to go, and you'll have a good time. I'm not really worried about the bikinis. Not that much."

He pressed himself against her, proof that he was still all turned on. "It turns out three weeks is enough time for me," he said. "I'd rather just not go."

She put a hand against his cheek and smiled at him. "Even a grand gesture like that wouldn't get you lucky tonight."

He shook his head. "I don't want to be away from you for ten days. I barely found you. What if stupid Ed comes around and somehow proves to you that he's worth another chance?"

"Can't happen," she said. "I hardly remember what he looks like. I'll be right here when you get back."

"What if I get so lonely and distraught I make love to some big-breasted nymphomaniac while I'm down there and come back to you all innocent, lying about it, just to teach you a terrible lesson?"

"I'd know."

"You didn't know with Ed," he reminded her.

"I know. I've been thinking about that a lot because it's been a real issue with me, that somehow I didn't know. I think Ed wasn't that important to me, or I would have been upset we had so little time together, and I wasn't. Wouldn't I have known something was *off* if he'd meant more to me? I don't think I cared as much as I wanted to. Lord, I think I would have married him even knowing he'd only spend two nights a week with me." She took a breath. "Maybe I would've married him *because* he'd only spend two nights a week with me." She ran her fingernails through the hair at Nate's temple. "But much as I fight it, Nathaniel, it's different with you." Then she smiled.

"In only three weeks?" he asked softly.

She was shaking her head. "It didn't take three whole weeks."

He took a breath, then groaned deeply just before he covered her mouth in a deep, hot, wet kiss that went on and on and on. When he finally lifted his lips from hers, he said, "Okay. We'll do this your way. We'll wait until you're ready. And when it's over and we're together forever, don't think you can boss me around like this."

"You've got a deal," she said, laughing.

Nathaniel called Annie twice before noon on Monday. First he wanted to know if there was anything he could bring to the farm. "I think we're throwing a couple of big pans of lasagna in the oven for dinner, and Mom is busy making bread. How about bringing some good red wine?"

The next time he called, he said, "I know you work on Tuesday. I'm leaving Tuesday afternoon. So tonight, if I pass the brother test, will you come home with me for just a little while?"

"For just a little while. And don't try that 'I'm going

into battle and you have to show your love before I leave'
trick. Okay?"

And he laughed.

That was the best part about Annie—her sense of
humor. No, he thought—it was her beauty. Her dark red
hair, her creamy, freckled complexion, her deep brown
eyes. But then a smile came to his lips as he recalled how
good she was on a horse. An accomplished equestrienne.
And while she would not find the term *sturdy* at all com-
plimentary, he admired that about her. Fortitude had
always appealed to him. Sometimes when he was holding
her, he felt like he was clinging to her as if she anchored
him to the ground. She had no idea how unattractive
flighty, timid, weak women were to him. Did such
women make some men feel strong and capable? Because
for Nathaniel, to be chosen by a woman of strength and
confidence met needs he didn't even know he had.

He had calls to make, ranches to visit, patients to see,
inoculations to administer, a couple of cows who had a
fungus to look in on, breeding animals who would deliver
early in the year to check. He phoned the vet from Eureka
who would cover for him while he was away, paid a visit
to a local winery to select a few bottles of good red and
finally made his way to the McKenzie farm.

When he pulled in, the place almost resembled a fair
in progress. Not one but two RVs were parked near the
back of the house, which probably eliminated the need
to borrow Annie's house for the family. There were also
trucks and snowmobiles on trailers. A bunch of cross-
country skis leaned up against the back porch. The
McKenzies were here to play. Kids ran around while
several sat on the top rail of the corral. Inside the corral,
Annie had a couple of young children mounted on her

horses. She held the reins and led them around the corral while they held the saddle pommels. Four men—her brothers and father—leaned on the rail, watching.

Nate wandered up to the fence and leaned his forearms on the top rail with the rest of them. "So," he said. "I'm here for the inspection."

The man next to him turned and his mouth split into a huge grin. "Hey, man," Beau McKenzie said. "I heard a rumor you were dating my sister. Good to see you, buddy." He stuck out his hand. "This true? You and Annie? Because I can tell you things that will give you ultimate control over her!"

"Nathaniel Jensen," the next man said. Brad McKenzie stuck out his hand. "I don't think I've seen you in twenty years! You finally made it over five foot six, good for you."

"Yeah, and beat the acne." Nate laughed. "How you doing, pal?"

"Jim, any chance you remember this clown?" Beau asked his oldest brother.

"I just remember this squirt from football," Jim McKenzie said, sticking out a hand. "Couldn't tackle worth shit, but you sure could run."

"I had to run," Nate said. "If anyone had caught me, I'd be dead. I was the smallest kid on the team."

"You take steroids or something? You caught up."

"Nah, I just got old like the rest of you," he said. "Thanks for letting me invade the family party. Annie's been looking forward to it so much."

"This is true, then?" Beau asked, Brad and Jim and even Hank looking on with rather intense gazes.

What had she said? That he'd have to be cool? Maybe she expected him to joke around the way they did? One side of his mouth tilted up in a sly smile. He supposed it wasn't cool, but could they beat him up for being honest? "She knocks me out," he said. "Where have you been hiding her? I didn't even know she was here! I bumped into her in a bar!"

"That's our Annie," Beau said. "Out tying one on."

Nate laughed again. "Actually, she rescued eight orphaned puppies. Mostly border collie, we think. Cute as the devil. How many you want?"

Beau put a hand on his shoulder. "Pass on the puppies, my friend. But we got beer, Nathaniel. And seriously, we can give you stuff on her that will give you years worth of control. Power. Mastery. Don't we, guys?"

"We do," said Brad.

"Indeedy," said Jim.

It was an amazing day for Nathaniel, though not exactly a brand-new experience. The venue was a little smaller and more crowded than his family gatherings, but the family interaction was pretty much the same as in his family. The men got a little too loud, the kids ran wild and had to be rounded up several times, the women had a little tiff about kitchen things like whether the bread should have garlic butter or not and whether the salad should be dressed or not. There was a lot of furniture moving to accommodate a dinner for seventeen. They needed the dining-room table extended, and two card tables. The youngest child present at dinner was three and the oldest fourteen, and they sat at the kid table, as it was known in both the Jensen and McKenzie households. Nathaniel felt at once a special guest and right at home.

The McKenzie boys had married well; their wives were attractive, fun, energetic, and there was a lot of family rapport—which always helped. The kids were mostly well behaved, just a couple of small problems that the mothers foisted off on the fathers. Mrs. McKenzie fussed over Nate in a welcoming fashion, maybe a hopeful fashion, showing her approval. Mr. McKenzie, whom Nate had only known as Hank for the couple of years he'd been practicing here, handed Nate his jacket and took him out to the front porch during the after-dinner cleanup. Hank gave him a cigar. None of the brothers joined them, so Nate knew this was the father-and-man-in-his-daughter's-life talk.

Hank lit Nate's cigar. "I don't have a whole lot to say about this. Always got along with you just fine, so I don't have any basic complaint," Hank said.

"That's good," Nate said, puffing. Coughing. He smoked about a cigar a year and never remembered to take it easy.

"Just a couple of things I want to say."

"I'm ready."

"I like Annie," her father said. "She's good people." He puffed. "Now that might not seem like much of a recommendation, but in my book, it's the best there is. She's just plain good. She'd never in a million years hurt a soul. But don't get lazy on her, because she's nice but she's tough. She can hold her own if there's some injustice, and she's not afraid of a fight. And smart? She could've run this dairy farm single-handed, she's that smart. That strong-willed. I offered it to her, too. Boys didn't want it, so I said, 'Annie, you could do it just fine, even if I dropped dead tomorrow,' and she said, 'Dad, if I stick myself out here with the cows, I'll never leave and never do anything else and I think maybe there's got to be more to my life. At least more people in my life.' That's what she said. So that's how it was. She bought that beauty shop and I sold off the Holsteins. You better be nice to her."

"Yes, sir," he said.

"Don't even think about hurting her, Nathaniel. I can handle about anything but seeing my girl, who I admire and respect, hurt."

"I promise," Nate said.

"Because if you do…"

"You'll shoot me?" Nate asked.

"Aw, hell, why would I do that? I'm not a violent man. I'll just spread the word that as a vet, you're not worth a crap."

Nate couldn't help it, he burst out laughing.

"The boys, though," Hank went on, "they're a tad violent. When it comes to Annie. So be nice."

Nate hadn't had a lot of dates in the past couple of years, but in the past ten he'd had quite a few. When he was tending Thoroughbreds in Kentucky and then in Los Angeles County, plenty of women were attracted to him. Socialites, daughters of rich breeders, women he'd met at parties, on ranches, at races. He'd never been talked to by a father, however. Not even Susanna's, not even when he'd given her a rock and carted her up to Humboldt County with the misguided notion of marrying her.

As father talks went, Hank's hadn't been stunning. But Nate liked it. It made him feel like a man with a job to do.

"It's probably way too early to talk about intentions," Hank said.

"No, sir, it's not," Nate replied. "I like Annie even more than you do. It's my intention to treat her very well while we're dating, and I think it might be a good match for both of us. I also think we might have a future, me and Annie. But you know what? She's a smart, stubborn girl—it's going to be up to her."

"Yeah, I reckon," Hank said.

"So. Could you at least wish me luck?" Nathaniel asked.

"You bet," Hank said, sticking out his hand. "Best of luck there, Nathaniel. Try not to screw this up."

"You bet, sir. Nice cigar, by the way."

"Yeah, not bad, huh? Have no idea where I got 'em. One of the boys, probably."

Nate wasn't sure, but he didn't think his own father had ever had one of these talks with his brothers-in-law or he would've heard about it. But right there, right then, he decided that if he ever had a daughter, he was going to do that. It was a good idea—take the young man aside, expound on the girl's wonderful qualities, threaten his life a little. It had merit.

A few minutes later Beau joined them, clipping off the tip of a cigar. Then Brad, then Jim. Nate leaned close to Beau's ear. "How'd you know he was done with me?" Nate asked.

"If he wasn't done, you weren't going to work out," Beau said with a shrug.

"Just out of curiosity," Nate asked, "has he had many of these talks?"

"I think you're the first."

"What about that loser, Ed?"

"Ah, Ed. I don't think Annie brought him around all that much. From what we heard, he was very busy. I met him once, I think, and not on a holiday. He did sell a couple of things to my dad, though. Farm things. Before he and Annie hooked up. Dad? We didn't like Ed much, did we?"

Hank just snorted and said something derisive under his breath.

"Just out of curiosity, why didn't you like him?" Nate asked.

"He swindled me on a hay baler," Hank said. "Said he had the best price in the county. Took me about a month to find all kinds of better deals."

"So, it didn't have anything to do with how he treated her?" Nate asked.

"Son, you really think if a man will swindle you on a hay baler, you can trust him with your kin?"

"I hadn't ever thought about it that way."

"I can't imagine another way to think about it," Hank said.

"Wow," Nate said, feeling more than a little privileged. *Yeah,* he thought. *I'm picking out my daughter's guy and giving him a talking-to.*

When the cigars were finished, the men wandered back inside where the women were sitting in the kitchen with coffee. Nate paused in the doorway and signaled Annie. "Got a second?" he asked her. When she stood before him, he said, "I'm going to get a head start. Spend as much time as you want with the family. I'll go home and make sure the puppies are fed and watered and their bedding is dry."

"I can come now."

"No, stay. I'll get the puppy chores done and when you get there, I'll have more time with you. By the way, are we all set on their care while I'm gone? We talked about it a little...."

"Not to worry, Nate. Virginia and I worked out the details. We're going to share the load and they'll be looked after. And if it's okay with you, I'll make sure the adopted ones are delivered on Christmas Eve. I think

Pam from the shop is going to take one, which brings us down to three left to place. I'll make sure they're okay."

"Tell anyone you take a pup to that if they bring 'em by in a couple of weeks, I'll check them over and give them shots, free of charge."

"That's nice, Nathaniel."

"Then I'll see you in a little while," he said, giving her a platonic peck on the cheek. "Thank you, Mrs. McKenzie," he said to Rose. "Nice meeting you all."

"Have a great trip, Nate," someone said.

"Good meeting you."

"Travel safe."

He shook the men's hands and was on his way.

Two thoughts occupied him as he drove home. He couldn't wait to get his arms around Annie. And he didn't want to be away from her for ten days. He didn't think a beach full of naked women could make him more inclined to leave right now. But he had packed his bags earlier, not leaving it to the last minute, and he would get this over with. Then, as far as he was concerned, it was full steam ahead with her. And she'd better not give him the slip, either. He was thirty-two and had had plenty of girlfriends, but he couldn't remember ever wanting a woman like he wanted this one. Heck, he wanted her whole family. He wanted to bring her into his. He wanted them to merge and grow.

He'd even been engaged without wanting all that. It was eerie.

He was barely home, the puppies slopping up their dinner, when the pager on his belt vibrated. He recognized the phone number of a horse breeder whose animals he took care of. His favorite patients, Thoroughbreds. This family was not nearby—they were over the county line in Mendocino.

He answered the call. One of their valuable brood-mares was miscarrying, and she was all freaked out, kicking at the stable walls.

He disconnected the line, but he held the phone. He took a deep, disappointed breath before he dialed the McKenzie farm and asked for Annie.

"Nate? What's up?" she asked when she came on the line.

"You don't know how much I hate to do this. I have to go out on an emergency. There's a mare miscarrying, and the stable is in the next county. It could be complicated. It could be late."

"Don't worry about the time, Nate. See about the horse," she said.

"Honey, you shouldn't wait here for me. I might be tied up until very late. There's a chance I'll be out all night with just enough time to come home, clean up, get ready to leave. But, Annie, I won't leave without seeing you—worst case, I'll stop by your shop on my way out of town tomorrow."

"You don't have to do that, Nate. If you find yourself pressed for time, just give me a call."

"But I *do* have to," he said softly. "I can't leave without holding you, without kissing you goodbye."

"That's so sweet. But if it doesn't work out that way, I understand. Drive carefully. I hope everything is all right with the mare."

Despite Nate's warning that he might not make it home until very late, she went to his house anyway. She could hear in his voice his desire to spend a little time with her, and what did she have to keep her away? If he wasn't back by early morning, she'd feed the puppies and go home to shower and get ready for work.

She was inexplicably drawn to the master bedroom,

though she had no real reason to go there. It was the sight
of a couple of suitcases open on the floor, filled with
clothing, that saddened her so deeply she felt a small
ache in her heart. Oh, she was going to miss him so much!
Disappointment filled her—she had looked forward to an
hour or two of cuddling before she had to give him up for
his ten-day adventure. Now it was probably not to be.

Suck it up, Annie, she said to herself. And with that,
she shucked her jacket and went to make sure the puppies
were taken care of. "Well, my little loves," she said to the
box of squirming, jumping, yelping, vibrating puppies.
"Ew," she said, taking a sniff. "Time for a refresh, I see."
And she set about the task of giving her little charges
clean fur and dry bedding. "Yeah, you're ready for new
homes. You have to be about six weeks by now. Close
enough, as far as I'm concerned."

Her puppy chores didn't take long. She wandered into
the family room and sat on that comfy sofa. That lonely
sofa. She hated to leave prematurely; she wanted to give
him time to get home, to catch up with her. As she looked
around the family room, it seemed so barren. At least
compared to the farmhouse, which was full to the brim
with food, decorations, people, laughter and happiness.

She turned on the fire to make it more welcoming for
him, and then on a whim she went to the garage and
looked through the storage cabinets that lined the walls
of the three-port garage. She smiled to herself. Nathaniel's mother had certainly made it easy. One entire cabinet
held boxes that were neatly labeled. She skipped the one
that said "ornaments" but opened another. And another.
And another.

She really only meant to bring a touch of Christmas
into the house for Nate, even if it was only for one night,

or just an early morning. First was a centerpiece for that long, oak kitchen table, then a couple of fat, glittery candles on a bed of artificial holly, which she put on the coffee table. She thought if she were decorating this house for real, there would be lots of fresh stuff and the smell of pine. And the aroma of hot chocolate and cookies.

She put her jacket on to go back into the garage and soon she had a garland for the mantel, stockings and brass stocking holders, and three-foot-tall nutcracker characters for a grouping in the corner. She found a large basket of red ceramic apples mixed with huge pinecones, a poinsettia with little twinkling lights. That gave her another idea, and she found some tiny tree lights in a box, which she brought in and used to adorn the house plants—a couple of tall ficus trees and a couple of lush philodendron and ivy. She tied thick, red velvet bows to the backs of the kitchen chairs.

A box labeled "Christmas dishes" was just too much to resist. Inside were some festive plates and cups. So she turned on the oven and poked around in the pantry, laughing to herself. Hadn't she said she wouldn't poke around? Well, Nathaniel obviously didn't do a lot of baking, and who knew how long that canister of flour had been there? And the brown sugar was like a brick. But he did have butter, sugar and M&M's. It took only thirty minutes to produce a plate of pseudo chocolate-chip cookies. She found chocolate-milk mix and fixed up a couple of cups with spoons in them, ready for filling. It was probably in her DNA—she covered the festive plate of cookies with plastic wrap.

"Christmas for a day," she said to herself, pleased.

She made sure all the boxes were stowed in the garage. Then she looked at the clock. Almost eleven, and she had to get up early for work. But it didn't take her a second to make her decision—a girl doesn't find a quality boyfriend every day. She turned down some lights in the house, took off her boots, reclined on the sofa in front of the fire with the throw over her legs and promptly fell asleep.

Six

Nate was physically tired and emotionally drained. By the time he reached the Bledsoe stables, the mare had miscarried a five-month foal and she was skittish. *Frantic* might be a better word. Indication was that the horse was sick, the cause of the miscarriage, though Nate had checked her over before she was bred and she'd been in good shape. Because he wasn't going to be around to follow up, he had called Dr. Conner, the Eureka vet. He tranquilized the mare to calm her, administered antibiotics, made sure the placenta was whole, and then transported the products of conception to Eureka so that Dr. Conner could follow up with a postmortem to try to determine the cause. Conner would probably choose to do an endometrial biopsy. Other horses in the stable would have to be examined immediately; Bledsoe had six breeding at the moment.

But that was not the hardest part. Not only was the mare valuable and the stud a champion, the owners' teenage daughter had raised this horse from a filly and it was her first foal. The girl was as distraught as the horse, and terrified her mare was going to die.

She wasn't going to die, but the jury was still out on whether she was a good broodmare. Some mystery problem or illness had taken its toll and caused her to drop the foal and suffer a considerable amount of bleeding. Time and follow-up would tell the story. But when Nate left the family, quite late at night, it looked as though the teenage girl was going to sleep in the stable with her horse.

Now that was something he could see Annie doing.

And to speak of the devil herself, when he pulled up to his house, it was dimly lit from inside and her truck was parked out front. The clock on the car console said two-fifteen. Lord, what was she doing? Half of him was so grateful he could burst, the other half wanted to spank her for staying up so late—he knew she had a long day in the shop ahead of her so that she could be closed the afternoon of the twenty-fourth and all day the twenty-fifth.

Annie, he had learned, was not afraid of hard work.

He entered the dimly lit house quietly. His first reaction was surprise, but pleasure quickly followed. On the breakfast bar a thick red candle flickered beside a plate of cookies and a couple of cups. There was chocolate powder in the cups, ready for hot milk to be added. Bows on the chairs, garlands strung around, table decorations, twinkling lights everywhere, and his girl, asleep in front of a fire. He chuckled to himself. Well, hadn't *she* been busy.

It was like really coming home. Holidays meant a lot to her. Her sense of love and family spilled over to everyone around her, and he felt so…embraced inside, like it was his first Christmas. He smiled to himself. In an important way, it was.

He took off his boots, belt and jacket in the kitchen. He blew out candles, turned off all but the twinkling tree lights and fireplace, and knelt down by the sofa, softly kissing her beautiful lips.

"Mmm," she murmured, half waking. "You're home. I must've fallen asleep."

"You were probably exhausted, digging through the storage," he said with humor in his voice.

"I'll put it all away before you get back," she whispered. "I should go, now you're home...."

"Are you crazy?" he asked. He slipped one arm under her knees, the other behind her back and stood with her in his arms. "We're going to get some sleep. It's almost morning, anyway. And this couch isn't going to do it. I want to hold you. I want to fall asleep with you in my arms. Now close your eyes and your mouth."

She hummed and snuggled closer to him. "Everything all right? With the mare?" she asked.

"It'll get sorted out. I'll tell you about it in the morning." He carried her to his bedroom and laid her gently on the bed. "Do you need the alarm?" he asked her. "I can set it for you."

"Nah. I haven't slept past seven in my life."

"Good," he said. He pulled back the comforter and crawled in, jeans and all, and she did the same. "Come close," he said. "All I want in life is to feel you against me. Mmm, just like that. Aaah, Annie, my Annie…"

Suddenly he knew that even as exhausted as he was, he wasn't going to sleep. He had a stunning thought—*this is what it feels like when you actually fall in love.* He'd thought that whole falling-in-love thing was some girl story that guys didn't experience. He was familiar with being attracted. Oh-ho, was he familiar with that! And of course he had known desire in all sizes, from warm to boiling. Wanting a woman, yes, that was a fairly regular occurrence. But this was all those things mixed together and yet something completely different at the same time.

He wanted to be only with Annie; if he were allowed one friend for the rest of his life, he would choose her. He wanted to come home to the kind of warmth she could bring to a room. He wanted to crawl in beside her and feel the comfort of her body, which fit so perfectly against his. He didn't want to be away from her; he wanted her for life.

He began unbuttoning her blouse. In spite of the fact that she seemed to be asleep, he was undressing her, knowing he shouldn't. But then he felt her fingers working away at *his* shirt buttons and he sprang to life, hard and ready. His hands went to the snap on her jeans while hers worked at his. Like choreography, they were slipping each other's jeans down and off and he pulled her hard against him, his shorts to her dainties. "God," he said. "God, God, God."

She pulled away just enough to shrug out of her shirt and remove her socks. She left the panties for Nate to handle, which he did immediately. "Let me have these," he said, clutching them in his fist. "Let me keep these for the rest of my life. Can I?"

She laughed at him and tugged down his boxers. "Sure," she whispered against his lips. "And you can keep your underwear."

He moaned as if in pain, his hand finding a breast. "Why are you wearing a bra?" he asked.

"Because you've been undressing me for five seconds and haven't gotten to that yet?" she returned. She un-snapped the clasp and it fell apart, just in time for his lips on her breast. He rolled on top of her, probing. "Con-dom," she whispered. "Condom, Nate."

"Right," he said. "Got it." And he leaped out of bed,

raced unceremoniously to the master bath, running back to the king-size bed with a packet in his hand, ripping it open as he went. He flopped on the bed and pulled her close. Then he froze. All motion stopped. Their thighs were pressed together, their lips straining toward each other, their hands pulling their bodies closer, and he said, "Annie? Are you ready for this?"

She didn't say anything and he couldn't see her face in the darkness of the room. She took his hand and captured the foil packet. She pulled his hand down between her legs where his fingers could answer his question.

He moved his hand up her inner thigh, opened her legs a bit, caressed her wonderfully wet folds. "Aaah," he said once more against her lips.

"Ready," she whispered. "Ready." And then she applied the protection.

"You know what, Annie?" he said. "Coming home to you, making love to you, it feels like the one thing I've always been ready for."

"Then let's not waste any more time," she said.

He fell asleep while still inside her, holding her close. Sometime in the night, they roused just enough to make love again. When he awoke in the morning, he was alone. There was a little puppy, whimpering, faint and distant.

He found her note in the kitchen:

Nate—you were so tired, you slept through puppy breakfast, which was noisy. I decided you should sleep. I want you to have the most wonderful time of your life on your trip. I'll take care of everything while you're gone and I'll put away the decorations. And thank you for last night. It was perfect. Love, Annie

He picked up the note and read it again and again. "It's awful hard to leave you, Annie," he whispered. "Especially at Christmas."

Nathaniel booked his flights to coordinate with the rest of the group—they were all meeting for breakfast in Miami. From there they would fly together to Nassau. He had to take a commuter from Santa Rosa to San Francisco. That meant a two-hour drive south to pick up the first leg of his trip. From San Francisco he would take a nonstop red-eye to Miami. He would be there in early morning. He'd have breakfast in the airport with his old gang. It brought to mind the breakfasts they'd had together after all-night study sessions, right before a big exam. Then they'd get to the Bahamas early in the day to begin their ten-day vacation.

He didn't mind driving, which was a good thing, since his practice had him running around the mountains and valleys of three counties looking after livestock. The drive from Humboldt County to Santa Rosa was beautiful and calm. But rather than enjoy the rolling hills and snow-covered pines and mountains, all he thought about was Annie.

Before he left Humboldt County, he had called her at her shop. "I'll be leaving in a couple of hours. Sure you want to let me go without you?" he had asked.

"This is your trip, Nate. Not mine," she said. "You planned it, you've looked forward to it, you paid for it—now go and enjoy it. I have family things to do. And puppy things. When you get back all the decorations will be put away, the puppies will be distributed to their new homes and you'll be tanned and rested. And it will be a whole new year."

"I hear cell reception is terrible there, but I'll try to call you while I'm gone," he said. "I want to see if you have any regrets about turning down an all-expense-paid vacation. And there's a note for you on the kitchen counter—my hotel info. Call me if you need anything. Anything at all."

When he said that, he had been thinking, *Me. Call if you need me. Call me if you miss me.*

But Annie had laughed cheerfully. "Now, Nate, what are you going to do if I need something? Catch a flight home? You'll be on the other side of the country! And you'll be with your friends—a reunion, Nate. Now stop worrying about stuff you can't do anything about. Just have fun. Besides, I can manage just about anything."

A few weeks earlier Nathaniel had been looking forward to this vacation with such enthusiasm. He'd built a few fantasies about girls in bikinis and low-cut sundresses. He saw himself inviting a beautiful woman out to dinner; maybe he'd be taking some lovely young thing sailing. He envisioned staying up late with his buddies, laughing, drinking and smoking cigars. He figured he'd be needed to rub suntan lotion on a bare female back.

None of those mental images were working for him now. Now all he could think about was how long the next ten days were likely to be. He hoped he'd at least catch an impressive fish or two. That's what he'd like to take home to her—a big, mounted sailfish. Maybe they'd hang it over the bed and remember their first Christmas. And their last one apart.

* * *

Annie had laughed brightly while on the phone with Nate, but melancholy stole her laughter away the moment she hung up. She supposed it was a combination of being a little bit tired and sad that he'd be away. She'd been up late decorating his house and baking him those awful-tasting cookies; he just didn't have the right ingredients on hand, and what he had was far from fresh. Of course she hadn't slept much in his bed; he'd kept her busy. And so satisfied. He was such a wonderful lover, but instead of leaving her sated, it left her wanting more of him.

And then she had to get up very early—she had to go home, shower and dress for work and arrange the Christmas gift baskets for the girls in the shop.

She wondered if he had felt her lips press softly against his before she'd left him. Had he heard her say, "Goodbye, Nate. Be safe. Hurry home"? He hadn't stirred at all.

She had been happy to hold him close, warm him and put him to sleep. She wouldn't mind doing that every day for the rest of her life.

She knew her mood had plummeted and she didn't want anyone in the shop noticing, so she grabbed up the appointment book and walked to her small office at the back of the little shop. But sure enough, Pam followed her. Pam stood in the doorway, looking at her.

"Don't worry, Annie. He'll be thrilled to get home to you," Pam said.

"Sure. Of course. I didn't say anything otherwise, did I?"

"You didn't have to," Pam said. "You laughed and joked with him on the phone, but the second you hung up, you got real sober. Serious. Maybe a little worried."

"Do you think it was a mistake to let him go?" Annie asked.

"The time will fly by," Pam said. "It's nice to see you like this. You love him."

"I love him," she admitted. Because he was sensitive but also very confident and strong, she thought. He was a sucker for a bunch of puppies even though they were such a pain to take care of. He didn't even have to think twice about whether to be out till two in the morning because someone had a problem with an animal. The way Annie had been raised, she'd come to accept that people who cared for animals had a special kind of soul, a precious gift. You weren't likely to get much back from animals except a lick on the hand or maybe a good performance in a competition. And in her family's case—the animals provided milk and meat, their roof, their very beds and clothes, their land and legacy. She had been raised with deep respect for animals and the physicians who cared for them. Those gifted doctors were men and women who knew the meaning of unconditional love.

"I love him because he's tender and strong and smart," Annie said. She smiled sentimentally. "And he's so cute he makes my knees wobble. But, Pam, I didn't tell him. I tried to show him, but I didn't tell him."

Pam chuckled. "You'll have your chance very soon." Pam stepped really close to Annie and made her voice a whisper. "Sweetheart, you're beautiful and smart. And I bet you make his knees wobble, too."

She smiled at her friend. "Thank you, Pam. That's sweet. The sweetest part is it wasn't just a compliment—I know you meant it. Did I tell you he asked me to go with him?"

"Ah, no. You might've failed to mention that. And you weren't tempted?"

"Sure I was tempted. But it's his trip and I have family things going on. But after this, if he feels for me what I feel for him, it's the last time I'm letting him get that far away from me without him knowing how I feel."

Pam gave her a fake punch in the arm. "Good plan. I've worked with you for five years, Annie, since before you bought the franchise on this little shop. Have you ever been in love before?"

Annie let go a huff of laughter. "Don't be ridiculous— I'm twenty-eight. I've been in love plenty of times, starting with Dickie Saunders in the second grade."

But never like this, she thought. Nothing even close to this. She wanted to massage his temples when he was stressed or worried, wanted to curl into him and bring him comfort, wanted to trust him with every emotion she had. She'd go into battle for him if he needed that from her, or better still, laugh with him until they both cried. It would feel so good to stand at his side and help him with his work. Or argue with him for a while before making up—she would have to promise never to have PMS again and he would have to pledge not to be such a know-it-all. *Green as a bullfrog,* he'd called her. She'd never had a man in her life who could see right through her so fast, who could read her mind, feel her feelings.

Realizing she'd been off in kind of a daze, she refocused and looked at her friend. She shrugged.

"That's what I thought," Pam said with a smile.

Nathaniel was pressed up against the cold window of a packed 747 all the way from San Francisco to Miami. Over five hours of nighttime flying. Three or four times he got up and walked around the dimmed cabin. Normally he could sleep on long flights, but not on this one. When he arrived at his destination at 7:00 a.m. on the morning of Christmas Eve, he had almost an hour before meeting his friends for breakfast in a preselected restaurant in the international terminal.

By the time he got to the restaurant, Jerry, Ron, Cindy and Tina were there, surrounded by enough luggage to sink a cruise ship. Missing were Bob and Tom and their wives. Jerry spotted Nate first and called, "Hey, look who just dragged himself off the red-eye. You look like hell, man," he said, grinning, sticking out a hand. "Get this man a Bloody Mary!"

Nate shook hands, hugged, accepted the drink, complete with lemon wedge and celery stalk, and raised his glass. "Great to see you guys," he said. "We can't keep meeting like this."

"Beats not meeting at all." Jerry looked at his watch. "We have an hour and a half." He looked around and frowned. "Nathaniel, did you manage to get your luggage checked through?"

"Nah, I left it with a skycap."

There was some head shaking. "Always has been one jump ahead of us," Tina said.

"Thing is—I can't make it. Sorry, guys."

Confused stares answered him. "Um, don't look now, buddy—but you're in Miami. Almost at Bahama Mama heaven."

Nate chuckled and took a sip of his Bloody Mary. "This was a good idea," he said of the drink. "I left my luggage at the airline counter with the skycap. They're working on a flight for me, but it looks bleak. Who would travel on Christmas Eve on purpose? Why are they booked solid? I'd never travel on Christmas Eve if I didn't have to, but I told them I'd take anything. I might end up eating my turkey dinner right here."

"What the hell...?"

"It's a woman," Nate said. He was shaking his head and laughing at himself. "I gotta get back to a woman."

Jerry clamped a hand on his shoulder. "Okay, let me guess, you got drunk on the plane..."

"Why didn't you just bring her?" Cindy asked.

"She couldn't come," Nate said. "She had all kinds of family stuff going on and she couldn't miss it. She's real close to her family—great family, too. So I said I'd stay home, but she said no to that. She said I should have my vacation. She insisted. And I let her."

"All right, bud, keep your head here. Give her a call, tell her you're miserable without her and you'll be home soon. Hell, get a flight out in two or three days if you still feel the same way."

"I have to go," Nate said. "I don't want to be sitting in a bar with you losers if they find a flight for me." He took another swallow of his drink. He stared at it. "Really, this was a good idea. So was the trip. Anyone game to try this next year? I shouldn't have any complications next year—that I can think of."

"Nathaniel, if she's the right one, she's not going anyplace," Jerry attempted.

He grinned. "That's the best part. She's not going anyplace. But you have no idea how much Christmas means to Annie. She's like the Christmas fairy." He chuckled. "Listen, I don't expect you to get this, but as much as I was looking forward to spending a few days with you guys, it hit me on the plane—I'm going to feel alone without her. I'm going to be with the best friends I've ever had, and I'm not going to have much fun, because she's not with me." He shook his head. "I know where I'm supposed to be right now, and I better get there."

"Nathaniel, this will pass," Ron said. "How long have you known this woman?"

"Oh, jeez—about three weeks. About three of the best weeks of my life. When you find the right one, you don't fly away and leave her wondering how you feel. See, Jerry, in case you ever find some brain-damaged female willing to throw her lot in with you, you'll want to remember this—you better not let her out of your sight and you better not leave her without telling her you love her. Got that?"

Jerry looked confused. "Isn't that why they invented florists? Don't you just dial up a big, expensive batch of flowers and—"

"Nathaniel, that is *so* sweet," Tina said. "I had no idea you were so sweet. Didn't we date once? Were you ever that sweet to me?"

With a laugh, Nate put down his drink, grabbed her, hugged her and gave her a kiss on the cheek. He gave his old pal Cindy a hug. He punched Jerry in the arm and gave Ron's hand a quick shake. "I'll be in touch. Have a good time on the beach. Thanks for the drink. Tell Bob and Tom I'm sorry I missed them. Merry Christmas." And he turned and strode away.

After closing the shop on the twenty-third, Annie had gotten right out to Nate's house to take care of the puppies. She'd gone back after dinner at the farm to make sure they were fixed for the night and then she'd stayed a while, enjoying her stab at Christmas decorations. Virginia had been good enough to check on the puppies on the morning of the twenty-fourth, as she had to look after the horses anyway.

Annie had purchased five decorated hat boxes at the

craft store, and on Christmas Eve she took one little pup—a female, Vixen—to work with her for Pam. Pam's mom would keep the puppy safe and warm until Christmas morning. They closed the shop at noon and Annie headed back to Nate's before going to the farm.

There was a long-standing tradition on Christmas Eve at the farm—Hank covered a hay wagon with fresh hay, hooked up Annie's horses and took the kids for a hayride while the women finished dinner. The winter sun was setting early, so they would have their hayride before dinner. The snow had begun to fall, so the wagon would have to stick to the farm roads. Seven kids, their dads and grandpa set out, singing and laughing.

And in the kitchen, the traditional prime rib was being prepared. In years past, it was their own beef, but now they had to buy it. From the kitchen window, Annie watched the hay wagon pull away from the house. Telling herself not to be moody, she briefly fantasized about sending Nate out with the kids and her dad and brothers. Well, there were years ahead for that.

Rose came up behind her and slipped her arms around Annie's waist. "You can go with them if you want to," she murmured. "There is *more* than enough help in the kitchen. Too much, if you ask me!"

Annie laughed at her mom. "I'm staying in," she said. "After dinner I have puppies to deliver on behalf of Santa. We're down to three boys. I think after Christmas, when things are quieter at work, I'll advertise. And I'll call the shelters to see if anyone they consider good potential parents are looking for a puppy."

Rose used a finger to run Annie's hair behind her ear. "Are you a little down this year?" she asked quietly.

"I'm fine," she said, shaking her head.

"It's okay to miss him, especially over the holidays," Rose said. "I like Nathaniel. He seems like a good boy."

Boy, Annie thought, amused. She couldn't tell her mother that he was all man. More man than she'd experienced in her adult life. And she hoped he pestered her as much when he came home as before he left. "Let's get everything on the table, Mom. They'll be back and freezing before we know it."

Of course the kids didn't want the hayride to end until they were blue with cold. Hank pulled right up to the back of the house to let the kids off so their mothers could fuss over them, warming them. Then with the help of his sons they unhooked the horses, took them to the barn and brushed and fed them. By the time everyone was inside, the house was bursting with noise and the smells of food, along with the scent of hay and horses. Stories from the ride, punctuated by laughter, filled the house while the meat was carved and dish after dish of delicious food was carried to the tables, then passed around.

The hayride wasn't meant for pure enjoyment; it was calculated to wear out the kids who might otherwise stay up half the night. After the main course and dessert, the women headed to the kitchen for cleanup and coffee, while Grandpa, Annie's brothers and the kids got out a variety of board games. That was when Annie took her leave. She had to go back to Nate's house, gather up her Christmas puppies and make some deliveries.

Bundled up and on the way to her truck, she wandered around the house to the back. The moon was so high and bright it lit up the farm. The weathered barn in rusty red stood quiet. She remembered when it was teeming with life—cows, horses, goats, chickens, not to mention people. Every single one of the McKenzie kids had had big parties at the farm. Her dad would dig a hole and fill it with hot coals to cook corn; hot dogs would be turned on the grill, and Rose would put out a huge bowl of potato salad and deviled eggs to die for. The kids who came to the farm from town would run wild through the pastures, barn and woods. They'd swing from the rafters of the barn on a rope and fall into a pile of hay, ride the horses, chase the goats. She could remember it like it was yesterday as she looked over the rolling hills and pastureland.

Someday, she thought, my own children and their friends will play here.

She climbed up on the hay wagon and lay down in the sweet hay, looking up at the sky. It was clear, black, speckled with stars. At the moment the house was throbbing with noise, but ordinarily it was so quiet in the country you could hear a leaf rustle a hundred yards away.

The sound of a car approaching caused her to sit up, and she recognized the Dicksons' truck, their nearest neighbors. Another country custom—people dropped in on each other, bringing homemade treats and staying for at least a cup of coffee. Of course the McKenzies didn't go visiting when the family was home—there were too many of them. A second truck trundled along behind the Dicksons'—looked like the whole fam-damn-ly was coming over. She plopped back down on the hay, hoping to be invisible. Once they all got inside, she'd take off. She wasn't feeling sociable.

There was only one person she wanted to be with right now. She hugged herself and tried to pretend his arms were—

"Annie? You out here?" Beau called from the back porch.

Don't answer, she told herself.

"Annie!"

But her truck was parked out front. "I'm looking at the stars, but I'm leaving in a second. What?"

"I just wanted to know where you are!" he yelled back.

"Well, go away and leave me alone! You're scaring the stars!" And then more quietly she muttered, "Pest."

Seconds later she felt the wagon move, heard it squeak and a large body flopped down next to her in the hay.

"Aw, Beau, you jerk!" she nearly yelled. She sat straight up, plucked straw out of her hair with a gloved hand and looked at the body next to her. Not Beau. Nathaniel lay facedown in the hay beside her. "What are you doing here?" she asked in confusion.

He turned his head to one side. "I came back to sweep you off your feet, but I've been either flying or driving or hanging around airports so long that I'm too tired to roll over, much less sweep you anywhere. And I didn't get much sleep the night before I left, either." He grinned. "Thank you very much."

"You didn't go?" she asked.

"I went. I made it all the way to Miami."

"And came *back?*"

He yawned hugely. "I realized halfway there that I couldn't go to the Bahamas without you, but they wouldn't turn the plane around."

She was quiet for a second. "You've lost your mind."

"Tell me about it," he said. "What have you done to me?"

"Like this is *my* fault? That you're a lunatic?"

He yawned again. "I was normal until three weeks ago," he said. "It's amazing how many people fly on Christmas Eve. I couldn't get a nonstop. I was up and down all day. I had to go from Miami to Lansing to Seattle to San Francisco. The last leg—I had to ride in the bathroom."

"You did not," she said with a laugh. She lay down in the hay beside him.

"Then I had to rent a car and drive to Santa Rosa to get my truck. Then drive home."

"Hey!" Beau called from the back porch. "You guys want the horses hitched up?"

Annie sat up again. "No, thank you," she yelled back. "Can you please go away?"

"You guys making out in the hay?"

"Go away!" they both yelled.

"Jeez." The back door slammed.

Annie lay back down. "Now, what do you have in mind?" she asked him.

"I had a plan," he said. "I was going to tell you I love you, then seduce you, put a really nice flush on your cheeks, but I'm not sure I have the strength. I do love you, however. And a little sleep tonight might give me a second wind, so brace yourself."

She giggled. "I have puppies to deliver," she informed him.

"Aw, you haven't done that already? I was so hoping we could just go home and go to bed...."

"Why don't I take you home to your house, then you can sleep and I'll deliver the puppies. I don't think you should be driving if you can't roll over."

"I'll be fine," he said, facedown in the hay. "You'll see. Any second now I'll perk right up."

"You love me?" she asked. "What makes you think so?"

He couldn't roll over, but he looped an arm over her waist and pulled her closer. "You are so under my skin, Annie McKenzie, I'll never be a free man again. Pretty soon now you'll probably want to say you love me, too. Hurry up, will you? I'd like to be conscious for it."

She laughed at him.

"Say it, damn it," he ordered.

"I love you, too," she said. "I can't believe you came back in the same day. Why didn't you just call? Or come back and tell me you had a miserable time? You could have had your vacation and then told me."

"Because, Annie—I realized if I stayed away from you, I'd be lonely. No matter how many people were around, I'd feel alone if I wasn't with you." He pulled her closer. "I wanted you to know how important it was to me, to be with you. I wanted you to know you were worth a lot of trouble. You aren't something I can put off till later. You're not the kind of woman I can send flowers to with a note to say how I feel—you have to be in my arms. I'm not looking for the easy way with you, Annie. I want the forever way. And I don't think that's going to ever change. Now can we please deliver the puppies and get some sleep?"

"Sure," she said, running her fingers through the short hair over his ear. "Merry Christmas, Nathaniel."

"Merry Christmas, baby. I brought you something. A diamond."

"You brought me a diamond?" she asked, stunned.

He dug in his pocket and pulled out a plastic diamond about the size of a lime, attached to a key chain. "Our first Christmas Eve together, and I shopped for your present in an airport gift shop. By the way, when I get the real diamond, I don't think it's going to be this big."

She laughed and kissed him. "You will never know how much I like this one."

"Wanna show me?" he asked, hugging her tight.

"I will," she promised. "For the next fifty years."

"Works for me, Annie. I love you like mad."

"You make my knees wobble," she said. "Let me take you home so you can start wobbling them some more."

"My pleasure." He kissed her with surprising passion for a man dead on his feet. "Let's go home."

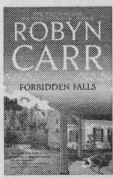

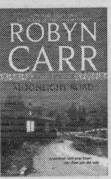

REQUEST YOUR FREE BOOKS!

2 FREE NOVELS
FROM THE ROMANCE/SUSPENSE
COLLECTION PLUS 2 FREE GIFTS!

YES! Please send me 2 FREE novels from the Romance/Suspense Collection and my 2 FREE gifts (gifts are worth about $10). After receiving them, if I don't wish to receive any more books, I can return the shipping statement marked "cancel." If I don't cancel, I will receive 4 brand-new novels every month and be billed just $5.74 per book in the U.S. or $6.24 per book in Canada. That's a savings of at least 28% off the cover price. It's quite a bargain! Shipping and handling is just 50¢ per book.* I understand that accepting the 2 free books and gifts places me under no obligation to buy anything. I can always return a shipment and cancel at any time. Even if I never buy another book from the Reader Service, the two free books and gifts are mine to keep forever.

185 MDN EYNQ   385 MDN EYN2

Name	(PLEASE PRINT)	
Address		Apt. #
City	State/Prov.	Zip/Postal Code

Signature (if under 16, a parent or guardian must sign)

Mail to **The Reader Service:**
IN U.S.A.: P.O. Box 1867, Buffalo, NY 14240-1867
IN CANADA: P.O. Box 609, Fort Erie, Ontario L2A 5X3

Not valid to current subscribers of the Romance Collection,
the Suspense Collection or the Romance/Suspense Collection.

Want to try two free books from another line?
Call 1-800-873-8635 or visit www.morefreebooks.com.

* Terms and prices subject to change without notice. Prices do not include applicable taxes. Sales tax applicable in N.Y. Canadian residents will be charged applicable provincial taxes and GST. Offer not valid in Quebec. This offer is limited to one order per household. All orders subject to approval. Credit or debit balances in a customer's account(s) may be offset by any other outstanding balance owed by or to the customer. Please allow 4 to 6 weeks for delivery. Offer available while quantities last.

Your Privacy: Harlequin is committed to protecting your privacy. Our Privacy Policy is available online at www.eHarlequin.com or upon request from the Reader Service. From time to time we make our lists of customers available to reputable third parties who may have a product or service of interest to you. If you would prefer we not share your name and address, please check here. ☐

BOB09